MW01526956

HUMPHREY'S MOTEL

EMILY B. KERROS

HUMPHREY'S MOTEL
Copyright © 2024 by Emily B. Kerros

All rights reserved. Neither this publication nor any part of this publication may be reproduced or transmitted in any form or by any means, electronic or mechanical, including photocopying, recording or any information storage and retrieval system, without permission in writing from the author.

This is a work of fiction. Names, characters, places and incidents either are the product of the author's imagination or are used fictitiously, and any resemblance to actual persons, living or dead, businesses, companies, events, or locales is entirely coincidental.

Printed in Canada

Soft cover ISBN: 978-1-4866-2474-4
Hard cover ISBN: 978-1-4866-2475-1
eBook ISBN: 978-1-4866-2476-8

Word Alive Press
119 De Baets Street Winnipeg, MB R2J 3R9
www.wordalivepress.ca

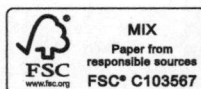

WORD ALIVE
—P R E S S—

MIX
Paper from
responsible sources
FSC
www.fsc.org
FSC® C103567

Cataloguing in Publication information can be obtained from Library and Archives Canada.

For Grandpa VanEgmond

CONTENTS

CONTENTS

"The muzzle of the Luger looked like the mouth of the Second Street tunnel, but I didn't move.

Not being bullet proof is an idea I had had to get used to."

—Raymond Chandler, *The Big Sleep*

SPRING

Fifteen years earlier

It was about eleven o'clock in the evening and the church was dark. Water came up past my ankles in the flooded basement, even higher on my shorter, dark-haired friend, but he didn't seem bothered by it. I knew him well enough to know he wasn't sober, even if he thought I couldn't tell. I could hear him wade through the water, searching for something. He finally found what he was looking for—two large steel shovels—and forced one of them into my hands before splashing back up the stairs.

I followed him between the pews and out the side door, where we cut across the grass to the adjacent cemetery. He stopped at a grave marked *Griffith* and plunged his shovel into the ground. I did the same.

"What if he skipped town?" I asked between shovelfuls. "We're never going to find him."

"I have money. I can find him."

"And then what?"

He was so focused on the dig that he didn't seem to have heard me. But then he stopped, dropped his shovel, and knelt down. I watched him brush away the last layer of dirt, not from an ornate coffin but from a large hunting rifle. He picked it up, and no sooner had he slung it over his back than we heard a siren, red and blue lights flashing between the dark headstones.

We did the only thing we could do: we ran, leaving the empty grave and full moon behind us. Only a glimmer of moonlight streaked across his face, like a camera snapping a photo—one I wouldn't soon forget, for the grin on his face was purely devilish, unlike anything I had ever seen before.

1

LOVELY LITTLE MOTEL

The dark-haired photographer from the *Gazette* wanted two Manhattans.

He sat alone at the bar, although I had watched him walk in with a woman: beautiful, blonde, and unfamiliar. He held the heavy glass door for her, pretending to be a gentleman, which he definitely was not. After all, I knew the man better than he knew himself.

He was a photographer, both for the newspaper and on the side, whatever that meant. He spoke three languages flawlessly and happened to be handsome—a stroke of pure genetic luck, I supposed. Strands of hair dangled over his face and he wore the same devilish grin as always while his dark beady eyes shifted around the room incessantly. A black tattoo creeped out from his shirt like a snake hissing at his neck.

His name was Logan Griffith and he was the same age I was—thirty-three. Not old, but definitely not as young as we used to be. And definitely not the friends we used to be. When he wrapped his arm around the woman, I had to look away.

The bar was called Humphrey's. It was dimly lit, which according to the photographer all the best bars were. The overhead fixtures fizzled and burnt out so often that the barkeep was tired of replacing the bulbs. The old granite bartop wrapped in a long L-shape from one end of the bar to the other, the barstools mostly mismatched. There were two cozy corner booths and several round tables and chairs. In another corner sat an old jukebox, which hadn't worked for years and no amount of tinkering was going to bring it back to life. It stayed because it had to; it was large and immovable, probably stuck to the floor.

A set of double doors behind the bartop led to the kitchen, and another, more subtle door led upstairs. The barkeep lived above the bar, which was common if not a little cliché. Perhaps that was exactly how the barkeep thought of himself: common, even a little cliché. I certainly wouldn't have argued with him.

There was nothing spectacular about his backbar, sparkling glass bottles of fine wines and distilled spirits that would have looked impressive were they not displayed on rows of rough wooden shelves. The only thing particularly peculiar was the stack of books, usually two or three at a time, left on the furthest shelf, which he would sneak off and stuff his nose into when the bar wasn't busy. He was a bookworm of sorts, and an old soul. He liked the classics.

Although the allure of alcohol didn't often appeal to me, I could appreciate the stack of books and supposed that if I had to choose a favourite bar, it would be Humphrey's. But only if I had to. Only if it was a matter of life or death. Or if I suddenly felt the urge to saddle up on a wobbly barstool and snap my fingers at the bartender for something tall and strong.

Ironically, something tall and strong would have suited me nicely. The tall part, anyway.

There were three bars in town. One stoplight. One grocery store. One church. Three bars. My mother once told me that the proportion was off, and she was right. I could think of at least two more intersections that would have benefited from a stoplight, or at the very least a roundabout, which were all the rage in Europe but apparently not in small towns.

In fact, I couldn't have agreed with her more, that there were too many bars, until one day everything changed. Whether I liked it or not, Humphrey's belonged to me.

In actuality, Humphrey's belonged to the Pearl Motel, a seedy hole-in-the-wall on the outskirts of town between the river and a thick forest of trees. Several of the windows were boarded up, two of the rooms had leaking sinks, and another was a risky overnight stay with its broken lock. Not that any of it mattered.

The town of Pearl didn't get a lot of visitors. Like its motel, Pearl was rundown, tired, and dead to the world, located out in the Canadian prairies. Back in my salad days, whenever I'd tried to find Pearl on a map, I couldn't, and I didn't suppose time had done it any favours. The lone stoplight was in the middle of Main Street where dust blew through on windy days and snow squalled in December. The dirt road to the Pearl Motel flooded every spring, forcing Humphrey's to close until the river calmed and the road became muddy but traversable. I watched the river rise every year like clockwork, and every year I let it entrap me.

Although lately, even though the river had already flooded and settled for the season, I still felt trapped. For better or for worse, I was stuck in Pearl. I had tried—and failed—to leave, bound by some imaginary force, and subsequently my window of opportunity had closed.

Before I'd known it, my old man had gone off and died, deserting Humphrey's and leaving the bar with my name on it.

Either way, the bookworm bartender was, in fact, me.

I hadn't wanted to be a bartender. I'd wanted to be something else entirely—the opposite of a bartender, whatever that was—but I had inherited Humphrey's like I'd inherited my blue eyes, and unfortunately from the same man. It was no secret that my old man had enjoyed his drink a little too much. That, along with his wild and weekly poker nights, had eventually been his downfall. He had taught me how to mix a Manhattan long before I was allowed to drink one and told me that it was one of the essential cocktails, right up there with the good old fashioned or Bond-style martini. And he passed down his secret ingredient—a homegrown whisky with a bronze label. It was probably the only good advice he'd ever shared with me, the only bit of truth, and it was how I had met the dark-haired photographer all those years ago. Now many a Manhattan had been mixed, and most of them for Logan Griffith.

I poured from a bottle of whisky and stirred it with bitters, dry and sweet vermouth, and ice, taking in the bittersweet smell. I stirred smoothly for about thirty seconds, watching the ice melt, and then strained the drink into a pair of tall cocktail glasses.

As I wiped a spill from the bartop, I checked over my shoulder to see the clock that hung above the kitchen doors. It took a while for me to make out the time: half an hour until midnight. Half an hour until I could head upstairs and finish the book I was reading, not one of the crime classics stacked on the edge of the shelf, but something new, an unfinished manuscript of sorts, sent to me for my unofficial opinion. I had left it upstairs, waiting for me in my armchair.

The old armchair was nestled next to the window where the slanted tin roof met at a peak. Relaxing there with a book was the only thing I liked about living above the bar. I didn't like being too tall to head up and down the stairs without ducking. I didn't like the brown, murky water that sometimes came out of the bathroom faucet. I didn't like the rusted-out fire escape that probably wouldn't hold me if the bar caught on fire, although I had already decided to just let it burn. And if that never happened, if I wasn't so lucky, I could always leave like my old man—throw one last poker night and never look back. His untimely death, of course, had thrown a wrench in any plans to leave, but perhaps my old man had been smarter than I gave him credit for.

I glanced at the photographer. He had nabbed his regular spot along what I called the sidebar, the smaller side of the L-shape closest to the kitchen. He was still alone, drumming his fingers impatiently. I looked around, but his mystery woman was nowhere to be seen. She had probably disappeared to the ladies' room, the only place the Manhattan Man couldn't follow her.

I decided to keep an eye out for her. Blonde, I remembered, and wearing something green.

I slid two chilled glasses garnished with an orange wheel in front of him. "So who is she?"

"Good to see you too, Humphrey," Logan deadpanned. He had a copy of *The Pearl Gazette* with him, tossed carelessly on the bar. He caught me stealing a glance at it and flipped it over.

"Does she have a name?"

Logan ignored me. He tested his Manhattan. "Is this Griffiths?"

Ah, the bronze label.

Logan Griffith had practically been raised on whisky. Granddad Griffith owned the swanky Griffiths Distilleries uptown. Barred by a family-crested gate and spread out over acres of land, it was home to one of the other two bars in Pearl, much fancier than Humphrey's. It had been our old stomping ground, before Logan had become the Manhattan Man, and I became just Humphrey. Going there had been magnificent, like leaving Pearl altogether. I could trade in the potholed streets for cobblestone, the cramped space above the bar for a three-storey mansion, and the plain Jane townsfolk for Logan's fascinating family. Wheelchair-bound Granddad Griffith had drunk whisky with his breakfast, and Logan's mother, who spoke a beautiful blend of French and Cree, told us stories before bed. All that wealth and whisky ran deep in Logan's veins, lingering even after he'd left it all behind to become a photographer.

Tongues wagged, of course, but I knew him. The photographer might have been slumming it in the world of small-town newsprint, but he was still a Griffith. Granddad hadn't completely cut him off, which at least explained the tailored shirts, waxed eyebrows, and the Bentley parked out front.

"You're losing your taste." I lifted the bronze-labelled bottle back up onto the shelf, feeling the embossed lettering: *Griffiths Fine Whisky, est. 1942*. "You know, you could have been a whisky king."

Logan narrowed his eyes. He chose his battles. Evidently not this one.

"Does she have a name?" I tried again.

"Out-of-towner."

"That's not a name."

One of his devilish grins. "Darling Daphne."

He took another sip from his Manhattan just as Darling Daphne returned. She slid onto the barstool next to him with ease, and I had to admit she was even more beautiful up close. Her pale skin was flattered by red lips and high and defined cheekbones. Her hair looked light as a feather, pulled back into a comfortable ponytail.

And I had been right—she was wearing something green: a green aviator jacket. Army green. Jungle green. Something like that.

"Is this mine?" She pointed to the second cocktail glass.

"Afraid not," I answered. "Logan always drinks two at a time."

She looked up at me. Green eyes too.

A slightly irritated Logan gestured towards me nonchalantly. "Daphne, darling, this is the bartender."

He called everybody darling—every woman, that is—and it wasn't the first time he had referred to me as simply *the bartender*. Nothing more, nothing less. Someone to serve the Manhattan Man. That was me. Somehow, even though I towered head and shoulders above him, Logan Griffith always made me look two feet tall.

"Nice to meet you, Daphne." I let her name roll off my tongue. It rolled off nicely. Easily.

We shook hands, her hand feeling soft against mine, and I held it a little longer than I meant to. I felt myself redden as I pulled back. Daphne either didn't notice or didn't care.

"You have a lovely little motel," she said. Her green eyes sparkled with interest. In me? That seemed unlikely. We had only just met.

"And you're a good liar," I replied, laughing at her particular choice of words. "Lovely?"

"Definitely little."

"Definitely a motel," I teased her.

There was a somewhat awkward pause and then Logan leaned closer to Daphne. "Darling, he doesn't own the motel. You'll have to talk to his landlord about the dead cat."

"Dead cat?" I repeated. I didn't particularly like cats, but strays were common in Pearl, especially during the spring and summer months. I had seen two scraggily black strays around the motel earlier, shooing them away from the dumpster out back. Just thinking about it made me shudder. I looked at Daphne. "Where?"

She grimaced. "Under the bed."

"We saw its filthy tail sticking out," Logan said, taking another sip.

We—as in Daphne and Logan, together at the motel. I tried to picture Daphne, a beautiful out-of-towner, staying overnight in a dark and dusty motel room, alone in the middle of nowhere, except for Logan and a dead cat.

I couldn't do it. The truth was, it made me feel a little sick.

I turned to Logan. "What did you do?"

"Nothing. I don't make a habit of touching dead cats, Humphrey." He downed his drink and slid the glass back to me with a trademark grin.

It was my cue to leave. Logan didn't want me there talking to Daphne about dead cats—or anything else, for that matter. I took his glass and stepped towards the kitchen when I realized that Darling Daphne hadn't ordered anything. Perhaps Logan didn't want me talking to her, but I was a bartender, after all, and Chef Seth's (say that ten times fast) menu was to die for.

I turned back, prepared to tell the *Gazette* photographer that I was doing my job, like it or not, and at that precise second, I didn't entirely dislike it.

I leaned on the bar. "Ah, Daphne, what can I get you?"

Logan disliked it. He moved on to his second Manhattan, tearing the orange garnish off the rim and dropping it into his glass. He didn't watch it sink. He watched me with a furrowed brow. Which made me like it even more.

"I'll just have a coffee," Daphne said eagerly.

I picked my battles too. "Coffee? At this hour?"

"Either the caffeine keeps me awake or the dead cat under my bed," she said, her eyes sparkling again when she looked at me. "Frankly, I don't see much of a difference."

Nobody said *frankly* anymore. I liked it.

Logan, on the other hand, looked as though he wanted to smack the smirk off my face.

I wandered to the kitchen and returned with the coffee. Black. Steaming. Daphne thanked me, wrapping both hands around the mug, and that was when I saw it—a large diamond on her left hand, glimmering even in the dimness of the bar. I couldn't stop staring at it, wide-eyed, even as she lifted the mug to her lips and took a sip.

"Humphrey."

It was the biggest diamond I had ever seen.

"Humphrey."

Surely it had cost a fortune.

"Humphrey!"

I looked at Logan.

"Why don't you talk to Tedd?" he asked.

Tedd Archer was the newest owner of the Pearl Motel and, perhaps more importantly, my new landlord. He owned several other properties in town, including his own antique shoppe, and I knew about as much about Tedd Archer as I wanted to. There were rumours floating around town about him and his part-time nanny, though not the sort of rumours one would expect. He dabbled in everything and was master of nothing. His wife ran Archer's Antique Shoppe while he bummed around collecting lease from the diner, the barbershop, and even the offices of *The Pearl Gazette*, which meant in an indirect way that he was Logan's landlord too.

I didn't like the thought of Humphrey's being the latest on Tedd's list.

Just two weeks ago, Tedd and I had met to go over the new lease. He was a man in his mid-fifties but his full head of grey hair and wrinkles around the eyes made him seem older. He had walked into Humphrey's as if he owned the place—which I supposed he did—and sprawled into the booth opposite me where I had been waiting, hands folded and clock ticking.

He was late, of course, and issued no apology. I shouldn't have been surprised. His voice was obnoxiously loud and he seemed annoyed, like a big bear poked awake from its nap. Still, I'd decided it was as good a time as any to fill him in on some of the finer, inner workings of the Pearl Motel.

"There's a leaking sink in Room 1 and it's seeping into my kitchen," I had said, matter-of-factly. The kitchen at the back of my bar shared a wall with Room 1, and Seth, who was not only the best chef in Pearl but also an old friend of my mother's, had grown tired of mopping up a puddle of water every day before his shift.

"Are you sure the leak itself isn't in the kitchen?" Tedd asked. Again his voice was obnoxiously loud, but his expression was bored, almost blank.

"I've overheard guests complain about the sink in Room 1."

His blank expression didn't change. "We don't get a lot of guests, Humphrey."

He said the word *guests* very loosely. Not that I blamed him. It was just a dumpy motel, after all.

But then he continued: "I'm not going to be bothered with a little leaking sink."

"So you aren't going to fix it?" I asked.

Tedd shrugged.

"Are you going to fix anything around here?"

Another blank stare.

"Fine. I'll fix it myself."

"That would be in violation of your lease," Tedd said loudly. "Need I remind you, Humphrey, that this isn't your motel?" He checked his watch. "Look, I haven't got all day. I just wanted to sign some papers. Make it official." He slid one of his papers across the table to me. "Dotted line, Humphrey. And quit stalling. I have places to be."

Apparently, he had procured an antique arcade whack-a-mole and promised his five-year-old a game. I watched him impatiently check his watch for the second time. He didn't strike me as a family man.

I stared at the dotted line, then slid the paper back to him. "I'm not signing this."

"Rather be homeless, Humphrey?" He said it loudly, as a joke perhaps, but it was obvious that he'd had enough.

He stood up, gathering his papers, and left as irritated and annoyed as when he'd arrived. The heavy door slammed behind him, leaving me stunned and a little regretful. Being homeless in Pearl was possibly the only thing worse than living in Pearl.

But after that meeting, Tedd had never come back, and I had never signed the lease.

I looked from Daphne to Logan, shaking my head. Even Darling Daphne, blinking her glorious green eyes, wouldn't be able to persuade me to poke that bear again.

"I'm not talking to Tedd," I said.

"Why not?" Logan had already downed half his drink.

"Because technically he is my landlord, but I never signed a lease."

Logan muttered something under his breath and then finished his drink, sliding his glass over to me. "I'll have another round."

It was his second attempt to get rid of me with a devilish grin, and I obliged this time. I set his dirty glass in the tub sink and got back to work, pulling the bottle of Griffiths whisky from the shelf and stirring another pair of Manhattans—all while keeping an eye on the two of them. I couldn't hear what they were saying, since they spoke quietly to each other. Every now and then Daphne would lay a hand on Logan's shoulder, laughing at something he had said. Of course, he must have said something funny, something charming. He wasn't obsessing about the ring on her finger. I could still see it, glimmering, out of the corner of my eye.

A sudden, rather frightening thought suddenly came over me: what if Logan had put it there? I shook my head. That couldn't be. I knew Logan, and he wasn't the settling down type. The marrying type, sure, but not the settling down type. Been there, tried that, hadn't worked out.

I poured both cocktail glasses to the brim, but this time I didn't bother to wipe the spill from the bartop. I slid the Manhattans, Logan's third and fourth, not that I was counting, in front of him. I motioned to the newspaper lying on the bar.

"So you're my paperboy now?" I said.

Underneath his composed devilish grin, I must have ruffled some feathers.

"I snagged tomorrow's edition for you, Humphrey. You're welcome."

I snorted softly. He had made it seem like it was difficult for the *Gazette* photographer to snag a copy of his own paper the day it was printed. *The Pearl Gazette* was the town's only newspaper and, like most of Pearl, hadn't changed in years. I could attest to at least thirty-three years firsthand. It was a weekly edition, still printed almost entirely in black and white, even Logan's front-page photos, preserving the charm and nostalgia of newsprint. Perhaps the only difference was that the newspaper had thinned over the years. Either there was less news or less interest in reading the news. I assumed it was the latter, although the *Gazette* still seemed popular among the townsfolk.

He handed me the paper. "As it happens, your new landlord made front page."

I flipped it over to read the headline and balked: "Pearl Motel Reopens — Tedd Archer, Our Very Own Town Hero." It seemed a bit of a stretch to call Tedd a "town hero." I scanned the article, written by *Gazette* reporter Magnolia Lee, all about the grand reopening weekend I had managed to avoid by flipping my sign to CLOSED and spending the day in my armchair with a book. Logan had snapped photos of the ribbon-cutting, Tedd Archer and Mayor McNally both holding a giant pair of scissors in front of the motel. Tedd looked tickled pink, although it could have been a sunburn, and Mayor McNally's poor spiked heels were sunk into the clumpy grass. Apparently they hadn't even bothered to trim the lawn before the reopening. It was overgrown with weeds and they seemed to have picked a cracked drainpipe to pose in front of. The ridiculousness of it all was exhausting.

I looked up from reading. "How was this a reopening?"

"It closed," Logan said dryly, "and then it opened."

"Does she actually think Tedd saved the motel?"

"Mag?" Logan shrugged. "I don't know. I didn't read it."

I tossed the newspaper back onto the bar. It didn't matter what Magnolia Lee thought. In newsprint, on the front page, Tedd Archer was be worshipped as a hero, yet it couldn't have been further from the truth. There was nothing grand about the Pearl Motel's reopening and, little did Pearl's townsfolk know, Tedd didn't plan on fixing or changing anything. He was only interested in two things: money and himself, two of the worst qualities in a man. I could attest to that too.

And if there was one thing I knew for sure, it was that I wasn't about to kowtow to the likes of Tedd Archer.

Nobody said *kowtow* anymore either. I almost wished I had thought it out loud.

"I'll take care of the cat," I said.

"You?" Logan choked.

I looked at the clock. "I close in ten minutes."

I would have scooped up a hundred dead cats for the smile on Daphne's face and the irritated expression on Logan's.

Midnight came and the nightcrawlers left, slowly disintegrating, one by one, out the door and to their cars, rumbling in the parking lot before their headlights disappeared down the road the way they'd come. When the last of them crawled away, Daphne helped me wash a dishrag over the bar while I started turning chairs upside-down on the tables. Logan lingered on his barstool, polishing off his Manhattans.

He patted his pockets. "Darling, do you have your room key?"

Daphne took his empty glasses and set them in the tub sink. "I thought you had it."

"I must have left it in the Bentley." He got off the barstool too quickly, losing his balance and almost toppling over before catching himself. He passed me on his way to the door and patted me on the shoulder. "Try not to bore Daphne while I'm gone, Humphrey." His words were a little slurred.

I ignored him and finished stacking the chairs. Daphne sat back down at the bar, twisting her ring around her finger as if by force of habit.

"So what brings you to Pearl?" I asked.

She hesitated. "Oh, I'm just here for … business."

She didn't bother to elaborate, so I piled a few more dirty dishes into the tub sink and replaced a few bottles on the backbar. Several minutes passed before Logan staggered back into the bar, spinning the room key on his thumb, an old-fashioned brass key with a beaded chain. He tossed it to Daphne with surprising accuracy and then wandered behind the bar. He ran his hand along the shelves, searching for something.

"I'll just take the bottle," he said, helping himself to the bronze label.

I didn't bother to tell him off. Letting Logan swig an entire bottle of whisky on a weeknight probably wasn't the best thing for a bartender to do, but I realized something as I watched him ease back onto his barstool and tip the bottle back.

"You're not coming with us?" I asked.

"I don't like dead cats, Humphrey."

I turned to Daphne. She only shrugged.

And just like that, I followed her out of the bar. I would gladly add the bottle to Logan's already lengthy tab. Nobody could tell me an almost whisky king wasn't good for a barkeep's bottom line.

When Darling Daphne had first walked into Humphrey's with the Manhattan Man, I never would have imagined we'd end up together, just the two of us, heading out to her motel room. The parking lot outside the bar was lit up but the sidewalk that stretched the length of the motel was dark, except for a small light above each of the room doors. I only counted six lights in the distance, which meant one of them must have been burnt out.

Daphne was staying in Room 3, so we didn't have far to walk. I trailed behind, letting her lead the way. Her hair swayed back and forth as she walked. She walked comfortably. Confidently. Even as an out-of-towner in an unfamiliar place. I found myself somewhat jealous.

The sidewalk jutted outwards around the motel office, a tiny extension of the building, where guests checked in and out. The desk clerk and cleaner, who happened to be one and the same, worked out of the office during the day. The motel hadn't had need for a night clerk in years.

As we passed Room 1, I couldn't help but wonder if the unattended leaking sink had finally flooded the whole room. I shook the thought away. It wasn't my problem, as Tedd had so kindly reminded me. I treaded one foot in front of the other, stepping over the cracked drainpipe. Weeds were growing through the cracks in the sidewalk and I tried stepping on them, squashing them childishly underfoot. It wasn't until I looked up and saw Daphne, already standing under the next light, that I realized how far I had fallen behind.

She politely waited for me to catch up and I shoved my hands into my pockets as I approached. Forced to walk beside her, my palms were suddenly sweaty.

"How long have you known Logan?" she asked.

"Too long."

She laughed.

I eyed her, feeling oddly ambitious. "How long have *you* known Logan?"

She thought about it. "Oh, three and a half hours."

"Still too long."

She laughed again. I liked her laugh.

As we approached Room 3, I stopped to inspect the window. The corner bricks were crumbling and part of the rickety windowpane was exposed. There was, in fact, a hole straight through into the motel room where the pane and a portion of the window itself were cracked.

"This is probably where it got in," I said to Daphne.

She peered into the hole before fumbling in her pocket for the room key. "Cats give me the creeps."

I had to agree. There was something about them. The beady eyes. The thin tails. The spikey white whiskers. Sometimes when I shooed a stray away from the dumpster, I swore it looked at me with the same devilish grin as Logan.

"Well, maybe it isn't dead." She fiddled with the lock. "Maybe it's just taking a catnap."

The door swung open with a loud creak. We waited for a scampering stray to emerge, but none came. It seemed we hadn't awakened anything from a nap, perpetual or otherwise. I followed Daphne in.

The motel room was small and dimly lit, much like at Humphrey's. The floor was a dark-sanded hardwood that had seen better days, draped with a dusty rug that matched the bedspread. The furnishings were minimal, with a table and two chairs by the window, a lamp, a small wardrobe, and two nightstands on either side of a rickety queen-sized bed. A large duffle bag had been flopped on the table. I assumed it belonged to Daphne.

Again I found myself wondering what had brought her to Pearl, of all places. She had said that she was here on business, but that could have meant a lot of things. She seemed to be one of those women I would learn absolutely nothing about unless she decided I should. Not untruthful or untrustworthy, but not forthcoming either. Perhaps not unlike myself.

Daphne crouched next to the bed, peering cautiously underneath.

"It's still there," she said over her shoulder.

I knelt on the other side and looked under. There it was, lying in a small heap of fur. Its tail was indeed poking out the side like a furry black snake.

I gave the cat a nudge with my finger. It didn't move.

"Dead?" she asked.

It wasn't breathing. There was no rise and fall of its chest.

"Definitely dead," I said.

I grabbed hold of it by the tail and dragged it out. It was lighter than expected, all skin and bones. I thought it likely that it had starved to death—that is, until I saw the blood, a red patch right above its hindleg, and it looked fresh.

My attempt to hide it from Daphne was useless. She moved around to my side of the bed and sucked in a breath when she saw the bloodied animal. She covered her nose with her hand and ran ahead of me to open the door.

Holding the cat at arm's length, I followed her outside. The fresh air was a welcome scent as we stood on the sidewalk, wondering how to dispose of the stray now that we had caught it by its tail.

I wasn't known for bright ideas. If I was known for anything, it wasn't anything remarkably good. So the idea that came to me, simultaneously exhausted from my shift and invigorated by the beautiful out-of-towner, all while clutching a dead cat, probably wasn't a good idea. But it was an idea nonetheless.

The Pearl River.

It ran through town and eventually crossed the dirt road within walking distance from the motel. The townsfolk loved the Pearl River, despite the monstrous flooding every spring. They swam in it during summer and played hockey when it froze over in winter. Fishing amateurs and enthusiasts alike took their boats out on it. And it was home to Pearl's odd infestation of bufflehead ducks.

But where else was I supposed to bury a dead stray?

Daphne stayed with me to the bitter end, trekking through the long grass and trees as their low hanging branches snagged and pulled at her hair. Finally we stood on the edge of the river. It was calm and the water was low. I tossed the cat over the riverbank and watched it tumble through the grass into the darkness of the night.

I listened for a small splash or some signal that meant it had hit the water, but everything was quiet. We lingered for a while, me and the out-of-towner, strangers with a common dislike of cats, particularly creepy dead ones, neither of us saying anything. Somehow it seemed like an inappropriate time to tell her, however platonically, that she was the most beautiful woman to ever walk into my bar. But as invigorated as I felt, I really was beat.

As we turned back to the motel, I couldn't help but look forward to reading the unfinished manuscript. And my armchair. And maybe even a good night's sleep. That was a rare occurrence these days.

"Humphrey?" Daphne stopped short. "What's that?"

It was the sound of a door creaking on its hinges, like Daphne's motel room only louder. She pointed to a light at the far end of the sidewalk, shining however dimly from the doorway of Room 7. The door had been left open and seemed to be swaying, although there was little breeze.

I had no way of knowing if Room 7 was vacant or occupied. It wasn't my motel, of course, and I didn't pay particularly close attention to its comings and goings, which mostly consisted of stranded truckers, lost tourists, and cheating couples. The fact that a light had been left on and a door left ajar was strange perhaps, but it wasn't any of my business. The motel was old, its guests few and far between. As it was, I didn't particularly care what went on outside my bar, but I supposed that strange things, when they indeed happened in Pearl, did tend to happen at the motel. Hadn't I just dragged a dead cat out of Daphne's room?

Perhaps it was all part of the small-town charm.

Daphne, obviously, didn't see it that way. The creaking door was creeping her out, much like the stray, and I agreed to follow her down the sidewalk to Room 7.

I assumed we would find an empty room, flick off the light, and shut the door. But as I stood in the doorway of Room 7, with Daphne peering over my shoulder, I found myself wishing it had been another dead cat.

Beggars can't be choosers, as my old man used to say. But that wasn't the only thing I thought of as I stood staring at the man who was lying on his back, his legs sprawled out. I recognized him immediately, with his grey hair and wrinkled eyes. Although somewhat shameful to admit, my first thought was what a sight it would be on the next paper's front page. I wondered what my new landlord would have thought about headlining the *Gazette* two weeks in a row.

Tedd Archer was dead.

Not just dead. Murdered. His body riddled with bullet holes, at least one in his forehead and some more in his chest, although it was difficult to tell exactly how many with the amount of blood pooled around him. He lay in the middle of the room, halfway between the door and the bed. The rug was stained deep red and drops of blood trailed all the way to the doorway. Blood still oozed from the bullet holes, soaking through his pinstripe pyjamas. His skin had turned a shade of grey, matching his hair, and his lifeless eyes seemed to stare at me in accusation. As if it was somehow my fault he had met a similar fate as the dead stray in Room 3—not a harmless catnap, but a permanent sleep. The big sleep, in fact.

I didn't know what to do. The two of us hadn't budged from the doorway and I could feel Daphne's quick breathing on my neck. After a long pause, she eased past me into the room. I watched her crouch next to Tedd and feel for a pulse. She shook her head.

Then she stood up, looking around the room. Room 7 was similar to her own motel room—small and cramped, dark as a dungeon, with an old queen bed in the middle and two chairs by the window. The small wardrobe was open, revealing an overcoat and blazer, each on its respective hanger. There was a clutter of things on the nightstand.

I had read enough crime fiction to know I shouldn't touch anything. Daphne, on the other hand, didn't seem to be as well-read, or at the very least she didn't seem to care. She rummaged through his things — an empty glass, a wristwatch, a handful of floss picks, a pack of minty chewing gum — and retrieved his wallet. I watched her thumb through its contents, opening my mouth to say something but nothing came out. I seemed to have lost my voice.

"Tedd Archer." She looked up at me. "This is your landlord?"

I nodded, still unable to speak.

"Somebody shot him," she said.

I could see that. I just didn't see how she could be so calm about it.

Daphne pulled a stack of cash from Tedd's wallet and counted ten hundred-dollar bills. "One thousand dollars. Who walks around with that much money?" She stared at the money for a moment, then quickly replaced it in the wallet and tossed it back on the nightstand. "Well, it wasn't a robbery."

I pried my eyes away from Tedd's, watching Daphne tiptoe around the blood-stained rug. I moved out of the way as she stood in the doorway. The lock on the door didn't appear to be broken. There was no blood on the sidewalk.

"Somebody shot him in the doorway and dragged him onto the rug." Daphne stared back into the room. "If he was shot here …" Her voice trailed as she wandered by the bed again and proceeded past the small bathroom on the other side of the room. The window was broken, the lower corner had been completely shattered and there was a hole large enough for a stray to fit through, but not much else.

"Is there glass?" I wasn't sure how my voice had suddenly returned, but I was grateful for it nonetheless.

I took a deep breath and tried to avoid Tedd's dead-eye stare, joining Daphne at the window. I ran my hand along the windowsill and the floor below it.

"See? Nothing. If a shot hit the window, there would be fresh glass," I said. "The window must have been broken before."

In fact, I would be hard-pressed to find a room at the Pearl Motel that didn't have a broken window or two.

"I didn't peg you for a Sherlock," she said, a curious look in her eye. "Well, your Moriarty couldn't have gotten far."

I must have looked confused.

"Moriarty. Sherlock's nemesis," she explained. "Whoever shot your landlord couldn't have gotten far. Those bullet holes are fresh."

"I know who Moriarty is," I said just as she lifted a hand to my mouth to quiet me.

We listened to the sudden fall of footsteps coming from outside. The sound of the footsteps quickened as they approached, then stopped short. We turned to find a figure standing in the doorway, directly where Tedd had likely stood when he'd been shot. The same spot where Daphne and I had stood only moments earlier.

It was a man. He stood tall, like a shadow, half in the light of the doorway and half in the moonlight. He paused, as shocked to see us as we were to see him.

"Who are you?" Daphne asked.

He didn't answer. He turned and ran, disappearing from the doorway in a split second.

Daphne looked at me, eyes wide. "Moriarty!"

I reached for her, but it was too late, or maybe she was simply too fast. She was out the doorway before I could so much as blink. I couldn't be sure, of course, but it looked like she had stepped in some of Tedd's blood, which was potentially worse than her fingerprints now being spread out all over the crime scene.

I didn't follow her right away. I hesitated, fixed to the floor, somewhere between confounded and dumbfounded. All I really knew was that I didn't want to be left alone in a dark motel room with a dead body.

I finally stepped outside Room 7, letting my eyes adjust to the dark. I could see Moriarty, as Daphne had dubbed him, running down the sidewalk back towards the bar. Daphne was on his heels, her jacket billowing like a cape behind her.

I ran too, my feet landing on the sidewalk with a rhythmed *thud-thud, thud-thud*. I ducked under the broken light dangling on a wire above Room 5 and almost tripped over the cracked drainpipe. I didn't think I would catch up and I wasn't sure I wanted to.

Fortunately, I didn't have to worry about it for long. Moriarty was stopped, rather unconventionally, by none other than Logan, who emerged just then from the bar, scanning the parking lot and sidewalk, his eyes glazed

over and a whisky bottle in hand. He saw Daphne in pursuit of Moriarty and
in one fell swoop swung the whisky bottle, smashing it over Moriarty's head
and knocking him to the ground.

A startled Daphne skidded to a halt, looking back and forth between
Logan and Moriarty. It was her turn to be speechless.

"Good grief," I gasped between breaths. So much for settling into my
armchair with a book. There I was, with the most beautiful—and bizarre—
woman I had ever met, a barrel-drunk Logan clinging to a broken bottleneck,
and not one but two bodies. If Daphne hadn't reached out to steady Logan,
there might have been a third.

2

SO LONG, VANCOUVER

"Good grief," I said again. This time I was close enough for Logan to hear. If he was startled by what had happened, he didn't show it. He moved towards me, shards of broken glass crunching underfoot.

"That," he said, pointing to Moriarty with his bottleneck, "is not a cat."

Far from it. And I couldn't make any sense of it either.

I left after that. I half-closed my eyes and stepped back into the bar, leaving Logan rubbing his head irritably and Daphne kneeling beside Moriarty, who was lying face-down in the gravel. She patted his cheek in an attempt to wake him.

I had three perfectly good reasons for leaving Logan and Daphne and our unidentified Moriarty to fend for themselves. For one thing, a drunk Logan was often an irritable Logan. It wouldn't be long before he started grumbling about a splitting headache. I wasn't heartless, but when it came to Logan and his whisky, I tried to be.

Second, I hoped the stillness and familiarity of the bar would help me calm down. It hadn't. But that, I supposed, was beside the point.

Third, I thought it was time to call the police. Tedd Archer was dead. And of all the people to find him, it had to be me and a beautiful out-of-towner.

I glanced out the window at Daphne and Moriarty, who appeared to have regained consciousness and gotten to his feet. He staggered into the bar, followed closely by Daphne, with Logan bringing up the rear. Logan found his barstool and saddled back up, resting his pounding head in his hands with a groan.

Moriarty was drenched in whisky and looked as drunk as I imagined Logan felt. He held one hand to the back of his head. Daphne pulled down a chair for him and helped—or rather, forced—him into it. He wasn't going anywhere. He had some explaining to do.

But even in the dimly lit bar, Moriarty was recognizable. And Moriarty was hardly Moriarty.

I blinked. "Riley Dugdale?"

Daphne looked at me. "You know him?"

I shrugged. "Everyone knows everyone in Pearl."

Riley Dugdale worked for Tedd Archer and his wife at the antique shoppe. He was a young man in his mid-twenties, tallish and lanky. He was dressed in a light-coloured button-down, which I supposed had suited him nicely when he'd first put it on, but now the front of it was roughened up with gravel and the back stained with whisky. He smelled like a mixture of sweat and booze. His curly hair was unkempt and his face flushed. He didn't look well, but that probably had something to do with seeing his employer dead in a motel room and being chased in the dark by a stranger, all before getting knocked out with a glass bottle. Thanks to Logan, a goose egg was already forming on the back of his head. I could see it from across the room.

I wrapped some ice in a towel and brought it to him. He thanked me with a nod—he had probably lost his voice too—and held the ice to his head. He winced a little, clenching his teeth.

I turned a chair around and sat next to him. His hands were shaking. There was dirt under his fingernails, which seemed unusual for his type of work, but maybe he was more of an outdoorsman than I knew. His left leg, the one closest to me, was shaking too, uncontrollably.

"What are you doing here, Mr. Dugdale?" Daphne asked as she pulled up a chair.

Riley looked at me, seemingly frightened of her. I couldn't really blame him. Everyone knew Pearl didn't get a lot of visitors. When we did, they typically weren't beautiful blonde women who stayed overnight in the motel and chased townsfolk around. He needed some encouragement.

"It's Riley," was all he said.

"Well, *Riley*, what are you doing here?" Daphne didn't so much as lean back in her chair. She wasn't willing to back down. This was the side of her I had caught a glimpse of in Room 7, when she had trodden over the crime scene like it belonged to her. Dogged. Whip-smart. Perhaps a little bit careless.

"I c–c–came to see Tedd."

"It's a little late for a visit, isn't it?" she asked.

Riley swallowed nervously and looked at me.

"Riley works for the Archers," I explained on his behalf. I turned to him. "At the antique shoppe, right?"

Riley nodded.

"Did Tedd ask you to meet him?" Daphne asked.

He shook his head, dropping the icepack on the table next to him.

"Then what are you doing here?"

"Tedd b–b–borrowed something from me. I j–j–just came to g–get it back."

He wasn't faking it. The stutter was real. Whether it was an actual impediment or a result of head trauma, I didn't know. I didn't really need to know.

Apparently neither did Daphne. "What did he borrow?"

"I d–d–don't remember." Riley wrung his hands together. "Is he really d–dead?"

Daphne shot me another look, harder to interpret.

"I'm afraid so," I said to Riley. His eyes enlarged and he took in a laboured breath, rubbing his head again. His leg was still shaking. I thought about Tedd wearing his pinstripe pyjamas, his belongings on the nightstand in Room 7, and his clothes in the wardrobe. "Riley, it looked like Tedd was staying at the motel. Do you know why?"

He shook his head. "I d–d–don't know. I d–didn't want to ask him."

Of course. Riley knew better than to poke the bear. That wasn't a surprise. He worked for the man, after all.

Daphne, on the other hand, seemed unconvinced. She eyed Riley suspiciously. There was something there, and it was more than just a playful game of Sherlock versus Moriarty. Much more. She knew what she was doing. She had done this before. What exactly, I didn't know.

"How did you know Tedd was staying here?" she asked.

Riley didn't even look at her. "I must have heard it around t–t–town."

"Were you at work today?"

Riley nodded.

"Did you see him?"

"He s–stopped by at lunch."

"How did he seem?"

"I d–d–don't know. Stressed out, k–kind of." Riley rubbed his head. "But he always s–s–seems that way. And there have been s–some th–thefts at the shoppe. Some antiques have gone m–missing."

Daphne inched forward in her chair. "You said he borrowed something from you?"

Riley nodded vigorously. Too vigorously. He probably had whiplash on top of everything else.

"But you can't remember what it was?"

"I d–don't know," he stuttered. "I th–think I'm just a bit sh–shaken up."

With that, Riley dropped his head into his hands, rubbing his eyes and taking another laboured breath.

As I watched him, it struck me: I could see myself in Riley Dugdale, albeit a much younger version of myself. Tall, long-limbed, and awkward. Easily anxious. Easily upset. He couldn't help it. The young man was in shock. I could understand that. I could understand him.

But Daphne frowned. She stood and grabbed me by the sleeve, pulling me over to the bar and lowering her voice.

"He drove out here in the middle of the night to get something back from his boss and now he can't remember what it is."

"So?"

"So you don't think that's strange?"

"I think he's in shock." I looked at Riley. He hadn't moved from his chair, wringing his hands together. His leg was still shaking. He had stumbled over a dead body, the same as Daphne and I had. Of course he was shaken up. I certainly was.

"He's lying," Daphne whispered.

"About what?"

"About why he came to see Tedd."

"How do you know?"

"I just know."

"You can't just know."

"I can see it in his eyes."

I could see it in her eyes too—the hint of curiosity. I shook my head. "I know him."

"How well do you know him?"

"I've met him a few times."

"Meeting him is not the same as knowing him," she said matter-of-factly.

"We live in the same town. I see him drive by. I know where he lives. I know him." I took a step back. "Who's on trial here?"

Riley let out a cough and we both turned. He was hacking gravel out of his mouth.

"The police can figure out if Riley is lying," I said, lowering my voice again. "It's none of my business."

Daphne let out a frustrated sigh. "It is your business. It happened at your motel."

"It's not my motel."

"Well, maybe not, but I can tell you care about it."

"You're wrong. I don't care."

Daphne didn't respond. She slid sideways onto the nearest barstool while I leaned on the bartop, a healthy distance between us as we waited. Waited for the police to arrive. Waited for Riley's memory to return. Waited for Logan to stop grumbling at the other end of the bar.

A minute passed.

"There's something else," Daphne said quietly. "Didn't Tedd live in town?"

I nodded.

"Well, was he married?"

I nodded again.

"It looks suspicious. A married man in a motel around the corner from his house."

"What do you mean?"

"Looks like infidelity."

I didn't want to defend Tedd Archer. I didn't care if he was sneaking around. I didn't care if Riley Dugdale was lying. I didn't even care if Daphne was a snoopy out-of-towner.

So I didn't know why I said what I said, but it was late and I was tired and I supposed the diamond on her hand had finally rubbed me the wrong way.

"I could say the same thing about you."

Her eyes widened in surprise and then settled into a green glare as she fingered the ring. I knew instantly that I had made a mistake. If there hadn't been a murder and if the police hadn't been on their way, she would have walked out of my bar right then and there.

Instead, she left me alone, finding her barstool next to Logan. She must have said something quietly to him because he looked at me with a drunken stare before spouting something in French, slurred and unfiltered.

It didn't matter. I hardly cared what Logan thought. I sat back down next to Riley, watching his leg shake. Daphne helped herself to a glass of water from the tap, sipping it like a stiff drink, leaving red lipstick marks around the rim. Besides the occasional groan from Logan, the bar was quiet. I could hear the clock above the kitchen door ticking as the minutes dragged by.

I have never been good at meeting new people. Exhibit A, of course, was Daphne. At first I had assumed she was Logan's latest love affair. But the ring, I had to admit, had taken me by surprise, although I wasn't exactly sure why. I didn't have to see the look on her face to know she was positively cheesed with me. Of course she was. I would be too.

Exhibit B: the unfamiliar man who walked through the door at precisely 2:15 a.m.

He had dark skin and broad shoulders. His thick eyebrows were hardly expressive; they didn't move at all when he talked. His whole face was weathered, like a soldier back from the battlefield, and he was dressed in a sleek black suit and tie. When he unbuttoned his suit, I caught a glimpse of a handgun in its holster.

He flashed his badge. "Detective Luther Maharmallo."

I'd had a few run-ins with the police, back in my salad days. The nearest city, Winnipeg, was over an hour away and, as such, the regional police force stationed in Pearl served the town and surrounding area.

But the detective was a new face. He introduced his uniformed sidekick, a sombre officer named Riggs. He had a matching gun and holster, a buzzing radio, and a pair of handcuffs all strapped to him like a ticking timebomb. I suspected the bomb would go off if any of us made the wrong move.

Needless to say, nobody moved, although two of us couldn't and the other two wouldn't. Logan didn't bother to look up from where he was resting his head on the bar. Daphne bothered, but all she did was sip her water. I couldn't tell if Riley was still soaked in whisky or if he was sweating profusely. It looked like the latter. As for myself, I remained firmly seated in my chair, hoping not to draw too much of the detective's attention.

"Which one of you is Neal Humphrey?"

So much for that.

I stood up. "That would be me."

"Come with me, please." Maharmallo motioned for me to follow him back outside.

The air had cooled significantly and a thick fog was settling in. As I stood next to the broad-shouldered detective, I realized that rapid fog and the cold weren't my only reasons for feeling chilled. I stuffed my hands in my pockets and glanced out into the parking lot, taking in Maharmallo's police cruiser, Logan's black Bentley, and a rusty old pickup that must have belonged to Riley.

Something crunched under Maharmallo's foot. He looked down. "Glass?"

"Logan broke a whisky bottle." I didn't feel like explaining it further and wasn't sure how much the detective needed—or wanted—to know.

"Logan." Maharmallo repeated the name with some bravado. "The dark-haired fellow at the bar?"

I nodded.

"Friend of yours?"

"Not really."

"You called about the body?"

I nodded again.

"You know him?"

"The body?"

"Yes."

"Tedd Archer. He was my landlord."

Maharmallo motioned to the crooked sign above the door. "You own the bar."

It wasn't a question. He didn't take a detective to figure out that a bar called Humphrey's belonged to a man called Humphrey. The sign itself needed replacing. It was falling off the iron rod above the doorframe. It didn't light up anymore.

"Whereabouts did you find him?"

"Room 7," I replied. "We saw the door was open and the light was on. We thought we'd check it out."

"We?"

"I was with Daphne. She's from out of town."

"Ah, the blonde."

Ah, indeed.

It was too dark and foggy to see all the way to Room 7, so Maharmallo stepped gingerly over the broken glass, motioning for me to follow him again. He started down the sidewalk to the furthest motel room.

"So you're not from around here either?"

Maharmallo shook his head. "Only arrived a couple weeks ago. Hardly had time to unpack," he said, almost under his breath. He neglected to say where he'd arrived from.

He eyed every window and door we passed, with one hand resting rather unsteadily on his holster.

"Tedd Archer was staying at the motel?"

I shrugged. "Apparently."

"What can you tell me about him?"

"Tedd and his wife have an antique shoppe in town, but he owns most of Pearl, like the diner and Rather Dapper—ah, that's the barbershop—and some other properties. He bought the motel two weeks ago. The reopening was last weekend."

The detective didn't scribble anything down in his notebook the way I imagined he might, although he seemed experienced enough. Likely he'd been trained to absorb and retain information like a sponge. He'd write it down later in some report.

Good grief, I suddenly thought to myself. I'd probably be in that report somewhere. Daphne and me. And poor Riley.

As we approached Room 7, Maharmallo stretched on a pair of blue latex gloves. The door was wide open, the way we'd left it, still creaking on its hinges. Somehow the fog made it even creepier.

He stepped inside and I waited in the doorway, though seeing Tedd's body for the second time wasn't quite as unnerving as the first.

"This is how you found it?" Maharmallo asked.

I nodded. I decided not to tell him about Daphne searching Tedd's wallet and the potential fingerprints she had left behind. Or footprints, for that matter.

Maharmallo knelt next to Tedd's body, carefully examining the bullet holes. They were more visible now that the blood had stopped oozing. There appeared to be two haphazard shots in Tedd's chest, but the shot in his forehead had hit dead centre.

After Maharmallo had gotten a thorough look, he got up and sifted through Tedd's belongings on the nightstand. He sniffed the empty glass. He opened the packet of chewing gum. He picked up the watch and set it down again. He pulled open the nightstand drawer, which was empty, except for a motel Bible. He checked the window, running his hand along the windowsill.

Great minds think alike, I thought to myself.

"Ah," was all he said.

Lastly, he opened the wardrobe, checking the pockets of Tedd's blazer and overcoat. His spent a lot of time looking at the overcoat, a leather trench coat of sorts, his fingers lingering on the foreign label. He then walked back to the doorway.

"Any idea who wanted him dead?" Maharmallo asked, ripping off his gloves and pocketing them.

"I don't know," I said.

"Do you know if he was wealthy?"

"Probably. He owned most of Pearl."

"His coat was handmade in Italy. Imported maybe."

I wondered what was so important about Tedd's coat being imported. It wasn't my business, I supposed.

"Why was he staying at the motel?" asked the detective.

I shrugged. I thought of Daphne's suspicion of infidelity but didn't mention it.

Maharmallo tried again. "You can't think of anyone who might have wanted him dead? Someone who held a grudge? Argued with him?"

I half-laughed. "This town worshipped Tedd Archer."

"What about you?"

"What about me?"

"Did you worship him?"

"Tedd? No." But I had replied rather quickly. Too quickly, I realized.

"What did you think of him?"

I hesitated. I thought about trying to backtrack, tread carefully, tell a white lie, but something about Maharmallo made me think he would figure it out sooner or later.

"I didn't like him." As I glanced outside, I could almost feel the thick fog settling on me, like snow on my shoulders, weighing me down. "Tedd Archer was kind of like fog. He was incredibly dense. He hung around like he was above everyone, better than the rest of us, and folks in Pearl believed it. You should see tomorrow's paper."

"I'd like to," Maharmallo said, "but I think you'll find that when a man like Tedd Archer is dead, the truth starts to surface."

"The truth?" I almost laughed again. "You don't know what it's like to live in a small town, do you?"

"Haven't the foggiest."

If it was his attempt at a witty joke, I couldn't tell. Maharmallo remained straight-faced. Then, for the first time since he had walked into the bar, his straight face fell away, replaced for a split second with a distracted expression. His eyebrows furrowed. His broad shoulders stiffened and released as he took in a stiff breath, like a shiver going through his spine. Then he was back, resting an unsteady hand on his holster. I wondered what had happened but thought better about asking. Maybe he had simply caught a chill. Maybe he wasn't used to the fog.

"Where did you say you were from again?" I asked.

"Vancouver." He turned and walked back to the bar, seeming to part the fog like the Red Sea.

3

HUMPHREY

Officer Riggs rounded up the motel guests, which, besides Daphne and the dead Tedd Archer, consisted of one man from Room 6. He had been staying for over a week. Obviously he wasn't scared of bedbugs or break-ins or dead cats.

He definitely wasn't scared of Riggs.

The bar door swung open and Riggs dragged the man, who was putting up quite a fight, by his elbow. He seemed to have dressed in a hurry, his shirt half-tucked as he fumbled with his Panama hat. He perched it on top of his head and tore his arm away from Riggs.

"Unhand me! Do you have any idea who I am?"

The bar fell quiet. He looked around and, seeing us, stood up straighter. He puffed out his chest and strutted towards Maharmallo like a rooster.

"Cosmo Clarke," he crowed. "Freelance reporter. You're probably familiar with my latest piece on polar bears. I spent six months up north writing it. I called it 'Prowler Bears.'" He flashed a toothy smile. "Extraordinary bears, really, and an extraordinary piece of writing, if I do say so myself. Published in fifty-two newspapers and magazines."

I, for one, had never heard of him or his piece on polar bears. From the unchanged look on the faces of Daphne and Riley, and the annoyed look on Logan's, I gathered neither had anyone else. Maharmallo's straight face was difficult to read.

"Fifty-two!" said the reporter. "Say, I just realized that's one for every week of the year."

Maharmallo ignored him. "Have a seat, Mr. Clarke."

"I'll take a seat, Detective, but don't ask me to remove my hat. Bed hair and all that. I'm still a bit train-lagged, I'm afraid, but then I didn't expect to be so rudely awakened." He shot a glare at Riggs. "I normally don't leave my room so shabbily dressed."

The longer I looked at him, the more difficult it was to believe he had spent six months anywhere with any bears. And the longer I thought of his name, the more I decided that Cosmo Clarke sounded like some sort of bad cocktail.

He seemed to notice Maharmallo was still ignoring him, so he perched on a nearby barstool with a dissatisfied grunt.

Outside, another car was pulling into the lot. The detective and his sidekick withdrew through the heavy door to meet it.

"Say, what's all this about?" Cosmo crowed.

Nobody answered him.

From my chair, I could see just enough to make out the yellow car. Two women, both familiar to me, were talking to Maharmallo and Riggs. The first was Madelaine Archer, Tedd's much younger wife. She seemed to have taken the news of his death remarkably well, without a single tear. She looked tired, dark circles formed under her eyes, but she wasn't so tired that she'd grown unattractive; that would be impossible. She had a classically pretty face and her brown hair fell to her collarbone, tucked partway into her long trench coat. As the detective spoke to her, she nodded slowly. I supposed he would need her to confirm that it was indeed Tedd's body in Room 7.

Beside her, the other woman looked as though she could be Madelaine's sister. She was in her twenties, maybe Riley's age, with a small nose and other delicate features. She too had brown hair, a similar shade to Madelaine's, but longer, and it was tied back with a trendy scarf. I recognized her as Madelaine's assistant. She worked at Archer's Antique Shoppe, but her name, although on the tip of my tongue, was lost to me.

Cosmo, becoming impatient, got up and strutted to the window. He cupped his hands around his face and peered outside.

"What's all this about?" he asked again.

I had a feeling Cosmo didn't like things that weren't about him.

The door opened and Riggs ushered Madelaine's assistant into the bar.

"Have a seat, Miss Grant," he said to her, motioning to a table.

Ah, that was it. Her name was Gwynn—Gwynn Grant. She picked the chair closest to me and slouched into it, so close that I could have reached out and touched her. I didn't, of course. She looked like she would rather be anywhere in the world but in my bar in the middle of the night.

I felt bad for her—that is, until I saw the look she exchanged with two of the other men in the room. The first was a cold stare towards Riley. She knew him, obviously, since they both worked at the antique shoppe, but the exchange appeared utterly unfriendly. The second involved Logan, who looked up immediately at the mention of her name and they locked eyes. If she was surprised to see him, she hid it well. Her cold gaze drifted around the room to Daphne and then, to my surprise, landed on me. I looked away as quickly as I could.

Finally, Maharmallo walked in with Madelaine and also motioned for her to have a seat. Riley stood up when he saw her, a little too quickly perhaps after his knock to the head, and he had to steady himself on the back of his chair.

"Maddy, I'm s–s–so sorry," he said, his eyes puffy and red. Either he was tearing up or his eyes were burning from the whisky.

Madelaine, smiling faintly, gave his arm a reassuring squeeze before settling into the chair next to Gwynn.

And so, a murder was afoot. Was that the saying? I didn't know. It certainly wasn't a saying my old man would have used. But something was afoot. Between Tedd's savagely shot body in Room 7 and the unlikely group gathered in my bar, it seemed like strange things did indeed happen at the motel. And I couldn't exactly disappear upstairs to my armchair and ignore it.

Officer Riggs took his place by the door while Maharmallo stood in the middle of the bar, focused on the group. Some of us were strangers, out-of-towners passing through town on business. Others were familiar with each other, but certainly not friends. I thought of the exchange between Gwynn and Logan. Perhaps some of us were more than friends. I didn't know. I didn't particularly care.

"Are you going to tell us what's going on?" Cosmo drawled, feigning nonchalance.

Maharmallo's face hardened. "I'm afraid a man has been murdered."

The freelancer sucked in a breath. "Murdered?"

"Mr. Tedd Archer. He was staying here at the motel in Room 7."

I glanced at Madelaine. She sat cross-legged, staring at her shoes. Even in the dimness of the bar, I could make out her large brown eyes and full round cheeks. A distinct scar under her left eye brushed upwards towards her temple, long and difficult to conceal, although she didn't seem particularly conscious of it.

"What happened?" Cosmo gasped.

"He was shot," Maharmallo replied. His voice seemed to bristle but he had no reason to be defensive. It wasn't as if he had shot Tedd Archer. It was highly unlikely anyway. I watched him inhale deeply and adjust his tie. "Did you meet him at any point during your stay, Mr. Clarke?"

"Cosmo will do." The freelance adjusted the hat, deep in thought—as deep as Cosmo Clarke could get. "As a matter of fact, I did meet the man. What was his name? Mr. Archer, you say?" No one responded. "I only met him once, outside the motel. He was wearing a wonderful overcoat. Full leather. I tried to ask him if it was vegan leather, but he was rather rude. Bit of an odd duck, no?"

Again, nobody said anything. All eyes seemed to fall on Madelaine, including Cosmo's.

"Say," he said suddenly, pointing. "His coat was just like that one."

Madelaine was fingering the lapel of her trench coat. I pictured her sitting like an old Hollywood movie star, legs crossed, smoking a thick Cuban cigar and imbibing a stiff drink. She might say her scripted line. She might make up her own. She looked perfectly indifferent, as if her husband hadn't just been murdered in cold blood.

She, in fact, didn't say anything.

To my surprise it was Riley who spoke, standing up again. "S–s–so what?"

Cosmo blinked. "So what? It was Italian leather, that's what! I've been in this drab town for a week and haven't seen a lick of sensible fashion until that odd duck and now this woman." He gestured towards Madelaine.

"That happens to be his w–w–wife."

"Fancy that! And what does that make you?"

But the outburst seemed to be all Riley had been able to muster and he collapsed back in his chair just as Maharmallo stepped between them.

"That'll be all, Mr. Clarke," the detective said, "unless you noticed something tonight that might be relevant."

"Cosmo, if you please." The freelancer held up a hand as he fumbled with his hat, tipping it forwards and then tilting his nose in the air. "And it just so happens that I did."

"What would that be?" Maharmallo asked.

"I heard voices in the next room."

"Room 7?"

Cosmo nodded sharply.

"When was this?"

"Sometime before midnight. I can't be sure when. I dozed off after."

"How many voices?"

"Two."

"Did it sound like they were arguing?"

"Not particularly, no."

"Men or women's voices?"

"Both men."

"You're sure?"

Cosmo cocked his head. "I'd smack the calfskin."

"Could one of the voices have been Tedd Archer's?"

"They were rather muffled."

"Then you couldn't hear what they were saying?"

"Afraid not, Detective. I stuck my ear against the wall and everything." Cosmo propped both elbows on the bartop behind him, proud as a peacock.

Finished with him, Maharmallo turned and gave a brief nod to Riggs, who was scribbling into a black book. Of course, I should have known. The best detectives had their sidekicks take notes for them.

"I want statements from each of you," Maharmallo said. "Once you've made your statement, you can go, but don't think about leaving town. Nobody talks about what happened tonight to anyone other than myself or Officer Riggs." He looked directly at Cosmo. "And we'll be searching all the motel rooms."

"Searching my room?" Cosmo exclaimed. "I don't think that's necessary."

Maharmallo seemed unbothered. "A man has been murdered, Mr. Clarke. Your cooperation is both necessary and appreciated, but if you like, Officer Riggs can return with a warrant."

The thought of Riggs manhandling his room must have horrified Cosmo, for he conceded.

"All right. You can search my room, Detective, but I'll have to tidy up a bit first. Not that I have anything to hide, of course. It's just that I'm a messy traveller, which is rather embarrassing to admit because I'm such a fabulous dresser." He flashed his toothy smile before realizing his shirt was still half-untucked. "Goodness! I suppose this is what happens when a man is awakened in the small hours of the morning—either he's murdered or might as well have been."

He stood up and strutted past Riggs with an indignant look.

Nearly everyone had left. From the window, I watched Daphne help a grumbling Logan into the passenger seat of his Bentley, apparently driving him home. I didn't know how she would be getting back to the motel. Maybe she would spend the night at Logan's. I supposed it was none of my business.

Cosmo Clarke was back in Room 6, probably sound asleep, while Madelaine Archer had left in her yellow car without shedding so much as a tear.

Riley Dugdale was now the last to leave. He had just finished giving his statement and I watched him rub the back of his head while he talked to Riggs, probably telling Maharmallo's sidekick what had happened outside with Logan and the whisky bottle.

As Riley left, Riggs scribbled down his last few notes in the corner booth. Outside I heard the young man's pickup rumble as he started it. I glanced out the window just in time to see the truck pull away, with someone in the passenger seat: none other than Gwynn Grant.

Of course, I assumed Gwynn, being Madelaine's assistant, had driven to the motel with Madelaine, but if she had come with Riley, she would have been at the motel all along. It seemed strange, especially considering the cold stare she had given Riley in the bar.

I watched the pickup drive off, unsure what to make of it.

And then there were two.

"Humphrey."

I turned to Maharmallo, who slid onto a barstool. "That paper you mentioned … could I see it?"

I looked around for Logan's copy of the *Gazette*, finding it at the sidebar. I handed it over to the detective. He scanned the front page and the article.

"So the great Tedd Archer, your town hero, is gunned down in his own motel."

"Something like that," I said.

"The two of you didn't get along?"

"Not really, no."

"What happened?"

"We had a disagreement over a leaky sink."

"How big of a disagreement?"

I shrugged. "I didn't sign my new lease."

Maharmallo nodded slowly. "Did you know him before he bought the motel?"

"Everyone knows everyone in Pearl."

"Tedd knew his murderer," Maharmallo said. "Whoever it was, he opened the door for them in the middle of the night. And they must have known he was staying at the motel." He folded the newspaper. "What do you think about Riley Dugdale?"

"I don't know that much about him," I admitted. "He works at the antique shoppe. As far as I know, the Archers and Dugdales have been family friends for years."

"Ah." Maharmallo nodded. "What about Cosmo Clarke?"

"I've never heard of him before today."

"Neither have I. I feel blessed, don't you?"

Both of us laughed a little. Tired laughs.

Maharmallo folded his arms on the bar. He seemed to be eyeing the place with the same careful scrutiny as he had the rest of the motel. I tried to see the bar the way he saw it—worn out and rundown, of course. It had never looked new, not even when I had been young, my clumsy feet pitter-pattering upstairs. The noise from below would travel through the thin floorboards until midnight and I would try to sleep, but I never could. I would stare at the cracked ceiling, listening to the wind whistle through the window and watching my mother read in the old armchair. If I closed my eyes, I could still see her. She was curled up with a pair of slippers on reading an old Raymond Chandler novel. She was always reading Chandler.

"Humphrey."

I opened my eyes.

"Where were you at midnight?" Maharmallo asked.

I motioned to the bar. "Here. I close at midnight."

"Was it busy?"

"Busy for a Wednesday."

"When did Logan Griffith show up?"

"Around eleven-thirty."

"Is he a regular?"

I nodded.

"He showed up with Daphne?"

I nodded again.

"Both of them were here until midnight?"

I nodded, then remembered Logan leaving to find Daphne's room key. "Actually, Logan left briefly, just after midnight. He went to get Daphne's key from his car."

"How long was he gone?"

I paused, feeling a little uneasy. "I don't know."

"If you had to guess?"

"Ten, maybe fifteen minutes."

"That long?"

I shook my head. "Maybe less."

"How did he seem when he came back?"

"I don't know. Normal. A little drunk."

A little drunk was normal for Logan, after all.

"And then you and Daphne went for a midnight stroll?"

Another pause. "It wasn't like that. I was helping her. There was a dead cat in her room."

Maharmallo's formerly stiff eyebrows shot up. "A dead cat?"

"Long story short, this motel is a dump." I let out a sigh. "That's why I didn't want to sign the lease."

"Was Tedd Archer angry that you wouldn't sign?"

EMILY B. KERROS

"I don't know," I replied. "He didn't give me a lot of time to look it over. He said he had somewhere else to be, and then he never came back."

"Did you argue with him?"

"I wouldn't say argue, exactly." I swallowed, my throat suddenly feeling dry. I couldn't remember the last time I'd had anything to drink, or eat. Probably before my shift, which had ended hours ago. I was tired. I was thirsty. I needed a drink of water, or really anything at this point. Beggars couldn't be choosers. Coffee. Whisky. Although I didn't particularly care for either.

Daphne had left her lipstick-stained glass of water at the end of the bar, but I didn't dare move. I could feel Maharmallo eyeing me. I wondered briefly if the detective drank. The shakiness I had noticed earlier, the jitters in the shoulders and unsteady hands, however quickly it passed … I had seen it with alcoholics. But surely a career detective wouldn't have a drinking problem.

"I need your help, Humphrey."

"I'm sorry?"

"You're right. I don't know what it's like to live in a small town. How am I supposed to unravel the lies and gossip from the truth?"

"You're a detective. Isn't that your job?"

"Ah. But I feel a little like an outsider here. Pearl is a lot different than Vancouver."

I had no doubt. Still, something didn't seem right.

"What are you saying?" Even my voice sounded dry.

"How long have you lived in Pearl?"

I shrugged. "Unfortunately, my whole life."

"You understand it. You see through the fog, so to speak."

He wasn't exactly wrong.

"And you're a bartender. You must hear things."

"I didn't overhear a plan to murder Tedd Archer, if that's what you mean."

"Maybe not tonight," the detective conceded. "But like I said, the truth will start to surface. And when it does, I want someone who knows Pearl inside-out and backwards."

"You want me to be your spy?"

"Just let me know if you see or hear anything."

"Why me?"

38

"Why not you?"

He was serious. He wanted me to eavesdrop on townsfolk at the bar. He wanted my opinion on them. He trusted my instincts. Or did he? Was it some sort of trap? What if this was his way of keeping me close, all because he thought I had murdered Tedd Archer, my landlord, over a pathetic leaky sink? Sure, I had been frustrated with Tedd, but maybe I hadn't hidden my frustration as well as I thought.

"I'm not interested in being a spy," I said.

He let it go. "I get it. You're not interested in the truth."

It wasn't a question.

He slid off his barstool, buttoning his suit jacket. Then he noticed the stack of books on the backbar. "You're a reader, Humphrey."

Another non-question. He already knew the answer.

"What's your poison?" he asked.

"Raymond Chandler," I replied when I realized we were still talking about books.

"Ah." He reached into his pocket, found his dirty latex gloves, and then searched through the other. He came up empty. "I seem to have misplaced my cards. I'll have Riggs stop by tomorrow with one. You can call the number if you think of anything else." He walked towards the door before turning to bid goodnight. With one look at the clock, he corrected himself. "Or should I say good day."

Hello, Neal.

I could almost hear my mother greet me at the top of the stairs. She used to wait for me as I climbed the narrow steps, exhausted after a shift, my back and shoulders sore from all the repeated motions. I had only been eighteen then, barely starting out. Learning the tricks of the trade hadn't come without growing pains. She'd rub my shoulders and tease me about my tousled hair, always a mess. It was the same colour as her hair, not blonde and not brown, but somewhere boring and in-between. Mine was, anyway. It didn't look so boring on her.

I recalled a picture on my bookshelf of the two of us. It had come to mind almost as soon as Maharmallo had exited the bar, the memory of her reading Chandler had resurfaced at the mention of "my poison." The detective, I supposed, was unaware that that particular poison was inherited.

I almost tripped over the landing before fumbling with the door and flicking on the light. I kicked off my shoes, feet sore, and looked around sleepily, my eyelids so heavy they might've closed any second.

The cramped loft-style apartment above the bar was also dimly lit, particularly at night. It had one large window and then a smaller window by the fire escape, both of which allowed for a lot of natural light during the day. Two bookshelves bracketed the large window, each one filled with books and overflowing into piles on the floor. The old armchair was nestled among the piles, upholstered in brown leather and patched in several places where the leather was softened and worn through.

I had lived above the bar my entire life. Our family of three, crammed into the tiny space, had somehow made it work. Only barely, now that I thought about it. There was a small kitchen and living room and bathroom, with no defined space for a bed. As such, I had spent most of my childhood on a fold-up cot in the corner where the tin roof met at a peak. It was there that I was tucked into bed while my mother would curl up with a book in the old armchair across the room, waiting for my old man.

My old man and my mother had been an unequivocally bad match. It had been that way right from the start, I assumed, though I obviously hadn't been around to spectate. But the entire town had known from the get-go. My mother—a Vancouver native, strangely enough—had been whisked away to Pearl when she'd married my old man. But her love of fiction … no, her love of crime fiction … had followed her. It was every bit a part of her.

And her collection of Raymond Chandler's seven hardboiled novels had been her unrivalled favourites. As such, she'd never minded waiting up for my old man as long as she had a book to read. As long as she had her armchair.

Besides her collection of poison, the armchair was the only thing she had taken with her from Vancouver. It had belonged to my granddad, who had passed long before I was born.

"Neal," she'd say to my ten-year-old self, "if anything ever happens to me, the armchair is yours. Your granddad would've wanted you to have it."

My mother was the only one who ever called me Neal. Sure, I had been Neal as a kid. Even, I recalled, as a teenager. But everything had changed the year I turned eighteen. After my old man left me the bar, everyone gradually began calling me Humphrey. Humphrey owned Humphrey's bar, after all. It was easier for them. And it was easier for me not to correct anyone.

My old man had always threatened to leave. But his threats, most of the time, were empty. He often threatened to throw us onto the street. He'd say the loft was too crowded. He'd say he never should have taken my mother out of Vancouver. He'd yell until he was red in the face. Sometimes he would count the cash from the register and say there wasn't enough to get by; in fact, we'd all be living on the street. Sometimes he would threaten to pour all the whisky down the drain. But he couldn't have done it if he'd tried.

And so, on one especially bad day, after he threatened to leave us, we didn't think much of it. My shift ended and I climbed upstairs, greeted warmly by my mother. A shoulder rub and off to bed. It was no life for an eighteen-year-old, barely finished high school, though I hadn't known it at the time.

My old man hosted poker nights, which had evolved to be loud, weekly affairs. The group of local men had slowly become larger, more unsavoury, and the drinks had become stronger. If I felt pressure to join in, I ignored it. I was too much like my mother in that respect; a book was always preferrable. She always waited up, though, until my old man would come stumbling up the stairs at the end of the night, blindly drunk, only to awaken the next morning a much richer or poorer man.

But one fateful night, he hadn't stumbled up the stairs.

We found him the next morning, passed out in the parking lot, tires marks across his back. He was dead. A poorer man, indeed.

The police had ruled it an unfortunate accident. Intoxicated, my old man had passed out outside the bar … and perhaps one of his poker players, more than likely drunk himself, had run him over. They asked us questions. Who frequented his poker nights? What time did it usually finish? How much money was on the table? None of which we knew the answers to. The only thing we knew was that my old man had finally made good on one of his threats. He was gone. He had left us.

They never called it a suspicious death, but Pearl was a small town. Word got around. At first, townsfolk were simply concerned about our loss.

Friends dropped off flowers. The mayor baked a pie. We had a service at the church and buried my old man in the cemetery, next to his old man and the one before that. I told myself I wouldn't end up in that line. In fact, I was bound and determined not to.

But my old man, to my eternal shock, had left me Humphrey's. I supposed the bar had been in the family for generations, so it was only logical for him to pass it on to me. I hadn't wanted it, the same as he, in all likelihood, hadn't wanted to give it to me. But he hadn't had any other children and hardly any other family, and his sudden death had occurred before anyone better had come along. Still, I had only just begun to learn the ins and outs of running a bar and, despite my mother's help and encouragement, I found myself struggling to stay afloat.

The rumours started only days after the funeral. From my newly minted position behind the bar, I overheard more conversations than I wanted to. It wasn't until the conversations shifted from my old man to my mother that I began to pay attention. Rumour had it she had "offed him," arranged an accidental death, inspired by her armchair reading. Certain rumours even implied that she had driven over him herself, finally freeing herself of his binge-drinking and petty gambling.

It wasn't true, of course. The police hadn't suspected her, not for an instant. His death had been nothing short of a drunken incident. But no man had ever come forward to admit his guilt.

It wasn't long before my mother heard the rumours. She was brave at first, holding her head high, waiting for the rumours to blow over. But they never did. Eventually she holed herself up in the loft. She couldn't live with the speculation, the scrutiny. She missed the city. She missed the mountains. She had begged me to go with her, but Vancouver wasn't my home. The only home I had ever known was the loft above the bar.

When she finally left, she made her dear friend Seth promise to take care of me. But the chef had never had a son of his own. If he couldn't turn me into one of his specialty sauces, then he hardly knew what to do. I hardly knew what to do with myself.

My mother's sister, Aunt Margot, had taken her in. She'd been there ever since. We were long overdue for a phone call, I supposed, though I was prone to being sentimental when I was tired.

I found the picture on the shelf, the one of my mother and me, and fingered the frame. Whenever I looked at it, I felt like I was looking at someone else entirely. I hardly recognized the young man. He was much taller than she was and had striking blue eyes, bright and happy. She gazed up at him, thirty years his senior, but with her young features she could have passed as his sister. Both of us looked happy, the candid moment captured at the time by a wannabe photographer.

I missed her.

Sometimes I even missed the wannabe photographer, though I didn't like to admit it.

I collapsed in the armchair, too tired to make it to the bed all the way across the loft. The bed was still unmade and the closet was open, revealing a row of short and long-sleeved Henleys, my bartending uniform of sorts.

I leaned back and closed my eyes …

… and only opened them when I heard a car start outside. I peered out the window at the parking lot down below and watched Maharmallo's police cruiser disappear down the dirt road into town.

You're not interested in the truth.

His words kept repeating in my head. It was the way he had phrased it—not as a question, but as fact—that bothered me. I didn't know what to think about Maharmallo. He seemed like a good enough detective, smart and thorough, but something seemed off. After all, why would an experienced detective from a big city like Vancouver end up settling in a place like Pearl? He probably thought of me as nothing more than a lonely, disgruntled bartender who disliked his town and everyone in it. Which wouldn't have necessarily been wrong.

Or worse, maybe he thought of me as Tedd's murderer. I could see it all now—me seated across from him in a bare white room. He would slam a heavy fist on the table. "Well, well, well, if it isn't the bartender who hated his landlord. Hated him enough to murder him, I should think. Shot him in the head and left him for dead. As a matter of fact, Humphrey, you don't really seem to like anyone, do you? Except for that author of yours … what was the name? Ah yes, Raymond Chandler. Rogue, hardboiled fiction. Murder mysteries, no less! That's it—plain and simple."

Good grief. He thought I was guilty.

Neal.

I thought of my mother sitting in the armchair. I pictured her gentle smile. Heard her voice. Felt her hands wrap around my sore shoulders. Even after everything she had gone through, she would have been interested in the truth. Wouldn't she want me to be too?

I stared at her old Chandler books, their colourful spines on the top shelf. I supposed I wasn't unlike Philip Marlowe, Chandler's private eye. Pearl was my seedy Los Angeles, and the bar was my lonely apartment. Unlike Marlowe, though, I was not a private eye. How did I search for the truth if I didn't know where to begin?

Neal. You know how.

I stood and picked a book from the top shelf, flipping through its well-read pages. It was practically in my blood. My mother had started reading Chandler to me at a young age, even back when my classmates had been reading chapter books. And when I was old enough, I had read Chandler on my own. She'd left them here, her favourite books, on the top shelf where only I could reach.

Top shelf. For the best booze and the best books.

Ah, I knew how. I was no Sherlock. I had no impressive skills in deduction. All I had was myself—alone, hard-up, bitter, and maybe a little too far gone. I was Marlowe through and through. And it hadn't mattered to Marlowe if the victim was a stuffy, stuck-up rich man or a greedy gangster. All that had mattered was the truth. He'd found it even when he didn't want to.

The truth always matters, Neal.

It had mattered once to me. My eighteen-year-old self had tried to figure who had run over my old man. I thought, of course, that if I found him, then my mother could return to Pearl and live happily. The police had said the man was likely a local, probably one of the men who attended my old man's poker nights. Yet I had deduced on my own that the tire treads seemed to match those of the police cruisers that drove around town. And there was only one police officer who my old man had been friendly with.

It had been Logan's idea to hunt him down. We hadn't had any desire to ruin a man's career, but justice needed to prevail. We would threaten him, turn the tables, force him to admit to his mistake. Once the townsfolk caught wind of it, my mother would be home free.

Logan had told me his hunting rifle was only supposed to be used for emergencies. He'd gotten it from his cousin who hunted big game, but his possession of the rifle had been unknown to his parents. Logan, being Logan, had come up with a foolproof plan to hide the weapon, buried underground in a fake grave. He hadn't had any use for it, until that fateful night, although retrieving it had attracted some unexpected attention. The lengths we had gone to for the truth ... only to fail ...

I still wondered if it had been worth it.

I put my mother's book back on the shelf. Maharmallo was wrong. Maybe I didn't particularly like Pearl, but I *was* interested in the truth, especially since Tedd's death had nothing to do with me. And once I proved that, I could go back to my lonely little life—my books and my armchair and my bottomless bar.

4

MRS. ARCHER

I woke up in the armchair. Sunlight filtered through the window as I stretched myself awake. I showered, dressed, and scarfed down a hastily fried egg before ducking down the stairs.

I left through the back door, startling a black stray by the dumpster. It scampered off as I walked through the alley behind the motel. I shoved my hands in my pockets, passing—and thoroughly avoiding—the large tarp-covered heap. There was a car under the tarp, another hand-me-down from my old man, parked in the alley for years. It was likely littered with strays. If not strays, probably field mice.

I knew the rumours, of course. That I didn't have a driver's license. That I could never get one. Pearl's townsfolk simply assumed it was one too many DUIs, and I had never bothered to correct anyone. But the truth was that the car wasn't mine and never had been. It had belonged to my old man, a classic Shelby fastback he had restored with his old man. He had only given me the keys on occasion and never willingly, never without endless warnings and precautions: "Don't scratch the paint" or "I just waxed the tires; don't go getting them dusty." Sometimes I wondered if he had loved the car more than me.

And anyway, I preferred to walk.

It wasn't a long walk down the dirt road into town. I did it all the time, rain or shine. It only took twenty minutes, half that if I put some effort into it and even less if I used the shortcut that helped me dodge most of Main Street.

The sidewalks on either side of Main Street were made of an unappealing brick, which over time had faded into a burnt red. On hot summer days, it reminded me of scorching desert sand. Tall lampposts ran along the sidewalk, looking like something out of a classic film, although I had yet to feel the urge to swing around one with an umbrella.

I took one of my usual shortcuts through the alley behind Rather Dapper and stopped under the awning of Bartel's Used Books. The owner, Bartel Smith, relied mostly on second-hand books, of course, but he also carried a small section of new titles, one of which was his own self-published memoir, *Born in a Bookstore*. I wasn't sure whether the title was literal, but according to Bartel it was a store bestseller. A bestseller that was somehow always stacked in untouched piles by the window.

I looked at the little bench under the awning, a welcoming reading nook even though I preferred my armchair. It just so happened that the bookstore was directly across the street from Archer's Antique Shoppe. The shoppe itself was an antique, constructed with a tastefully preserved brick and mortar, and it didn't appear to be open. The interior looked dark and the sign on the door was flipped to CLOSED even though it was well after nine o'clock.

Of course no one was there. Tedd Archer had just been murdered, after all, and it would be far from business as usual. I thought about sitting there, under the awning, watching to see if Madelaine Archer or Riley Dugdale eventually showed up. It seemed like something Marlowe would do. Observe. Listen. Wait.

"Humphrey?"

The door of the bookstore jingled open. I turned to find Bartel Smith himself. He was an old man, almost eighty, with a pointy nose and big ears.

"Humphrey?" He shielded his eyes from the bright morning sun. "Is that you?"

I didn't bother telling him that it was indeed me.

"I finally found that Chandler book," he said, figuring it out on his own. "I've been holding on to it for you."

"Is it *Playback*?" I asked, already knowing the answer.

"Huh?" He fiddled with his hearing aid.

"*Playback*," I said again, louder.

He looked down at the book in his hand and shook his head.

Out of the corner of my eye, I caught a glimpse of something moving across the street. One of the rocking chairs in the window of the antique shoppe was moving, as though something—more likely, someone—had bumped it.

"Bart, did you see anyone go into Archer's this morning?"

"Huh?"

"There." I pointed. "Has anyone been in or out?"

The old man looked confused, but I didn't have time to explain. I left him standing there, fiddling with his hearing aid as I jaywalked across the street.

I tried the door of the shoppe and found it locked. I peered at the window display: antique mirrors, authentic Griffiths whisky barrels, and half-price Persian prayer rugs—the big spring sale. I stared at the rocking chair, still swaying back and forth. Someone was inside. I knew it.

I went back to the door and knocked, patiently at first and then harder.

The door opened a crack. A pair of cold eyes stared back at me. "What do you want?"

I recognized the eyes. They belonged to Gwynn Grant, of course, and from the sounds of it she wasn't thrilled to see me.

"I'm looking for Mrs. Archer," I said.

"Madelaine's not here."

She tried to close the door, but I moved quickly, shoving my foot between the door and the frame. She slammed the door twice, rather force-fully, on my foot. When she realized I wasn't budging, she stepped back.

"We're closed," she hissed. "Go away."

"I have some questions about what happened last night."

She tried to slam the door again and this time I couldn't help but flinch. I hoped she hadn't noticed.

"It must be horrible," I said. "Tedd being murdered, I mean."

She laughed a petulant sort of laugh. "Tedd was horrible. I don't miss him."

I shouldn't have been surprised. I hadn't liked Tedd, of course, but I wasn't used to hearing others speak poorly of him. Sure, there had been the incident with the nanny, but even that had blown over in a matter of days.

"Why?" I asked. "What did he do?"

"He thought I was stealing stuff."

"Stealing?"

She looked me up and down and swore. "You're tall."

"I don't mean to be."

"You're a friend of Logan Griffith's?"

I shrugged. "I don't mean to be that either."

She laughed at that, bitterly this time, and then let me in.

I hadn't been inside Archer's Antique Shoppe since Madelaine's previous sales assistant, a pushy professional who'd commuted from out of town, had tried to sell me a stylish armchair in perfect condition. Apparently she figured my current armchair was worthless and should have long ago been heaved into a dumpster. Needless to say, I hadn't bought anything that day.

Gwynn, in a somewhat strange way, was the opposite of pushy. As soon as she let me in, she seemed to disappear, swallowed up inside the shoppe, which was stacked to the roof with antiques. I tried to follow her, squeezing past a dozen half-price Persian rugs, all rolled up and leaning against each other. There was a large wooden trunk in the middle of the shoppe stacked with old wireless radios, their antennas poking out in all directions.

"So Tedd thought you were stealing?" I called out, unable to see her. Every now and then I saw her brown hair bobbing up and down as she manoeuvred through the chaos.

"He threatened to fire me. As if."

"But he didn't?"

"Madelaine stopped him."

"What do you think of her?" I asked just as I knocked over a stack of vinyl records.

She stopped amidst a forest of tall switch lamps. She turned, backtracking through the lamps, and stared at the mess I had made. She started sliding records back into the covers, not necessarily the right ones.

"I adore Madelaine," she said firmly. "I would never steal from her."

I helped her clean up the rest of the records. We stacked them in a precarious pile and then I followed her further into the shoppe. After dodging two carts full of novels, comic books, and dog-eared classics that would give Bartel a run for his money, we reached the counter, where Gwynn resumed tagging a vintage luggage set. I pressed a key on a nearby piano. It was badly out of tune.

"Did you see Tedd at all yesterday?" I asked.

"He stopped in around lunch."

"Do you have an alibi for last night?"

"I already told the detective."

"I saw you leaving the motel with Riley."

Gwynn scowled. "So what's wrong with that? We worked late and went out after for a few drinks. We're not friends. He just owed me one."

So they weren't friends, but she seemed awfully defensive about it.

I tried a few more keys, each one sounding even more painful than the one before, like it was out of tune on purpose, something out of a horror film.

"Where did you go?" I asked.

"Pope's." She fixed me with a cold glare. Pope's was a bar on Main Street, the third bar in town. "Will you stop that?"

I ignored the not-so-subtle jab, both at her choice of bar and my piano playing. "Why did Riley make a pitstop at the motel?"

"Tedd borrowed something from him and he wanted it back."

"Did he say what it was?"

Gwynn shook her head. "Only that he wouldn't be able to sleep if he didn't get it."

Riley had also mentioned the thefts from the shoppe, and he had seen Tedd stop in around lunch. Their stories seemed to be consistent. But if they were each other's alibis, then that was no surprise.

"Did Tedd say what was stolen?"

She shrugged. "I overheard him talking about a typewriter. I don't know what else."

I peered around the counter, behind which were two closed doors. One of them, half-hidden by a rack of vintage postcards, had an old-fashioned nameplate that read *Tedd Archer*. It must have been his office.

"Is Riley coming in today?"

Gwynn laughed. "I doubt it. He'll take any excuse for a day off."

"He did seem a little shaken up."

"Shaken up? No, Riley's just a couch potato. He didn't like Tedd any more than I did."

I was beginning to wonder if anyone liked Tedd Archer. So far he didn't seem to be very popular with his employees. Was this what Maharmallo had meant by the truth starting to surface?

"Do you like your job?" I asked.

Gwynn's face pulled into a frown. At first I thought she wasn't going to answer, but then she shrugged and said, "I guess so. I mean, I adore Madelaine, but someday I'd like to live in the city. I don't want to be stuck in Pearl forever."

She was referring to Winnipeg, dubbed "the city" by Pearl's townsfolk. And I understood how she felt. Being stuck in Pearl forever sounded like a nightmare.

She led me back through the maze and then unlatched the lock to let me out. I turned to thank her, but she spoke first.

"By the way, Humphrey, I'm not interested."

I blinked. "Interested in what?"

"Don't think I didn't notice you gawking at me last night."

Gawking? Had I gawked? I didn't remember gawking. But before I had a chance to say anything, the door slammed behind me and I was back on the street with my hands in my pockets. Finding my inner Marlowe was going to be a little harder than I thought.

The Archers lived uptown, on Lilac Lane, aptly named for its lilac trees that elegantly lined both sides of the street in full bloom. It was a neat neighbourhood and the Archers' house was the tallest on the block, with a white picket fence, immaculate lawn, and at least two lilac trees in the front yard alone.

Madelaine's yellow car was parked in the driveway, meaning she was likely home. I lifted the heavy doorknocker, no doubt a priceless antique, and knocked it against the door.

I knocked again, but there was no answer.

The door opened just as I was about to leave.

"Hullo?"

It was the Archers' five-year-old son, a boy much smaller than I would expect a five-year-old to be. He stared up at me with big round eyes, brown like Madelaine's. In fact, he was the spitting image of his mother. Perhaps the only thing he had inherited from his father was his name: Tedd Archer Junior, or Teddy for short. He was wearing a navy-blue T-shirt, his forearms

EMILY B. KERROS

covered in bruises of a similar colour. It wasn't until I really looked at him that I noticed the side of his face was bruised too, and quite badly. It looked fresh, maybe two or three days old, just beginning to turn deeper shades of purple.

"Who are you?" He was holding a stuffed animal by the leg, dangling it at me. I couldn't tell what it was. A bear. Maybe a monkey.

I knelt next to him. "Neal Humphrey. Is your mom around?"

"I'm not supposed to talk to strangers. I thought you were Wiley."

"Ah," I replied, somewhat confused.

Just then, someone ran up behind the boy. "Teddy!"

It was the boy's nanny, a young woman, little more than twenty, named Agnes Swope. She was the granddaughter of the Archers' next-door neighbours and as such had gotten the job rather by default. The rumours about Agnes and Tedd Archer were not the kind one might expect, such as an illicit affair. It was rather simple. Tedd, in a fit of rage, had one day thrown a kitchen knife at her, missing her by a long shot but shattering Madelaine's treasured antique wine cabinet. Rumour had it he'd been fed up with the nanny, who was prone to being somewhat ditzy, but he had apologized and the whole thing had blown over in a few days.

Although if I had been Madelaine or Agnes, I wasn't sure I would have been so forgiving.

The young nanny reached for Teddy, pulling him back by his shoulders.

"You're cute," she said, giggling at me as her cheeks blushed. "You kind of look like Riley, but Riley has curly hair. Curly hair is cuter."

I didn't know what to say. "You must be Agnes."

She giggled again. "Yes."

I didn't know what was so funny. Poor girl had a giggling habit.

"Is Mrs. Archer home?" I asked.

"Yes." More giggling.

"Can you let her know Humphrey is here to see her?"

She battered her eyelashes at me. "That's a funny name."

"So is Agnes, if you think about it."

She didn't giggle at that. She tucked a strand of dark hair behind her ear. "You ... you're making fun of me."

"Uh-uh. Mrs. Archer?"

"In the kitchen," she pouted, but she pointed me in the right direction.

She dragged Teddy off, somewhat reluctantly, as he carried the stuffed animal behind him. A dog? No, I was fairly sure it was a rabbit. Perhaps with an ear missing.

The kitchen was beautiful and modern, with crisp white walls and lots of natural light, the sun bouncing off the polished gold hardware. It was completely spotless, except for the hints here and there of a resident five-year-old. There was a half-eaten banana in the fruit bowl. On the windowsill rested a pot holding a bean plant, decorated with coloured markers and a pair of googly eyes. Another crafty masterpiece was displayed on the fridge: a drawing of three stick people and, as I suspected, a one-eared rabbit.

I spotted the wine cabinet, Madelaine's prized antique, tucked in the corner of the room. It was fairly tall, with refurbished glass doors and a polished latch between them. If Tedd had indeed damaged it in a fit of rage, it seemed to have been repaired flawlessly.

I wasn't exactly sure what I had expected to find at the Archers' house, but it certainly wasn't Madelaine, the old Hollywood movie star, seated on a barstool with her bare feet propped up on the kitchen island. She didn't belong in the room. She was dressed in a fluffy bathrobe—perhaps I had called on her too early?—and was drinking from the biggest wine glass I had ever seen, especially before noon. It was already half-empty, although I supposed it was five o'clock somewhere.

"Mrs. Archer?"

"Humphrey?"

"Sorry to bother you at home." I wasn't really sorry. It was just something to say.

She blinked at me, unchanged from the night before, still indifferent to her husband's murder, refusing to play the part of a grieving widow.

She didn't look tired anymore. The dark circles under her eyes were gone. She looked surprisingly well-rested and was even more attractive in the daylight, despite the long scar I'd noticed at the bar.

She took a sip of wine as if it was a typical Thursday brunch. She had the decency to lower her feet from the island, crossing one leg over the other as she leaned back. She might as well have had a string of pearls and elbow-length gloves, blowing smoke rings in the air.

"What are you doing here?" she asked.

"I just have a few questions about last night."

"The detective already talked to me."

"Ah. Maharmallo is thorough."

She swirled her wine around. "Have you taken up sleuthing?"

"Something like that." I managed a nervous laugh. "How are you doing?"

"I'm fine, Humphrey. Peachy." She took a sip of wine.

"Do you have an alibi for midnight?"

"Depends what you call an alibi."

"What did you tell Maharmallo?"

"That my alibi is my five-year-old who was sound asleep."

She seemed to be wary of me, not that I blamed her. We didn't really know each other. Not personally anyhow. She was Madelaine Archer, Tedd's young business-minded wife who ran an antique shoppe, and I was a bartender at a bar she never drank at. Evidently, she drank at home.

"I was just at your shoppe," I said. "Gwynn mentioned there have been some thefts."

"Hmmm." She took another sip.

"And Tedd accused her of stealing."

Her lips curled, almost into a smile. "Gwynn is no thief."

"Is that what you told Tedd?"

She nodded slowly.

"Did you argue about it?"

"We argued about lots of things. Do you want a list?"

"A list of the missing antiques might be helpful."

She looked at me, blinking her big eyes. "You think you're helping me?"

"Don't you want to know who murdered your husband?"

She pursed her lips. "I can't pretend to care."

I thought that she very well could.

"Aren't you afraid you might be next?" I asked.

"Why would I be? I wasn't mixed up in his affairs."

"What affairs?"

"How should I know? I wasn't mixed up in them."

"Do you know what he borrowed from Riley Dugdale?"

I watched her swirl her glass, contemplating her last sip. "Tedd wasn't the borrowing type."

"What type was he?"

She hesitated. "The type that takes."

"So you think he took something from Riley?"

"I don't know, Humphrey. I really don't." She stood up, taking her glass with her, cradling it in her arm. She wandered over to the window and stared out at the back yard, where Agnes was pushing Teddy on a rope swing.

I moved closer to her. "Why was Tedd staying at the motel? Why wasn't he home?"

Slowly, her indifference withered away. I watched her eyes, fixed on Teddy, as she tried unsuccessfully to fight back tears. A single tear trickled down her face, then more followed. They weren't sad tears, but angry tears.

"He hurt Teddy."

That was it. Something had happened to Teddy. She had pretended to be indifferent, but she couldn't be. She hadn't loved her husband. She hadn't even cared about him.

I glanced sideways at the drawing on the fridge, picturing Teddy's bruised face. He was just a boy. Small. Helpless. Big doe eyes like his mother. He deserved the happy family in his drawing.

I looked back at Madelaine, her angry tears subsiding as quickly as they'd come, and I couldn't help but wonder just how angry she really was. Was she angry enough to murder her husband?

"I'm sorry, Mrs. Archer," I said, almost in a whisper.

She wiped a tear from her face and downed the last of her wine in one gulp. She set her glass on the island with a shaky clatter, then mustered every ounce of composure she had left. Which as it turned out was quite a bit.

"Mrs. Archer died with Tedd. You can call me Madelaine."

Madelaine's next-door neighbour happened to be Pearl's mayor, Cynthia McNally, who also happened to be the grandmother of the Swope sisters, the oldest of which was Agnes. Cynthia and Madelaine had become fast friends when Madelaine first moved in. It had started with friendly chats over the fence, then chats over wine. When Madelaine was pregnant with Teddy,

Cynthia had been the first person to know. Madelaine didn't have any family in Pearl, but Cynthia felt like family.

The problem was that Cynthia wasn't exactly known for being tight-lipped. The whole town had known that Madelaine was having a baby, probably before Tedd.

Cynthia reminded me of all this when I bumped into her after leaving the Archers' place. She was scurrying up the driveway as fast as she could go in her heels. She almost dropped her handbag twice as she blew her nose into a wad of tissues. When she saw me, she squished me into one of her giant hugs.

"It's just dreadful, what happened," she blubbered. There was a pink stripe in her hair, probably left over from Wacky Hair Day at the middle school where it was a longstanding tradition for the mayor to participate. She wore clunky hoop earrings and her eyebrows looked different than usual. Maybe she had taken a page out of Logan's book and gotten them waxed.

I tried to wriggle out of the hug, but she squeezed even tighter.

"Oh, Humphrey." She patted my back. "I heard you found him. How dreadful!"

It had been dreadful, but not nearly as dreadful as being stuck in Cynthia's clutches. "Mayor McNally, I can't breathe."

She released me like a spring. "That's what Brigid Dugdale said when I talked to her this morning. She said it was like she couldn't breathe. That's how dreadful this is. It reminds me of ... oh, never mind. I shouldn't say."

It reminded her of my old man's death. I could see that, even if she couldn't bring herself to say it. Admittedly, the similarities were striking: an unhappy family, a problematic husband and father conveniently taken out of the picture.

"It's so rare, these types of things," the mayor continued. "Pearl's such a safe town. When I talked to Brigid, I told her it was one in a million."

"Wait," I interrupted. "You heard about it from Brigid Dugdale?"

"No, no, dear." Cynthia shook her head vigorously. "I heard about it from Madelaine. She called me sometime around two in the morning to watch Teddy while she ran to the motel. Not ran, literally. Drove. Oh dear. It's just dreadful!"

This was followed by even more blubbering.

"How was Madelaine? Did she seem different?"

"Different how?"

"I don't know. Just different."

I immediately regretted my insinuation. Just like with my old man's death, I had fallen into the town's inevitable suspicion of Madelaine. But Cynthia defended her friend.

"Oh no, Madelaine had a proper alibi," she said. Referring to her husband, she added, "Pope was on neighbourhood watch last night, so he would have seen her drive off. He was sitting right there on the porch." She pointed over the picket fence to her house, where their front porch indeed seemed to have an excellent vantage point of the Archers' house.

"You have a neighbourhood watch?" I asked.

Cynthia nodded. "We formed it last fall after two houses on the street got egged."

"I remember. One of them was yours."

She looked astonished. "How did you know?"

"You told me about it. It happened on Halloween."

"That's right! We got egged on Halloween.'

I half-laughed. "If you don't hand out candy, you get egged."

"Don't be ridiculous! We handed out candy." She stuffed the wad of tissues in her handbag. "I was out of town that weekend, but I put Pope in charge."

I couldn't picture Pope McNally handing out candy to children. Which meant they definitely got egged.

"Either way, it's vandalism and this neighbourhood is historic property, which makes it even worse," she said. "Since forming the watch, we haven't had any incidents involving eggs."

"Was Tedd Archer on your neighbourhood watch?"

Just like that, Cynthia was blubbering all over again. She unravelled the wad of tissues from her handbag and blew her nose. One of them fell to the ground, but she didn't notice.

"Oh, no," she blubbered. "Tedd wasn't much interested in … bettering the neighbourhood."

Of course not.

"Oh dear, I shouldn't speak ill of the dead." A flustered Cynthia stuffed the wad of tissues back in her handbag. She reached out and gave my shoulders another squish. "Oh, did you meet Agnes? Isn't she the sweetest girl?"

"The sweetest."

She lifted the doorknocker. "Humphrey, I must say you are in better spirits than I thought you would be. Brigid says Riley is in dreadful shock. He has something called traumatic amnesia. She googled it."

"Traumatic amnesia?"

"Didn't you hear? Logan Griffith slugged him outside your bar. Apparently he thought Riley was you." She shook her head sadly. "Really, Humphrey, the two of you are grown men. I think it's about time you put the foolishness behind you before somebody else gets hurt."

5

MANHATTAN MAN AND A PRIVATE EYE

The offices of *The Pearl Gazette* were quiet on Thursday mornings. The usual hustle and bustle, rumbling of the photocopier, and gurgling of the watercooler all died down midweek after the newspaper was printed and mailed. The first thing I noticed when I climbed up the steps and pushed open the door was a rather large box stacked on the front desk. I moved it so I could peek around the side, but no one was sitting there. In fact, there didn't seem to be a living soul in the whole office. I glanced into the small sitting room with three uncomfortable fold-up chairs but didn't feel like waiting.

I was about to leave when someone came down the hallway. If she was older than me, it couldn't have been by much. I pegged her to be early thirties. She had sleek jet-black hair that fell to her shoulders, and she wore a pair of clear-framed glasses that accentuated her almond-shaped eyes. When she smiled, the glasses slid down the bridge of her nose and she pushed them back into place.

"Can I help you?"

"Neal Humphrey," I offered.

She smiled again. "I know who you are."

I knew who she was too: Magnolia Lee, the *Gazette*'s star reporter. I would have to be completely oblivious not to know who she was. Besides her name being on every front page, Logan talked about her incessantly, especially after a few Manhattans. According to Logan, she was "Mag the Nag," too demanding and too much of a perfectionist. It appeared she was Logan's greatest nemesis, seconded perhaps only by me. I supposed we had that in common.

"I'm here to see Logan Griffith," I said.

Apparently the feelings were mutual, because her friendly smile turned into a frown as soon as I mentioned his name.

"Good luck with that. Logan's an absolute wreck this morning," she grumbled. "He showed up late, threw up in the break room, and now he's sitting in his office doing nothing."

That sounded like Logan.

"I don't know why he bothers to show up when he's just going to slack off," she added.

If I had wanted to cut the slacker some slack, I would have explained that Logan had been up half the night getting drunk to impress a beautiful out-of-towner, only to break a whisky bottle over Riley Dugdale's head and be questioned about the murder of Tedd Archer.

I wondered how much Mag knew. "I just want to talk to him about last night."

Her eyes lit up. She knew. Of course. I shouldn't have been surprised. She was a reporter, after all. It was her job to know everything that happened in Pearl.

"Is this about the murder?" Mag lowered her voice to a whisper. She peered over her shoulder, making sure no one else was around. Her eyes flicked back to me. "Or the private eye?"

I looked at her. What private eye?

Mag's face flushed as though she had made a mistake. She looked away, pushing her glasses back up her nose and mumbling something under her breath. She quickly recovered, pointing down the hallway.

"Second door on the left."

She hastily scooped up the box of newspapers and nodded goodbye, turning back the way she had come and leaving me properly puzzled.

I knocked on the door, second to the left, with Logan's name printed on it. The office was lined with windows, but all the blinds were drawn, so I couldn't see inside. I knocked again with no answer.

I let myself in. The door swung open and hit the doorstop with a *bang*.

Logan didn't even flinch. Slouched in his desk chair, he faced the opposite wall with his head tipped towards the ceiling. His eyes were closed, but he inhaled melodramatically as though picking up my scent like a dog smelling dinner. He had probably heard me talking to Mag through the thin walls.

"Humphrey," he said with a sigh. Apparently he liked pretending he had a sixth sense.

"So you puked in the break room?"

"Who told you that?" His eyes popped open. "Mag?"

I stepped into his stuffy office. It was a mess as usual. Sticky notes surrounded his laptop in a colourful perimeter. There were two cameras on his desk, both expensive models with wide zoom lenses, and at least four more on top of the filing cabinet in the corner. His trash bin, next to the filing cabinet, was overflowing. The entire wall behind his desk was covered with photographs and newspaper clippings. Hanging on the opposite wall was a red-barrel dartboard.

I sat in the chair across from him and eyed the mug on his desk, filled with a green liquid. "What is that?"

"Matcha."

I raised an inquisitive eyebrow.

"It's supposed to help with hangovers. I told her I don't drink tea, but she doesn't listen."

"Mag?"

"It needs a shot of whisky. You wouldn't happen to have some Griffiths on you?"

"Does this look like a bar?"

"Unfortunately not."

"Then I'm not your bartender."

Logan spun around slowly. "You know, if I didn't get a headache from the whisky, I would have from that freelancer."

"Cosmo Clarke," we both said, shaking our heads. At least we could agree on something.

I picked up one of his cameras, but he tore it out of my hands with surprisingly fast reflexes, especially for a morning after downing an entire bottle of Griffiths.

"So you thought Riley Dugdale was me?" I asked.

"Did Mag tell you that?"

"Mayor McNally."

"How does she know? I told that to Wick to get him out of my hair."

"You talked to Wick Dugdale?"

Wick Dugdale was Riley's old man, a former policeman. It was Wick who had been friendly with my old man, who we had tracked down and threatened. It hadn't ended well for us. Needless to say, Logan and I steered clear of the man every chance we got.

Logan leaned back again. "He called the *Gazette* this morning to complain about me. Said I deliberately hit Riley."

"You did."

"I was drunk. That's not deliberate."

"So you told him you deliberately meant to hit me."

"Why not? Riley's tall. He kind of looks like you." Logan grinned. "It's nothing I haven't done before."

"Unfortunately not," I said, echoing him from earlier.

I eyeballed Logan's other camera, then picked it up. He let me turn it on and shuffle through the photos.

"Mayor McNally knew about Tedd's murder," I remarked.

"If Cynthia knows, the whole town will know."

I clicked through the photos absentmindedly. "Don't suppose you mentioned it to Mag."

"Me tell Mag? Are you kidding?" He scowled at me with his bloodshot eyes.

I paused on a photo of Cynthia at a peewee hockey game, standing centre ice for the puck drop. It looked familiar. Maybe it had made the front page at some point.

"Fine. I might have told Mag," Logan admitted, "but she kept nagging me about being late. On and on, it never ends. She's awfully annoying, Humphrey. I don't know how her husband puts up with her, whatever his name is. I met him once at a Christmas party. Poor guy."

I ignored him. "Maharmallo told us not to tell anyone."

"I only told Mag."

"Right. You only told a reporter."

"That's your problem, Humphrey. You always have to follow the rules. Look where that's gotten you." He propped his legs up on the desk. "I break the rules."

I was about to ask where that had gotten him but was too distracted by the photos. I'd gotten to a crop of photos from the motel's reopening. There were more photos of the ribbon-cutting and several featuring the crowd of townsfolk gathered to listen to Tedd's speech.

"Who was at the reopening?" I asked.

He shrugged.

"Were the Dugdales there?" I thought I could see Wick in one of the photos, his back turned to the camera, standing beside a brown-haired woman that could have been his wife, Brigid.

"I don't know. Probably."

"Who do you remember?"

"Tedd, obviously." He rubbed his head. "Cynthia was there to cut the ribbon. She brought the whole McNally family tree—kids, grandkids, everybody. So that's like half of Pearl. Bart was there, I think. And some of the other old-timers. And Mag was there. She came with me." He paused and then added awkwardly, "Madelaine Archer's assistant. What's her name again?"

"Gwynn Grant."

He nodded. "She was there."

"What about Madelaine?" I didn't see her in any of the photos.

"I don't think so."

I set the camera back on his desk.

"You weren't there either, Humphrey, if I remember correctly. What's with the sudden interest?"

"I'm just curious."

"Curiosity killed the cat." Logan lifted the matcha tea to his nose. He made a face and put it down, dangerously close to his expensive cameras. "Speaking of cats, whatever happened with Daphne's dead roommate?"

"I threw it into the river."

"Ouch. What did that river ever do to you?"

"You're right. I should have put it under your bed."

"I should have hit you with that whisky bottle."

I rolled my eyes. "What about Daphne?"

A devilish grin. "What about her?"

"What's she doing in Pearl?"

"What does it matter to you?"

"It doesn't matter." I slouched in my chair, trying to seem nonchalant. I could feel it—something suspicious going on between Daphne and Logan.

Of course, Logan wasn't going to tell me about it. He was enjoying the secrecy too much. He knew it bothered me.

I tapped my fingers on the arm of my chair, eyeing Logan. By the time I got up to leave, I had almost forgotten a rather important question.

"What's this I hear about a private eye?" I asked.

"Private eye?"

"Mag mentioned it."

Logan leaned his head back and sighed. "Mag is a nuisance."

"So there's no private eye?"

"I have no idea what you're talking about, Humphrey." Logan closed his eyes. "Do you mind getting the light on your way out?"

I did just that, flicking off the light and slamming the door behind me—a little harder than I'd meant to—leaving the Manhattan Man alone in the dark with his matcha.

Logan was right. By nightfall, the entire town knew about the murder of Tedd Archer. The news spread like wildfire, consuming everything and everyone in its path, and it was much too late to smother the flame underfoot. It was difficult to say who exactly had started the fire. Whether it was Cynthia or Logan, I supposed it didn't matter. Perhaps I had started it by finding Tedd in the first place.

Regardless, the gossip had begun, especially back at the bar, with Riggs and several other uniformed officers snooping around the motel all day. A strip of yellow police tape stretched across the doorway of Room 7. The officers went in and out with clear plastic bags. I overheard a couple of old-timers swapping stories about what was in the bags. One of them, a smooth-talker with a Bogart-type lisp, swore he had seen a knife in one of the bags, long with blood on it. He was having a hard time convincing his friend, a balding man who was downing drinks like there was no tomorrow. But after another beer or two, I had no doubt Baldy would believe anything Bogart told him.

A familiar figure walked into the bar around happy hour. Most of the nightcrawlers ignored him. While he was familiar to me, he wasn't yet familiar to most of Pearl's townsfolk, and he didn't look like a police officer. He was dressed in the same sleek black suit as the night before and approached the bar casually, no different than Bogart or Baldy had before him, like a man in need of a drink. He slid onto one of the mismatched stools with ease. It happened to be the same one he had sat on the previous night, right across from the clock and the kitchen doors.

"Ah, spying becomes you," Maharmallo said.

If spying meant listening to two old-timers debate the length and amount of blood on a fictional knife in an evidence bag, then the detective had been right after all. I wasn't interested.

Maharmallo looked better than the last time I'd seen him. Somehow his face was less weathered and his eyes less distracted. He had no nervous shudder in his shoulders. His hand didn't hover unsteadily over his holster. And had he smiled when he saw me? Perhaps I had imagined that.

News about the detective had been spreading around Pearl along with the usual amount of newcomer gossip, accelerated perhaps by the rumours associating him with Tedd's shocking murder. I'd happened to pick up a few things walking through town. His wife, Tess, was apparently quite the looker. She'd been spotted more than her husband, usually at the grocery store and once or twice at the library. Their teenage son, Ethan, was finishing up eleventh grade. They had bought a house on Second Avenue, their back yard apparently bigger than the one they'd had in Vancouver, and they had planted a garden, which was doing so-so. The tomatoes needed watering.

He slid his card across the bar to me. "You can call that number if you hear anything."

I picked it up. "I thought Riggs was going to stop by."

Maharmallo shrugged. "It's on my way home."

I shoved the card in my back pocket. The motel wasn't on anyone's way home.

"Have you been keeping your ears peeled?" he asked.

Of course. That was it. He was checking up on me. I supposed it was only fair. I wanted to tell say I'd heard plenty about him. I thought better of it. "Actually, I did hear something strange today."

He waited for me to go on.

"Something about a private eye."

Maharmallo nodded. "I dealt with a few private eyes back in Vancouver. Whenever our cases crossed paths."

"It's probably nothing," I said.

"Probably."

Next to Maharmallo, Bogart and Baldy were arguing about how many times Tedd had been stabbed with the alleged knife. Five times, Baldy said. Bogart thought it must have been more, judging by the amount of blood.

I couldn't tell if the detective was amused by their conversation, but I certainly was.

"Can I get you something to eat?" I asked.

I didn't offer him anything to drink. I wasn't sure if he was on-duty or off-duty. He didn't strike me as an alcoholic, but I had seen enough in my unwanted career to know the signs, and shaky hands were among the most common.

Maharmallo shook his head. "Thanks, but no. Tess is making my favourite. Grilled salmon. I'm preparing myself for the fact that the salmon here might not be as good as on the west coast."

"It's Pearl-good," I said. "You'll get used to it."

He changed the subject and continued on, but I barely heard him, still distracted by Bogart and Baldy discussing the knife. According to Bogart, it was a fishing knife. He then proceeded to list the names of all the fishermen he knew in town. He thought a few of them could be murderers, but he didn't know for sure. Baldy nodded along in agreement now that the beers had settled in.

Maharmallo smiled a little. I hadn't imagined it.

"I should get going," he finally said.

I turned to get back to work, taking the dishrag from my shoulder and tucking it under the bar. But the detective didn't leave right away.

"Incidentally, Humphrey, you don't strike me as a gravedigger."

I paused to look at him. "You did a background check?"

"It's called a criminal record check, and yes, it's standard procedure for anyone involved in a homicide investigation."

Good grief.

"Disturbing a gravesite is a serious crime," he added.

If we had disturbed a real grave, I would have agreed.

"Ah," I said. "How does Logan's rap sheet look?"

"Besides spending one too many nights sobering up in a jail cell, better than yours."

He left after that, and somehow, even though there was no clear battle between us, it felt like he was winning.

Daphne was a sight for sore eyes if I had ever seen one. She walked into the bar shortly after the detective had left. I was in the middle of polishing a cocktail glass when I saw her enter behind a rowdy group of twenty-year-olds. She wore her aviator jacket with her hair pulled into a ponytail. She had ditched the red lipstick, and apparently the ring, since her left hand was noticeably bare.

I hadn't expected Daphne to set foot in my bar ever again, but there she was.

She found an empty barstool near Bogart and Baldy, the tipsy old-timers watching her with dazed, overeager expressions. They smiled, almost too politely, and Bogart handed her his menu. I overheard him say that Seth's famous brownie-waffle sundaes were "heavenly tasting, humanly speaking." Which wasn't a lie. But it was a line if I'd ever heard one, sure to be followed by something vaguely inappropriate.

I willed myself to swoop in before they offered to buy her a couple rounds of beer. I didn't think she would want to play the guess-how-long-the-knife-is game.

"Dinner or dessert?" I asked, tossing the dishrag over my shoulder.

She looked up at me with her green eyes. "Both. But I'll start with a coffee."

I brought it to her in the biggest mug I could find and served it with a much-needed apology.

"I'm sorry about last night. Coffee's on me. Dinner's on me. Everything's on me."

"Humph—"

"Everything tomorrow is on me."

"Humphrey, it's—"

"And the day after tomorrow."

EMILY B. KERROS

"Humphrey, it's just—"

"And every day that you're here. How long are you here? It doesn't matter. It's all on me. If it were up to me, you wouldn't have to pay for your dumpy room either."

She sipped her coffee. "It's all right, Humphrey. Really."

"I shouldn't have said ... uh, what I said."

"You didn't know."

I still didn't know. I didn't know why she'd been wearing a diamond ring last night and why she wasn't wearing one now. I didn't know who she was or what she was doing in Pearl. I didn't know why her relationship with Logan, whatever it was, had to remain such a secret. I also didn't know why it bothered me so much.

I watched her browse Seth's menu.

"How good is the brownie-waffle sundae?" she asked curiously.

"The word *heavenly* didn't convince you?"

"I want to know what you think."

I folded the menu for her. "I think you should order dessert first."

She smiled again, and suddenly it came to me—her relationship with Logan. It had nothing to do with the ring. It had nothing to do with anything except perhaps Logan being Logan. Too much money. Too much time on his hands. It all made sense now.

But if I couldn't get Logan to admit it, maybe I could get her to.

"I saw Logan today," I said, waiting for a reaction.

Nothing. She sipped coffee.

"He mentioned something about a private eye."

"Did he?"

Still nothing. I leaned on the bar. "I know who you are."

She set down her mug. "Have you been spying on me, Sherlock?"

If she only knew. "You know, I prefer Marlowe to Sherlock."

"Marlowe," she repeated. She made a show of looking me up and down. "I see it now."

"You don't know who Marlowe is," I teased.

She laughed. "Absolutely not."

"Maybe I'll lend you a book."

"Maybe I'll just have to help Marlowe catch his Moriarty instead."

68

I didn't have the heart to tell her that Marlowe didn't have a Moriarty. "Marlowe's a private eye."

She took another sip of coffee. I waited. No sneaky smile. No sparkle in her eyes. She hadn't so much as flinched.

"He isn't charmed by beautiful women," I explained.

"Sounds lonely."

"I mean he isn't tricked by them."

She set down her mug. "Who's trying to trick you, Humphrey?"

"You are. You and Logan. Think I don't know what's going on?"

She laughed. "Not for a second. Well, who am I?"

"You're a private eye," I said.

"Me?" She raised both eyebrows. "I thought *you* were Marlowe."

"Metaphorically."

"But *I'm* a private eye?"

"Definitely."

She leaned closer to me over the bartop. "How about you meet me in Room 3 when you close up? We'll figure out which one of us is the real Marlowe."

I must have seemed taken aback because she laughed and patted my arm.

"Relax, Humphrey. I'm not trying to trick you. Not anymore."

6

DAPHNE

Midnight came sooner than expected, and for the second night in a row I closed the bar and wandered outside in the dark instead of going upstairs to my book and my armchair. I stuffed my hands into my pockets and headed down the sidewalk to Room 3. There was no fog and the moon shone clearly. Everything was still and quiet, except for an owl hooting from the trees nearby.

But I was exhausted.

Exhaustion, it seemed, ran in my blood. My old man had been exhausted every day of his life. I couldn't remember a day when he hadn't been exhausted, worn out, sighing here, sighing there. Perhaps exhaustion and Humphrey's bar went hand in hand. Some things just went together. A bartender who was always tired but couldn't sleep. I supposed it was yet another thing I had inadvertently inherited from my old man, although I liked to think I tolerated it better.

When there was no answer from inside Daphne's room, I knocked again. Nothing. I looked into the parking lot, spotting what must have been Daphne's beat-up SUV with a windshield cracked into a spiderweb and chipped paint on the hood. A dreamcatcher hung from the mirror. Somehow I couldn't quite picture her behind that wheel. It seemed much too dull. Too boring. Too old. She was none of those things.

"Humphrey!"

Hearing her voice, I turned to see her approaching from further down the sidewalk. She was standing under the light by Room 7 and waved me over enthusiastically. As I headed towards her, I watched her duck the police tape. She fished her hand into the pocket of her aviator jacket and pulled out two paperclips, straightening each into a long wire and inserting them simultaneously into the lock, tampering with it until she heard a click.

Just like that, she opened the door. Quick and easy. Fast and simple. She never ceased to amaze me. Or confound me.

Despite it all, I ducked the tape and followed her in. I hardly had a choice in the matter. I was pretty sure I would have followed her anywhere.

Once inside, Daphne flicked on the light and shut the door behind us.

"What are we doing here?" I asked. Room 7 looked different. For one thing, it looked empty. Tedd's body was gone and so was the blood-stained rug. The wardrobe was bare, except for a few wire hangers. Tedd's things had disappeared from the nightstand too, probably sealed one by one into evidence bags.

Daphne ran a hand through her hair. Still no ring. "Remember Tedd's wallet?"

I nodded.

"One thousand dollars, in bills."

"What about it?'

She sucked in a breath. "Logan is being blackmailed."

I blinked. "Our Logan? Logan Griffith?"

"The one and only."

"I don't get it," I said, shaking my head in disbelief.

Daphne reached into her pocket and handed me a crisp white business card that read *Daphne Holland* underneath bold lettering: *Redhill & Holland Private Eye Inquiries*. There was a downtown Winnipeg address with two phone numbers and a magnifying glass logo in the corner.

"Logan hired me."

"So you *are* a private eye?"

"Well, Marlowe, you caught me," she teased, perching herself on the edge of the bed.

I sat next to her, fingering the card in my hand. Good grief, I had been right. Daphne Holland, private eye. That explained a lot, but certainly not everything.

I was so lost in thought that I forgot she was still talking.

"Logan's blackmail letters each demand exactly one thousand dollars."

"You think Tedd was blackmailing Logan?"

"It's too big of a coincidence."

I felt some hesitation. "But ..."

Daphne sighed. "But Logan doesn't think it was Tedd."

"Why not?"

"His blackmailer knows a lot about him."

"Such as?"

"Well, it's someone who knows that he's wealthy."

"Everyone in town knows Logan is wealthy," I pointed out.

"Someone who knows about his ... side hustle."

I blinked. Side hustle? Is that what he was calling it now? I shook my head. The kind of photography Logan chose to do on the side was none of my business. I could look the other way, and very often I did. I had a feeling most of Pearl's townsfolk did. Logan's hobby might not have been public knowledge, but it wasn't exactly a secret.

"And there was something about his marriage ... I don't remember. I got the impression it didn't last long."

Good grief. Logan's month-long marriage to Ginny Russel certainly wasn't public knowledge. He'd been irrepressibly young, as had Ginny, and the two of them had gone off and married on a whim, starting and ending it without their family's consent. I had only known about it on account of being caught in the middle, the two of them being my best friends. The entire affair had taken place after my old man's death and my mother's departure for Vancouver. The marriage, if it could indeed be called that, had ruined our friendship and, with the exception of Seth, I had been left entirely alone. It seemed so long ago now.

"It's got to be someone who knows, or knew, him well," Daphne was saying. She stared at me on the edge of the bed. "Someone like you."

I stood up. "Me? You think I'm blackmailing Logan."

"Well, you were his best friend."

"Is that what he told you?"

"He told me something happened when you guys were eighteen."

I stuffed her card into my back pocket and sighed. "Good grief. What *didn't* happen."

It wasn't a question. I didn't really want an answer.

"Don't tell me you fought over some girl in high school," she teased.

"I won't tell you."

She stood up too, so close that I could smell her. She had a lemony scent, almost like a whisky sour, but better. I hadn't mixed one of those in a while. I inhaled deeply as she started pacing, a thoughtful expression on her face. I watched her ponytail sway back and forth. Her worn-out running shoes squeaked whenever she turned around.

"Suppose Tedd was blackmailing Logan," Daphne began. She stopped short. "I've never worked on a murder case before."

"Really?"

She shook her head. "People usually hire us for the regular, run-of-the-mill stuff. Blackmailers. Cheating husbands. Stolen dogs. Someone once hired me to tail their grandmother on Friday nights because they thought she was gambling their inheritance away."

"Was she?"

"She had joined a book club."

I let out a laugh, but admittedly it was a tired laugh. If it hadn't been the exact bed where Tedd Archer had been lying before his murderer knocked on the door, I might have been tempted to collapse and fall asleep right then and there.

I looked at Daphne, suddenly recalling something the detective had mentioned.

"Maharmallo said that Tedd likely knew his murderer."

Almost in a daze, she went to the door and fiddled with the knob. Then she fiddled with the lock. She swung the door open and shut. "No forced entry."

"Besides you. Where did you learn to do that thing with the paperclips anyway?"

"My first foster home."

I watched her stand on her tiptoes and look through the peephole. She opened the door again, this time stepping outside. She closed the door. A moment later, she knocked three times.

Ah, I thought to myself. *A re-enactment of sorts.*

I peered through the peep hole. A familiar face. I opened it.

"Tedd could have seen who was at the door," Daphne said.

I nodded. "So he let his murderer in. Or was he shot in the doorway?"

"I think so." Daphne made a finger-gun. "Bang, bang, bang! Three shots, close range, to the chest and the forehead. He would have died almost instantly, dropped dead in the doorway. But the murderer couldn't close the door, so they dragged his body beside the bed, hence the trail of blood."

"But they didn't close the door. And they left the light on."

"Well, it was a sloppy murder."

"Maybe they wanted us to find Tedd."

Daphne bit her lip. "Didn't Cosmo say he heard voices?"

"Apparently," I said. When it came to Cosmo as a witness, I wasn't entirely convinced. "Assuming he's right, Tedd wouldn't have been shot right away. Whoever came to see him wanted to talk to him first."

"Who was it—his wife? She didn't seem very upset last night."

"She isn't." I proceeded to tell Daphne about my visit with Madelaine and how she had thrown Tedd out of the house after an incident with their son. "Didn't Cosmo say he heard two male voices?"

Daphne shrugged. "She still could have visited him."

"According to Mayor McNally, she has an airtight alibi."

"How airtight?"

"Pope McNally's neighbourhood watch. He didn't see her car leave the driveway."

"Did you talk to him?"

"I don't think I've ever talked to Pope McNally."

Daphne flicked off the light as we stepped outside. I waited for her to duck the police tape, curiosity creeping into my thoughts. Logan was right: curiosity had killed the cat. But apparently they also died minding their own business in motel rooms, so what was wrong with an inquiry or two?

Somehow I mustered up the words: "Logan's so-called side hustle," I began, feeling my face redden. "You never, uh … I mean, you haven't …"

"Posed for pictures?" Daphne finished, a hint of laughter in her voice. "No. Logan hired me to find his blackmailer. That's all."

I breathed an inward sigh of relief. I should have known. She was smarter than that.

"Actually, Logan hired my business partner, but he was busy working on another case. And I wasn't, so here I am." She gave a faint smile.

I smiled back. Suddenly, something rustled and emerged from the long grass, darting across the sidewalk in front of us with a hissing noise. Startled, I jumped back, grabbing hold of Daphne as a small black shadow scampered around our feet.

It was only a stray cat.

I let out a sigh of relief before realizing that Daphne was laughing under her breath. She was laughing at me, no doubt, for allowing myself to be spooked by a stray, especially after handling a dead one. The expression in her eyes, though, was sympathetic.

"I think I'm going to have to get to know Pearl a little better if we're going to solve a blackmail-murder case," she said to me when we were back at Room 3.

"We?"

"How else are we going to figure out who the real Marlowe is?"

"It isn't you. You don't even know the difference between Marlowe and Sherlock."

She laughed. "How about this? I'll read Marlowe if you show me Pearl."

I had no choice, since I would have agreed to anything. I promised to take her on a proper tour of Pearl in the morning, before Humphrey's opened.

"It's a date ... uh, a deal," I said.

We shook on it. This time she held my hand a little longer than she meant to. "Good night, Humphrey."

"Good night, Daphne."

I almost tripped over the cracked drainpipe on the way back to the bar and forgot to duck on the stairs, but I slept considerably better than the night before.

I had a dream about a blonde woman. She wasn't as beautiful as Daphne, which was easy to say since I never saw her face. In fact, she was completely faceless, but she laughed like Daphne. She also drank whisky sours. An awful lot of whisky sours. I tried to get her coffee, but the bar wasn't mine. It was some strange bar I didn't recognize and the whisky wasn't Griffiths and there was a black cat running around.

Despite it all, it was still one of the best sleeps I'd had in a while.

When I woke up, sunlight had already filled the loft, which meant I had slept in. I dressed quickly and headed downstairs, half-expecting Daphne to be waiting for me, but the bar was empty. The empty bar happened to be one of my favourite things.

I walked over to the bar phone, an old landline that still hung on the wall just behind the backbar, above the cellar door. It had been there for forever, only used when I made a long-distance call to my mother in Vancouver—substantially cheaper with the old grandfathered plan—or I wanted to use a number that wasn't easily traced back to me. I fished two cards out of my back pocket and called the number on the first card.

"Maharmallo."

"It's Humphrey."

"Ah, Humphrey." He even sounded straight-faced over the phone.

"How was the salmon?" I asked.

"Pearl-good. But I liked it." He seemed busy. I could hear him rustling papers. A door slammed.

"So I found out who the private eye is."

"Ah. Did she walk into your bar?"

I paused. "How did you know?"

"She told me. I'm a detective, remember?"

Good grief. "So what do you think?"

"Think about what?"

"Is she really a private eye?"

"One of my guys found her office in Winnipeg. Redhill & Holland Private Eyes. Looks legitimate."

I thanked him and ended the call, hanging up the phone and glancing at the clock. Humphrey's didn't open until twelve o'clock, just in time to drag through the lunch rush, happy hour, and midnight burnout. We still had plenty of time.

I waited for Daphne, thumbing the second card in my hand while running my finger over the two phone numbers. She hadn't told me which number was hers—or, for that matter, whether they both were.

Hesitating, I picked up the phone again and tapped it on the hook at eye level. I glanced at the door, then back at the phone. I punched in the first number and waited for it to ring.

Someone picked up almost right way. It was a man's voice. "Redhill & Holland."

I swallowed. "Hello. Is Daphne there?"

"Sorry, she's out of town on business. Anything I can do for you?"

"No ... uh, thanks," I stammered. "It's not important. I'll call back."

He waited for me to hang up first.

I wasn't sure how long I sat there, fingering her name on the card, thinking about the man on the other end of the phone. So Redhill & Holland were the real deal. Maybe even a private eye couple like Nick and Nora Charles. I pictured Nick, or Redhill, or whatever his name was, in a downtown office, the window cracked open, with his feet up on the desk, snoozing under a wide-brimmed hat until the phone rang with his next case. He had sounded nice on the phone. Friendly. Honest. The type of guy who would buy a beautiful woman like Daphne an expensive diamond ring.

I must have been thinking for a long time. When Daphne showed up, I didn't notice until she rested a hand on my shoulder. I walked alongside her all the way to Main Street, so lost in her green eyes, gentle laugh, and lemony scent that I forgot all about Nick and Nora. All I could think about was her.

7

TALL TALE TOWN

"This is the infamous *third* bar?" Daphne asked.

"If we're going to rank them," I supposed.

Pope's on Main Street was indeed infamous. Infamous for its two seasons: winter, when it was closed if there were more than twelve inches of snow, and fishing season, when it was closed as long as it wasn't raining buckets.

So on a sunny spring day, the start of fishing season, I wasn't surprised to find the doors locked. The two of us peered in the window so Daphne could check out the place without actually having to experience it. Pope's belonged to Pope McNally, the mayor's husband, and it was the old-timers' favourite spot. Old farmers. Old fishermen. Old carpenters. Sometimes all three at once. They liked the pool tables and neon signs and tiled floor that looked like a giant checkerboard. The granite bartop was even older than mine, crumbled on one end from too many arm wrestles, bar brawls, and fistfights—the kind of stuff folks couldn't get away with these days. The windows were in desperate need of a wash, but we could make out the chairs stacked atop tables and the sparkling backbar. The building was a single-storey shack nestled between the laundromat and Rather Dapper.

Rather Dapper was Guy Russel's barbershop, another establishment. For years it had been simply called Guy's and was combined with a hair and nail salon called Dollie's, named for Dollie Russel, Guy's on-again, off-again wife whose half of the building was covered in polka dots and pink flamingos. When a marketing buff from the city had gotten hold of Guy's and buffed it up, his half got renamed Rather Dapper. They'd wanted to call it Guy's and Dollie's, but, as that was already the name of a moving company.

As I walked past the barbershop and caught a glimpse of myself reflected in the window, I had to admit I was starting to look a little dishevelled. It was probably time for a haircut.

Across the street from Rather Dapper were the *Gazette* offices, right next to the diner. It was the only diner in town and, aside from Humphrey's, one of the only places to get a good meal. It was where Daphne and I were headed for breakfast and coffee. The first official stop on the tour.

We reached Pearl's lone traffic light and stopped at the crosswalk, watching the morning traffic, which consisted of two cars cruising through the green light. Daphne perched herself on the edge of the street like a New Yorker, quite unnecessarily.

"Is the coffee as good as Seth's?"

"I don't know." I shrugged. "I don't drink coffee."

She looked at me the way Logan had looked at me when I'd told him I didn't drink whisky—with utter shock.

The diner was bustling as always, with townsfolk crammed wall to wall. There was a lineup for takeout orders and waitresses with magnetic nametags buzzed past us carrying loaded trays.

We found an unoccupied booth at the back, beside the kitchen and next to the washrooms. It was probably the worst spot in the diner, but at least it was private. I didn't need the whole town gossiping about Daphne and me sharing breakfast.

But as soon as we slid into the booth, we were spotted. Across the diner, Bartel waved from the takeout line and I waved back sheepishly.

Daphne peered over her shoulder. "Who's that?"

"That's Bart. He owns the bookstore."

"Your favourite place in town, I'm guessing."

"Uh-huh." I smiled. "He borrowed a book from my mother years ago and lost it. Probably sold it accidently. But now he thinks he owes me."

"A specific book?" Daphne asked.

I nodded. "The final Raymond Chandler novel, *Playback*."

"And he's been trying to find another copy?"

"Not just any copy. The exact same book he borrowed."

"How will he know it's the same book?"

"My mother always wrote her name on the inside cover," I explained. "The problem is, it's been so long that Bart doesn't even remember what he's looking for. Every time he comes across one of Chandler's books, he saves it for me, but it's always the wrong one."

She laughed. "The man who cried Chandler."

"Something like that." I laughed too.

Our waitress, a friendly young woman with dark hair, came to take our order. I recognized her as one half of the Swope sisters and one of Pope and Cynthia's many grandkids. The name on her tag read Sara. She resembled Agnes, I supposed, but other than appearances she was nothing like her older sister. Sure, she talked a lot, complimenting Daphne's "cute jacket" as she pulled out her notepad and scribbled down our order, but she hadn't giggled once. She nudged us towards two heaping breakfast sandwiches and, of course, coffee. She came back right away and left Daphne the whole pot.

As Daphne picked up her sandwich, I couldn't help but notice the ring still missing from her left hand.

"What do you think of Pearl so far?" I asked.

"I think it's lovely."

"You think everything's lovely."

"Well, what do you think?"

"Boring."

She bit into her sandwich.

"Gossipy," I added.

She nodded, fairly.

"Plain Jane."

She thought about that one.

"Seedy—"

"Humphrey?"

I stopped and looked at her.

"Have you ever been antiquing?"

There wasn't much else to see on the so-called tour. If Daphne stood in the middle of town, where the main intersection crossed with a through-road, she could pretty much see all of Pearl at once. Directly across from the diner was the tallest building, the town hall, and together they made up one half of the intersection's four corners, with the gas station and old theatre making up the other half. Just down the street from the diner was the *Gazette*, the post office, bank, library, another vacant building, and then Archer's Antique Shoppe across from Bartel's Used Books.

Daphne let me lead the way to the antique shoppe. She eagerly pushed the door open. Or tried to. The door only budged enough for us to squeeze through. Blocking the doorway were row upon row of rolled-up prayer rugs, overflowing from the window display. Each had a large sale tag dangling from it. They were nearly taller than me, and Daphne had to inch up onto her tiptoes to see over them.

"You're back."

Gwynn had emerged from the wall of rolled rugs. She stood with her arms folded, even less thrilled to see me than before, if that was at all possible.

"Is Madelaine here?" I asked.

"Why? Are you stalking her too?"

Gwynn turned and I moved quickly, motioning for Daphne to follow as Gwynn led us through the depths of the shoppe. I kept my eyes fixed on her as she expertly weaved through the maze of antiques.

We found Madelaine at the counter, busy logging something into a giant leatherbound book in front of her. She wrote swiftly. The point of her pen scratched the paper.

"Humphrey," she said without looking up.

"Madelaine." I gestured towards Daphne. "This is Daphne Holland. You might remember her from, uh, the other night at the bar. She's a—"

"A friend from out of town," Daphne interjected. "I love your shoppe. Antiquing is actually an interest of mine. I just love antique mugs. You wouldn't happen to have any, would you?"

Madelaine blinked at Daphne. "Gwynn, show Humphrey's friend where the mugs are."

Daphne gave me a look before following Gwynn off to some dusty nook and cranny. The floorboards creaked as they wandered further into the store. I peered over the piles of stuff, trying not to lose sight of Daphne. If they weren't back in a few minutes, I was going to stand on that piano, antique or not.

I turned to Madelaine. "About those missing antiques …"

She stopped writing. "I thought I told you to leave me alone."

That wasn't quite how I remembered it.

Madelaine, on the other hand, seemed to think the matter was settled. She appeared unfazed, flipping a page in her giant book and continuing to copy down items from an apparent receipt.

"Madelaine, we think Tedd was blackmailing someone. Do you think that's possible?"

"If he was, he didn't tell me." Madelaine sighed. She continued writing as she talked. "But he didn't tell me much. Did you know he didn't tell me when he bought the motel?"

"No."

"I found out about it from Cynthia." She shook her head, then put down her pen and made eye contact with me. "Who was he blackmailing?"

I hesitated. "Logan Griffith."

"Hmmm," she murmured, nodding slowly. "Then maybe Logan Griffith murdered him."

She wasn't wrong. Good old-fashioned blackmail was an excellent motive for murder. Nonetheless, I was taken aback. Sure, Logan had disappeared just after midnight, but that had only been to get Daphne's motel key from the Bentley. Besides being drunk, he couldn't have had time to murder Tedd in Room 7, ditch the murder weapon, find Daphne's key, and return the bar … all in ten, maybe fifteen, minutes.

I thought about Maharmallo. *That long?* the detective had said. Did he think Logan was guilty?

No. I knew him. Logan was a lot of things, but not a murderer.

"More likely it was whoever was stealing from the shoppe," I said. "That's why a list of missing antiques would be helpful."

Madelaine let out another sigh. Without saying anything, she turned and went into one of the back offices. She returned with a sheet of paper and handed it to me.

"Everything on that list went missing in the last four weeks," she said. "I log everything as soon as it arrives. I keep good ledgers. If it's in the shoppe, it's in here." She motioned to her leatherbound book as she picked up her pen. "It might look unorganized, but I know when things go missing."

I scanned her list. She had scribbled it down quickly, but her handwriting was a neat and straight cursive.

I didn't get very far before fixating on one of the missing items.

"*The Big Sleep*?" I asked.

"A 1939 first edition. I'd say it's worth about thirty thousand."

I took in a breath. An original edition of Raymond Chandler's first novel. No wonder Tedd had been stressed out. Someone had stolen thirty thousand dollars right out from under his nose. Compared to that, Logan's blackmail seemed a trifle.

Just then, Daphne and Gwynn returned, emerging from behind an old sandy-coloured armoire. They spoke in low, comfortable voices and I wondered if the quest for the perfect antique mug had somehow resulted in a friendship.

I doubted it. They were complete opposites.

If I needed any proof of that, it came as soon as the two of them saw me. The scowl returned to Gwynn's face while Daphne smiled, holding up a creamy ceramic mug shaped like a giant teacup.

"Isn't it lovely?" she said.

"Lovely," I agreed. I stuffed the list in my pocket.

Madelaine ripped the price sticker off Daphne's mug.

"Is Riley here?" I asked while we waited.

Madelaine shook her head. "I fired him."

"You fired him?" I repeated.

"He was stealing."

"Really? Riley?"

Madelaine pursed her lips. "It's not like I had a long list of suspects, Humphrey. It was either Riley or Gwynn, and it wasn't Gwynn."

"Tedd seemed to think it was."

"He was wrong," she replied. "It was Riley."

"Did Riley admit to it?" Daphne asked.

"No, he tried to tell me he didn't do it." Madelaine tucked Daphne's mug into a small brown bag, then handed it to Daphne with an extended arm. "Turns out Riley Dugdale is a thief and a liar."

"What's on the list?" Daphne asked as she walked beside me.

I had to admire her cleverness. I hadn't thought she'd noticed the piece of paper Madelaine had given me, but evidently she had, and she had waited until we were well on our way down Main Street, about to turn off towards Riley Dugdale's on Second, before mentioning it.

I shrugged a shoulder. "I don't know if it matters."

"You don't want it to be Riley."

"What?"

"Riley. You don't want him to be the thief."

"Ah. Is it that obvious?"

Daphne smiled. "Well, he may not be. Madelaine has no proof."

"Gwynn, then?"

She bit her lip.

"Did Gwynn say anything to you?" I asked.

"Not much. She asked me what it was like living on my own in the city."

"What did you say?"

"Who says I live on my own?" She held up her bag. "She also said I had bad taste."

"A pocketful of sunshine, isn't she?"

Daphne laughed as I pulled the crumpled list from my pocket and handed it to her.

"A 1970s typewriter," she read aloud.

Gwynn had mentioned that one. No surprise there.

"Almost a dozen of those prayer rugs," she continued. "Authentic prayer rugs would be worth a small fortune."

"Do you know what else is worth a small fortune?" I pointed to the next item on the list.

"*The Big Sleep*. What's that?"

I stopped short. "Chandler's first novel. Marlowe. You've never heard of *The Big Sleep*?"

She shook her head. "Is it like *Playback*?"

"Bigger than *Playback*. It's a crime classic. Madelaine thinks a first edition is worth about thirty thousand."

"You're kidding."

I shook my head. "I'd die for that book."

"Would you murder for it? That's the rub."

"That's the rub," I agreed.

A truck rolled past us and honked. I waved. Bartel. Good grief, the man was everywhere.

A sign in the window of Dollie's read *Curtain Bangs Are Back*, whatever that meant. The door to the laundromat opened and two women walked out, cackling like hens, their eyes wandering to Daphne, who had settled into a steady albeit fatigued pace beside me. One of my strides was nearly two of hers.

She half-smiled at me. "This minimalist lifestyle of yours is exhausting! Next time I'll drive."

"Your vehicle seems to be on its last legs ... uh, wheels."

"Says the man who *walks* everywhere."

"I have a car."

"Really. Where?"

"Back at the bar. In the alley. Chances are it's filled with strays."

"Dead or alive?"

"Probably both. Should we sink it in the Pearl River?"

She laughed, but then she looked at me rather seriously. "I don't think so, Humphrey. How are you ever going to get out of Pearl if your car is at the bottom of a river?"

Riley Dugdale lived with his parents, Wick and Brigid, who were for the most part ordinary folks. They lived in an older part of town, a quiet neighbourhood. Their house was small and square with a detached garage and fenced-in back yard. They were high school sweethearts and had been married for almost thirty years. Wick was a family name, passed down from a long line of Dugdales. But although Wick had wanted to carry on the tradition when Riley was born, Brigid had thought Riley didn't quite look like a Wick. He looked more like a Riley. And so Riley it was. He was their only child, and as their only child Brigid often worried that he was lonely. Once she adopted a chocolate Labrador to be Riley's companion, but that didn't last long. Wick didn't like dogs, or any pets for that matter.

Wick was a retired police officer, but that didn't mean he was old. He'd been forced into early retirement because of his bad back. It was so bad that pain medication didn't work anymore, and sometimes he couldn't bend into his favourite chair on the porch. Brigid thought it was because he was overweight and should eat healthier. She'd read somewhere that he just needed to go on a diet, so she'd printed off a list of recipes and pinned it to the pantry door. She even tossed out all of Wick's favourite snacks, all while Wick sat on the front porch, sullen and bored.

Of course, I didn't know all this firsthand. I'd heard rumours here and there, at the bar, at the diner, at Rather Dapper. I had never had reason to visit the Dugdales before. In fact, I had every reason to avoid them.

I had neglected to fill Daphne in on my history with Wick Dugdale, the man I thought responsible for my old man's death and subsequently my mother's absence. It was complicated, after all, and I worried Daphne might have perceived me differently. We talked about other, less ominous, things: how the diner's coffee was not nearly as good as Seth's, how she adored Pearl's infestation of bufflehead ducks, how she could get used to a quiet life in a small town.

Surely, she hadn't meant that.

Our voices travelled ahead to the covered porch on Second Street. It had a large shrub on either side of the teetering steps, planted in patches of hearty soil. Wick looked up from his chair, shielding his eyes from the sun with one hand. He was a heavyset man with a chiselled jaw and a square face.

"Humphrey," he said.

I nodded. "Mr. Dugdale."

If there was still animosity between us, it was Wick Dugdale who had put it there. He had known my old man, a regular at the bar fifteen years ago. But since my old man's accident he hadn't set foot inside. The tire treads on his police cruiser matched the treads across my old man's back. And he'd been there that night. I knew it. Yet I had been powerless to prove it.

My run-ins with the police following my old man's death had been mostly Logan's influence and pretty much every officer back in the day had known it. I might not have been a minor anymore but I had been young, and after a few overnights in jail they'd encouraged me to make better choices.

Wick was another story. He had seemed to have it out for us, me in particular. Although I supposed it was retaliation for what we had tried to do.

We'd hunted him down in his own town, tracked him off-duty. Logan had even pointed the rifle in his face, briefly. A criminal offense, Wick had told us. Up to five years in prison. But he wouldn't admit his guilt to two unstable eighteen-year-olds. Still, if he had dragged us down to the station, he would have risked us talking. And he couldn't risk losing his career over one drunken mistake.

So he made life miserable for us. Any minor infraction and he hauled us in, seating us down in front of his senior officers. His favourite line? "Get comfy, Humphrey." He said it every time he'd stuffed me headfirst into the back of his police cruiser. I could still feel his large hand on my head, hear the sneer in his voice.

"Is Riley around?" I asked.

"Why do you want to know?" the former policeman grumbled. He got up slowly and tottered to the edge of the porch, hands on his sides.

"We just wanted to make sure he was all right after last night."

Wick frowned. "Why? What'd he do this time?"

Before I could answer, the screen door swung open and Brigid Dugdale popped out. She was about the same height as her husband with soft-looking skin and curly brown hair. When she opened the door, I caught a strong whiff of something delicious coming from the kitchen.

I couldn't help myself. "That smells amazing."

"Cashew butter muffins," Brigid said, beaming. "Fresh out of the oven."

Wick perked up. "Butter muffins?"

"Cashew butter. It's healthier."

Wick muttered something under his breath. Brigid ignored him and turned to introduce herself to Daphne.

"Brigid Dugdale. And you must be the young woman who gave our Riley quite a scare."

Flustered was a new look on Daphne. She straightened her stance, trying to regain her confident composure. "Oh, I'm sorry. With everything going on, I wasn't—"

"Nonsense," Brigid replied, batting a hand. "Riley needs his exercise, otherwise he'll end up like his father."

Wick muttered something else.

"Are you staying at the motel then? What brings you to Pearl?"

Daphne glanced at me before turning back to Brigid. "I'm a friend of Humphrey's."

I added a smile for authenticity. Wick added a snort.

"How's Riley doing?" I asked.

Brigid looked at her husband, and Wick looked at Brigid—sort of.

"He's all right, considering," Brigid finally said. "I'm afraid it's been quite the shock."

"You're friends with the Archers, isn't that right?" I asked.

"I thought so," Wick snorted.

I glanced at Daphne. "We heard Riley was fired. Madelaine said he was stealing."

Wick narrowed his eyes into slits. "Riley didn't steal anything!"

"Of course not," Brigid chimed in, patting her husband on the shoulder. "It's all a big misunderstanding. Madelaine will come to her senses. She always does."

"But some things have been going missing," I said. "Who else would it be?"

"Probably that Gwynn Grant," Wick sneered, eyeing me. "She's a menace."

It took one to know one, I supposed, realizing all at once that my appearance at Wick Dugdale's home might have been a mistake. He wasn't bound by the law anymore. He didn't wear a uniform or flash a badge.

Then again, I wasn't some green eighteen-year-old anymore either. He couldn't lay a hand on my head now. I would have liked to see him try.

The deadeye stares between us hadn't gone unnoticed, for Daphne had fixed her attention on our strange, silent interaction. The fact that everybody knew everybody in Pearl was no doubt taking on a whole new meaning to her. But she knew better than to say anything in front of Wick. I could feel her prying eyes, private-eye mode activated.

Brigid, on the other hand, was entirely unaware. She was the next to speak, her voice perfectly polite. She didn't want any trouble.

"We don't mean to speak poorly about Gwynn. I'm sure she's a lovely young woman, but to be perfectly honest, the two of them haven't gotten along terribly well."

"Gwynn and Riley?" I asked.

Brigid nodded. "Riley started working at the shoppe before Gwynn, yet she seems to be getting all the perks."

Wick snorted. "Madelaine's little pet."

"Riley's always had a hard time making friends," Brigid added. "He tried with Gwynn, but things got ... complicated. She isn't the easiest to be friends with. What?" She looked at her husband.

"She's a menace," Wick said. "You should never have encouraged him."

"Honestly, Wick, I thought I was helping him. It's better than video games."

Video games? I glanced at Daphne, feeling strangely like the two of them were on the verge of an often-recurring fight.

"Is Riley here?" Daphne asked. "I'd love to see him—you know, apologize in person."

I smiled to myself. She was good. Quick-witted. I had to admire it.

"Of course," Brigid said with a nod. "Come on in. He's downstairs."

Any objection Wick had was muttered under his breath as he rose from his chair, a hand to his back as an audible *crack* rang out. He swore something fierce—like a sailor, my old man would have said, although he hadn't been any better in that department.

Brigid welcomed us in and led us through the screen door. She commissioned Wick to take us downstairs while she veered off to the kitchen, promising to bring down some muffins. The former policeman groaned and swore the whole way down, though it was unclear if the cause of his petulance was his bad back or his wife. More likely it was me, Get-Comfy-Humphrey, inside his house.

The basement was mostly dark, lit only by a big-screen TV in the corner. Riley was slouched on the couch directly across from the TV, wearing an elaborate gaming headset, his arms jerking left and right, absorbed in the figure on the screen, who appeared to be shooting his way through a burning building, dodging explosions left and right. He didn't notice us until Wick gave his head a stiff smack.

"You have visitors."

Riley paused the game. "As long as you d–d–didn't bring your other friend with you," he consented, seemingly relieved that Logan was nowhere in sight. He observed Daphne with caution.

"How are you doing, Riley?" I asked.

"I don't know."

"Sorry to hear about your job."

A shrug.

"You didn't steal anything?"

Riley shook his head.

"How long have things been going missing?"

"A m–m–month maybe. Maddy had a list."

Maddy. It was a nickname he had used the night of Tedd's murder. Clearly, he was comfortable with it. And yet no one else seemed to call Madelaine by that nickname. Not Gwynn. Not even Cynthia.

I glanced at Daphne, wondering if she had noticed, but she was still watching me, eyebrow raised.

I pulled the crumpled piece of paper from my pocket. "Did it look like this?"

Riley pulled his headset off one ear. He scanned the list. In fact, he barely had to look at it before handing it back to me.

"Yeah, exactly."

"Tedd thought it was Gwynn?" I said.

Riley nodded. "He wanted to f–f–fire her, but Maddy wouldn't let him."

Wick snorted again.

Riley looked at his old man, angrily. "What?"

"She should've been fired. You took the fall for it, son."

This was followed by some more colourful words. Riley ignored most of them, rolling his eyes. He flipped his headset back on and unpaused the game, shooting his way off what looked like a rooftop with a large machine gun.

"Sometimes that's what friends do," I said to Wick.

The former policeman scoffed. "That's not a friend. That's a coward."

"You'd call your own son a coward?"

"If he took the fall for something he didn't do." Wick rubbed his back, grimacing. "He needs to man up. He and Gwynn, they aren't friends."

"So you keep saying."

"You can't take the fall for something you didn't do, Humphrey. That just wouldn't be right. Even if someone were to, let's say, point a gun in my face, I don't think I could tell a lie. Honesty, I find, is always the best policy. I've tried to teach my son the same." Wick leaned in closer, gripping a large hand on my shoulder. "It's all right, Humphrey. I know your friend, Logan Griffith, was the real menace." He eyed Daphne. "Looks like you traded up in the world."

With that, he headed back towards the stairs, muttering something about his back and popping some pills.

Daphne watched him leave before turning to me. She seemed about to say something when Riley flipped off his headset again.

"Is he gone?"

I nodded. Frankly, I was too stunned to speak.

"I d–d–didn't want to s–say anything in front of my dad." Riley sighed. "He can be …"

"I get it," I said. "My old man was the same."

"But I d–d–don't think it was Gwynn."

"What makes you say that?"

"A f–few weeks ago, I accidently walked in on Gwynn in Tedd's office. He was accusing her of stealing and t–told her she was fired. He said she'd never work anywhere in this t–t–town again." Riley shrugged. "I d–don't know. She just s–s–seemed really upset. She said she d–d–didn't know what he was t–talking about. I just don't th–think it was her."

"Who do you think it was?" I asked.

"I th–think Tedd was stealing from himself," Riley replied. "He knows where to s–s–sell stuff and he has a good insurance policy. And I think he t–t–tried to pin it on Gwynn."

"Why Gwynn?"

"I d–d–don't know, but he d–didn't like her. He didn't really like anyone."

"You and Gwynn aren't friends?" I asked.

"I don't know. Not really."

"But you were together the night of Tedd's murder?"

"Yeah."

"Why?"

"We worked l–late, s–s–setting up another rug display. I owed her one."

"Where did you go?"

"Pope's."

"So you have an alibi for midnight."

He looked a little confused. "Yeah. You and the b–blonde."

I glanced at Daphne. She took no offense.

"That was after midnight," I said. "What about Gwynn?"

"Right, Gwynn. We were probably at Pope's until about m–m–midnight." Riley's hands were sweaty around his controller. He set it down, wiping them on his pants.

"And then you drove to the motel?"

Riley nodded.

"Why?"

"I already told you. Tedd borrowed s–s–something from me and I wanted it back."

"Are you're sure you don't remember what it was?"

"I'm s–sorry. I wish I did."

"Did you tell Gwynn what it was?"

He shook his head.

"But you told her you wouldn't be able to sleep if you didn't get it back."

"I d–d–don't remember that."

The basement fell quiet. I looked at Daphne again. She had positioned herself near the bottom of the stairs, listening to the voices travelling down from the kitchen. Wick's voice was deep and bellowing, easily audible. Brigid's, not so much. They were arguing. Something about muffins and murder and Madelaine.

I turned back to Riley. "Whatever you forgot would have been among Tedd's things when the police bagged it up. Have you asked the detective? It might jog your memory."

Riley shook his head. "I'm not th–the biggest f–f–fan of talking to cops."

With an old man like Wick Dugdale, who would be? I glanced at Daphne, who procured a crisp business card from her pocket and handed it to Riley.

"I'm a private eye," she said. "It's possible Tedd's murder might be related to a case I'm working on. If you think of anything …"

"Th–thanks. I'll add it to my collection." Riley took the card and placed it on the couch on top of a card that looked like Maharmallo's.

Meanwhile, the argument upstairs had escalated.

"You let him into our house!"

"Wick, how was I supposed to know?"

"You should know. You're so darn nosy all the time."

"I am not nosy!"

"So is that *friend* he brought with him. I can see it in her eyes. They're up to something."

"Nonsense!"

"I know a menace when I see one!"

Brigid was laughing now.

"What?"

"You didn't know Tedd was a menace."

A snort. "Tedd was no saint, but he wasn't that bad."

"And Madelaine?"

"You're the one who said she would come to her senses."

"I said I would try, Wick. I can't work miracles."

That was our cue to leave. I took the stairs behind Daphne and scrambled up them two at a time, just as Riley pulled the plug on his headset, flooding the basement with gunfire and explosions to drown out his parents. I batted open the screen door and held it briefly for Daphne.

We hustled back down the driveway towards the quiet street, without bothering to say goodbye to Wick or Brigid. Neither of us turned back to peer over our shoulders in case they might have noticed we were gone. I thought I could still hear their voices, but I couldn't be sure. It might have just been Riley blowing stuff up.

It was nearly noon by the time we headed down the dirt road to the motel. The bar would be opening soon. Seth was probably already there, busy prepping the kitchen. He would have noticed I was gone. He might even be concerned. I was never late.

"Do you believe him?" Daphne asked.

"Riley?" I shrugged. "I have no reason not to. You don't?"

"I think he knows more than he's letting on. That's why I left him my card. If he won't talk to the police, maybe he'll talk to me."

She made a good point. Given the choice between the two cards, Riley was more likely to pick up Daphne's than Maharmallo's. I had forgotten

EMILY B. KERROS

Daphne's card and my awkward phone call with the mysterious Redhill, but now I was curious again about the man I'd spoken with earlier.

"So who's Redhill?" I asked.

If she was surprised by the question, she didn't show it. "My business partner."

Of course. I had assumed as much. "And the two numbers on your card. One is his?"

His. She noticed the slipup. There had been nothing on the card to suggest her business partner was a man. I shouldn't have known he was a man unless I'd talked to him.

"One is my office number in Winnipeg," she said after a moment. "He'll answer it sometimes if I'm away."

"Isn't that a little confusing?"

"We're partners."

Ah.

"It doesn't matter which one Riley calls," she added, falling further behind.

Neither of us said anything else until we reached the bar. It wasn't Riley I was worried about.

94

8

THE STRAY CAT SCRAWLS

"You did what?" Logan paused mid-sip.

"I told Humphrey about the blackmail," Daphne said, seated next to him.

I stood on the other side of the bar with a dishrag over my shoulder, sucking on a lime. It was a taste test; Seth had insisted. He had switched his supplier and wanted to know if I could taste the difference.

I spit it into the tub sink. A lime was a lime.

Humphrey's was busy, which wasn't unusual for a Friday night. There were still a few empty seats at the bar, but all the tables were full. A group in one of the corner booths was ordering up round after round. It sounded like somebody's birthday. Between the rounds Daphne and I had been going over suspects: blackmail suspects and murder suspects and the likelihood of it being one and the same.

When Logan arrived after work for his usual happy hour, Daphne filled him in.

"If I didn't like you so much, I would fire you," Logan said.

The private eye laughed. She looked absolutely radiant with her classic red lip and gorgeous green eyes, refreshed from our morning tour of Pearl, after which she had disappeared to her room for a few hours. In the middle of my shift, she had brought in a list of suspects written on a notepad, which reminded me of Riggs. I teased her about it and then she asked why I was so curious about her partner, Redhill. I came up with an awkward excuse.

"It's a different name," I said lamely. "Not from around here."

And of course I consented to the fact that she wasn't going to tell me anything about Redhill—or the diamond ring, for that matter. Either she didn't want to or she didn't know me well enough. I hoped it was the latter; at least we could change that.

Daphne's suspect list was now lying on the bar next to the uncrumpled list of missing antiques. Logan scrutinized the list of names Daphne had scribbled down.

"I really don't think it was Tedd," he said, taking another sip of his Manhattan.

"What about the money in his wallet?" Daphne reminded him.

Logan set down his glass. "It doesn't make sense. Why would he blackmail me?"

"You're easy to blackmail," I replied. "You're crazy rich and you do dumb things."

Ah, that definitely ruffled a feather or two.

Daphne cut in before he had a chance to retaliate. "What if Tedd was struggling? Financially, I mean. Big spender. Bad gambling habit. He had no other choice. He needed easy, untraceable money, so he resorted to blackmail." She tapped her pen on the bartop. "It goes without saying that he would pick the richest person in town."

"Second richest. You're forgetting Granddad." Logan took another slow sip.

I shoved another lime in my mouth and mulled it over. Sure, it was possible that Tedd and Madelaine's antique shoppe wasn't doing so well, especially with the recent thefts, but the longer I thought about it the less sense it made. The Archers had always seemed well-off, or at least comfortable. Hadn't Riley said that Tedd was insured? And if Riley was right and Tedd was indeed the mastermind behind his own thefts, didn't that rule him out as Logan's blackmailer? A thousand dollars here and there was nothing compared to antiques worth thirty thousand or more.

One thing was certain: I couldn't ask Madelaine about it. She seemed more than a little fed up with me and I didn't think she would be very forthcoming about their financial situation. Besides, she had mentioned more than once that Tedd hadn't involved her in his affairs. I needed to ask someone who knew the Archers. Preferably someone who knew the Archers but also liked me. Even better if that someone also happened to be the town gossip.

I spit out the lime, realizing that I was overdue to visit Cynthia anyway.

"Tedd *was* a big spender," I said to Daphne, suddenly remembering something Maharmallo had said. "His coat was imported."

"Italian."

I nodded.

Logan shook his head. "It's impossible. Tedd hardly knew me. The closest I ever got to him was taking the photos at the reopening."

"So who knows you well enough?" I asked.

"You, Humphrey, for starters."

"Besides me."

Logan sighed. "I suppose my evil twin."

"Your evil twin?" Daphne half-laughed. "Oh, you're serious."

He was serious all right. Logan's twin sister, Lennon, as it happened, was no laughing matter. She had tormented us, but mostly me, throughout our childhood and teenage years, hence why Logan had dubbed her his evil twin. It suited her, I supposed, since her devilish grin was worse than Logan's and her beady eyes were dark and cold as ice. She was a bartender now—at Griffiths Distillery, if I wasn't mistaken. It was a little funny, the irony of it all.

"Lennon," Logan said to Daphne, who added her name to the list.

I stuck yet another lime in my mouth. I wondered, briefly, if Lennon taste-tested limes. Another shudder.

"Lennon doesn't know where you live," I said.

Logan lowered his drink. "That's right. I gave her a fake address when I moved onto Cigare Street."

Logan's house, on Cigare Street, was the oldest and largest house in town.

"You gave your twin sister a fake address?" Daphne raised a curious eyebrow.

"I don't like visitors," he deadpanned. He took a slow sip, swirling the orange slice around the bottom of the glass. "But Lennon wouldn't waste her time blackmailing me. She has an endless supply of funds. She hasn't been disowned."

"You say that like it's a bad thing."

Another lime spit into the sink. Another ruffled feather. Sometimes I liked watching Logan squirm on his barstool.

The photographer looked at me with his devilish grin. "I guess we're back to you."

"I don't see my name on the list," I said.

"That's because Darling Daphne made it."

Daphne didn't look up, but her face turned a blushing pink. I chose to ignore it. Remarkably, so did Logan.

"So what exactly does your blackmailer have to know about you?" I asked.

Logan ran his finger around the rim of his sweating glass. "I do some other photography on the side—"

"Uh-huh," I interrupted quickly. No need to dwell on that any longer than we had to. "What else?"

"Ginny Russel. Montreal."

Just like that. Three simple words. Ginny Russel. Montreal.

Back then, we had told each other that whatever happened in Montreal stayed in Montreal, although unfortunately what happened to Logan in Montreal had eventually followed him to Pearl. They'd gotten married, the two of them, and a month later, after the glamour of the vacation had worn off, they'd gotten divorced. Somehow, even years after the fact, I didn't think the folks around town would be very understanding. I almost felt bad for Logan.

Almost.

"That was the first letter," he went on. "I thought it was a prank so I didn't pay up, but then someone told Guy about Ginny. He didn't take it very well."

Guy and Dollie Russel were Ginny's grandparents. Her own parents had been largely absent, so Guy and Dollie had practically raised her and her brother as their own. I pictured Guy, who had always been especially protective over Ginny, running after Logan with a threatening pair of scissors.

"Is Ginny the girl?" Daphne asked, looking back and forth between us.

"What girl?" This from both of us, at the same time.

"The girl you two fought over in high school."

"We didn't fight over a girl," Logan said with a devilish grin.

"I tried to tell her," I added.

A smile pulled at Daphne's mouth. She seemed unconvinced.

Logan took another sip of his drink and continued, "When the second letter showed up, I didn't know what to do. I paid up and then I got a third letter. That's when I hired Daphne."

"Why didn't you just go to the police?" I asked.

"Granddad Griffith always says secrets should be handled secretly."

"Ah. Brilliant." I turned to Daphne. "So that's how you got mixed up in all this."

She laughed, shrugging her shoulders. "Well, I didn't have any other cases."

"And here I thought you really cared. Knife to the heart, darling," Logan said, sipping his Manhattan. "Knife to the heart."

Around ten o'clock, Cosmo Clarke strutted into the bar. The freelancer was considerably more put together than the last time we had seen him, dressed in a collared shirt and light-coloured pants with his Panama hat tipped fashionably forward. He found an empty barstool next to Logan and Daphne, rested both hands on the bar, and tossed the three of us the sort of smile usually affixed to the face of a fraudster. I didn't trust him as far as I could throw him. Another one of my old man's sayings.

"What can I get you?" I asked.

Cosmo eyed Logan's drink. "How about one of those?"

"A Manhattan?" I reached for a cocktail glass.

"Yes. A Man–hattan." He pronounced it as if it were two words. "Seems like a manly drink, and I do love hats." He chuckled to himself as he added, "Why, I think a Man–hattan is my perfectly suited cup of tea, or perhaps I should say tea–quila."

"Whisky," Logan corrected, his voice dripping with annoyance.

"Whichever." Cosmo removed his hat and ran his fingers along the brim. "Speaking of hats. I happen to be a collector. Fedoras. Indianas. All sorts. I've even been known to wear the odd bowler, but the Panama is my favourite. The straw is what makes it lightweight and breathable. This particular one was handwoven in Ecuador. I bought it the same day I finished my article—you're probably familiar with it—on the giant tortoises of the Galapagos, their natural habitat—"

"Mr. Clarke," Daphne interrupted.

"Cosmo," he insisted.

She tried again with a faint smile. "Cosmo, I'm surprised you're still in town."

"Oh, I can't leave. Detective's orders, I'm afraid. In fact, I've just been to see him."

"You've been to see Maharmallo?" I asked. "Why?"

"I seemed to remember something. Thought I'd better share it."

"About Tedd's death?"

The freelancer blinked. "Who?"

"Tedd Archer. The man in Room 7."

Still nothing.

"The man with the trench coat."

A long, unnecessary pause. "Goodness! That's right. He did have a fab-ulous trench coat. I'd nearly forgotten. Odd of me. Anyhow, I went down to the station today to talk to the detective, but he gave me the cold shoulder. All I got was that measly officer of his."

"What did you tell him?" Daphne asked.

"Only that I remembered what the voices were saying. Say, bartender, where's my drink?"

Ignoring my irritation, Daphne pressed on. "So you did hear voices. You're sure it was midnight?"

"Positive. I'm a bit of a restless sleeper. Prone to writer's block, which is just kryptonite for greatness, I know. But I went to bed at eleven-thirty and had just dozed off when they woke me up. They were arguing rather loudly."

I slid a Manhattan in front of Cosmo. "You told Maharmallo they weren't arguing."

"Goodness! That's right, I did. Oops."

"Oops?" Logan added dryly.

"Perhaps I fudged a little." Cosmo took a sip.

"So it was two men arguing?" I clarified.

"Come to think of it, it might have been a man and a woman. I can't be sure, you see, because I'm partially deaf in one ear. I'm afraid I was prone to infections as a child and my—"

"Cosmo," Daphne interrupted again. "One man or two?"

He shot her an indignant look. "There was definitely one man.".

Logan muttered something under his breath.

Daphne leaned forward. "What were they saying?"

"It was quite muffled, and as I said, I'm partially deaf in one ear, so really it's quite a miracle I heard anything at all ..." Cosmo scratched his chin. "But I did make out a few peculiar phrases."

"Such as ...?"

"*Give me the money!*" Cosmo crowed. He waved his drink so exuberantly in the air that he almost fell off his barstool.

"Anything else?"

Cosmo cleared his throat. "*She doesn't love you!*"

This time, Cosmo's outburst caught the attention of almost everyone in the bar. Logan drowned himself in his Manhattan, Daphne leaned back slightly, and I awkwardly tried to look busy. Where was a lime when I needed one?

Cosmo, unaware of our audience, took another sip. "If you ask me, I'd say the phrase 'She doesn't love you' implies that someone didn't love Tedd Archer." He waved a dismissive hand. "I'm afraid I don't know what the money thing means."

Good grief.

"Did you hear any gunshots?" Daphne asked, her voice hushed.

"Gunshots?!" He shook his head. "Oh no, nothing of the sort. I would have told the detective if I had heard gunshots."

"Maybe you lied," Logan said between sips.

"I am not a liar." Cosmo looked at him, eyes wide. "Fudging isn't lying."

"Beg to differ," I muttered.

Irritated, Cosmo downed the rest of his drink and slid the empty cocktail glass back to me. Then he balanced his Panama hat back on his head and strutted out of the bar without throwing so much as a toothy smile our way.

"Freelancers," Logan muttered, shaking his head.

But he was right about one thing: what else had Cosmo Clarke fudged about?

Give me the money.

> *She doesn't love you.*

Two more relatable phrases had arguably never been uttered. Whether or not Cosmo had actually heard them was another story.

I fingered the pages of the unpublished manuscript, trying to focus on reading, but all I could think about was what Cosmo had heard that night. I leaned back in my armchair and had just closed my eyes when I stiffened rather suddenly.

I sat up. There was a strange scratching noise, presumably coming from outside, yet I was on the second storey. There was only one place it could be coming from.

I wandered over to the fire escape. That's when I spotted it: a black cat, scratching at the window. I shooed the stray off, then watched it dash down the fire escape and disappear into the night.

I suppose the thing about cats is they always come back.

Cynthia's office was just like Cynthia—somehow cluttered and organized at the same time. An organized mess. Admittedly, it drove me a little crazy, which is one reason I didn't visit very often. There were lots of reasons, not least among them the fact that Cynthia had added to the rumours surrounding my mother after my old man's death. It wasn't just Cynthia, of course; it had been the whole town.

As the years passed, though, the mayor seemed to be trying to make up for it.

I scaled the lengthy set of stairs to the top floor of Pearl's town hall, an old brick building with barely any windows. I knew the way like the back of my hand. I could have done it in my sleep. I probably had, at one point. Even the paint chips in the walls, and the tear in one of the framed paintings, were familiar to me.

The only thing unfamiliar was perhaps Pearl's new deputy mayor, Randy Something-or-Other. I couldn't recall his last name. He poked his bearded face out of a door to remind me that Cynthia had a meeting in T-minus twenty minutes, so I had to be "quick about it." The conference room behind him was being set up, with a giant projector on one end of a long board table overflowing with boxes of doughnuts and coffee from the diner.

Quick about it? Randy Something-or-Other obviously didn't know Cynthia.

The mayor welcomed me into her office with another one of her hugs. The pink stripe was still in her hair. It appeared the damage was permanent and she wasn't going to be able to wash it out anytime soon—certainly not before the meeting across the hall. It didn't seem to bother her.

With high heels clicking, she walked over to her desk and settled behind it. She motioned for me to have a seat, accidently toppling over a photo on the side of the desk. It landed facedown. She reached to set it upright and smiled, turning it so I could see. It was a family photo, Pope and Cynthia with all their kids and grandkids.

"Isn't our Sara so grown up?" she asked.

I spotted Sara in the middle, right next to Cynthia, and I could almost feel the favouritism oozing from the frame.

"We're so proud of her," Cynthia went on. "She's a straight-A student."

I tried to look interested but found myself distracted by the half-eaten yogurt tipped sideways on the desk, a spoon sticking out of it.

"I seem to remember you being top of your class, Humphrey."

Top of the class and bottom of the popular list, I thought to myself. Either way, Cynthia had been mayor for too long.

"She's waitressing at the diner now," Cynthia said, still talking about Sara. She clapped her hands together, then leaned towards me and lowered her voice as though she was about to tell me a secret. We were the only ones in the room, although I didn't suppose that would have made a difference. A secret was a secret, after all. "Maybe you saw her there yesterday morning. I heard you and that out-of-towner were getting pretty cozy."

I swallowed stiffly.

"She's drop-dead gorgeous," Cynthia went on. "Blonde and blue-eyed. Like a supermodel."

"Green," I corrected before I knew what I was saying.

Cynthia scrunched her nose. "Green? Sara said they were blue, but not as blue as yours."

I fidgeted uncomfortably. The last thing I wanted to think about was Cynthia gossiping about me with her teenage granddaughter. Thankfully, she shifted the conversation to something slightly less uncomfortable.

"Did you settle things with Logan?"

"It looks like he meant to hit Riley Dugdale all along," I said.

Cynthia raised both eyebrows in surprise. "Whatever for?"

I shrugged. "You know Logan. He drank too much whisky."

"Oh dear!" Cynthia shook her head with a disapproving frown. "That's what happens when you stop going to church on Sundays."

She gave me a look that suggested she wasn't only talking about Logan. I repositioned myself in the chair. Head high. Shoulders back. I didn't need the gossip. I would have rather been squished in another of Cynthia's hugs. That was saying something.

I had come in pursuit of the truth. Marlowe would grit his teeth and bear it, and so would I.

"Mayor McNally, I—"

There was a sharp knock at the door.

"Come in," Cynthia answered, much louder than she needed to. I nearly sprung out of my seat.

Randy Something-or-Other poked his head in. "The electricians are here to check the corner outlet. Should I let them in?"

Why not? It wasn't like they were interrupting anything. I propped my elbow up on the armrest and rested my head in my hand. I was going to be here for a while. I could feel it.

"Of course, of course." Cynthia nodded, bobbing her head up and down heartily.

Randy swung the door open and ushered in two men dressed in matching grey shirts. He directed them to the corner behind me where they hovered over a perfectly normal-looking wall outlet.

"I heard a strange buzzing noise coming from that one," Cynthia said. "I had Randy call someone right away. We can't have subpar electrical. Town hall is a historic building, you know, like the motel and Great Pearl."

By Great Pearl, she meant the community church, which was anything but great. It was a small church situated on a little hill on the east end of town. She stole a sideways glance at me when she mentioned it.

The two electricians hovered over the outlet, listening for the buzzing noise. Cynthia and I sat in silence, lending an ear to the apparently better-than-subpar electricians.

"Listen!" Cynthia said suddenly. "Do you hear that?"

We all listened. I peered out into the hallway.

"That's Randy humming," I said. At least I thought I said it. Nobody seemed to hear me.

"You need a new outlet," one of the electricians said.

The other one nodded. "We have one in the van. We'll go down and get it."

They left the door open when they trudged back through the narrow hallway and disappeared down the stairs. They moved slower than snails, but somehow I didn't think it would be long before we were interrupted again.

I turned back to Cynthia, who had resumed eating her yogurt, scooping the last spoonful into her mouth. She proceeded to lick off the spoon before setting it down and folding both hands in front of her.

"Now, Humphrey. Where were we?"

I steeled myself. "Cosmo Clarke is a freelancer. He was staying in the room next to Tedd and it's possible he heard a man and woman arguing the night of Tedd's murder."

"A woman? Oh, it wasn't Madelaine." Cynthia shook her head. "I told you. Pope would have seen her leave."

"I understand that Madelaine is your friend, Mayor McNally, but her husband was just murdered and she doesn't seem to be very upset by it."

Cynthia pursed her lips. "I really shouldn't say anything. I don't like to speak ill of the dead ..."

I waited.

She peered down the hallway. No Randy. No electricians.

"There was an ... incident with Teddy," she said.

"What happened?" I asked, leaning forward.

The two electricians returned. They had brought another, older man with them. They could have been his sons. Maybe it was a family business.

I stifled a yawn.

"Are you getting enough sleep, Humphrey?" Cynthia asked. "With everything that's going on …"

"There was a stray cat scratching at my fire escape all night."

"Oh dear! Poor thing is probably just hungry. You should talk to Pope. He has a knack with animals. That's why he's such a wonderful fisherman. He always catches and releases."

I nodded absentmindedly.

Good grief, I thought to myself. *How many electricians does it take to change a wall outlet?*

"Pope is taking Sara fishing when school's out. It's become a little tradition. Last year they caught a walleye in the Pearl River. This long." Cynthia spread her arms as far apart as she could.

Finally, the electricians finished up. Cynthia thanked them, told them to help themselves to doughnuts on the way out, and then watched as they left.

"What happened to Teddy?" I asked once we were alone again.

Cynthia shook her head. "I can't tell you."

"Why not?"

"Madelaine wouldn't want me to."

I pictured Madelaine's five-year-old. How small he was. His bruised arms and face. It wasn't hard to imagine a terrible incident.

"Do you think Tedd could have been involved in blackmail?"

Cynthia sucked in a breath. "Blackmail. How so?"

"We think he was blackmailing someone."

"Oh dear! Who? Why?"

I shrugged. "Money. Were the Archers struggling?"

Cynthia thought about it. "I don't think so. Madelaine never mentioned it."

"How about the shoppe?"

"No. It's always been a success, and Tedd owned a lot of places in town," Cynthia said. "I don't know how much you pay for overhead at the bar, Humphrey, but I bet it's a pretty penny."

I had to agree with that. "Did Madelaine ever mention any thefts at the shoppe?"

Cynthia looked worried. "Now, she did mention that. Things going missing."

We were interrupted again, this time by Cynthia's phone vibrating loudly on her desk. She looked at me apologetically and picked it up.

"Hello."

I could hear a man's voice on the other end, but not what he was saying.

"Oh dear! Madelaine?"

Again, a muffled voice.

"I'll be right there." She set down the phone with a shaky hand, her face as white as a ghost. "Madelaine's been poisoned."

9

RULES OF MURDER

"Poisoned?" Officer Riggs, looking sombre as ever, stood outside Madelaine's room at the nearest hospital, an hour away from Pearl. He looked back and forth from me to Cynthia. "Mayor McNally, I told you it was anaphylaxis."

Cynthia had insisted I come with her to the hospital, as she was in "no state to drive." If she had heard any DUI rumours about me, she had clearly forgotten them when she tossed me the keys to her car and crawled in, high heels and all, leaving Randy Something-or-Other in the dust.

She was also in no state to talk to police officers. She looked like she was ready to pummel Maharmallo's sidekick with her handbag if he didn't get out of her way.

She wriggled a finger in his face. "If someone gave Madelaine cashews, she was poisoned. Everyone knows she's allergic."

I hadn't known, but I supposed that was beside the point.

"We don't know if it was deliberate," Riggs replied.

"How could it not be?" Cynthia objected. "Tedd was just murdered."

She tried to push past Riggs into Madelaine's recovery room, but he stopped her.

"Mayor McNally, she's been through quite a shock. We suggest you avoid that particular topic of conversation."

He let Cynthia through after she promised not to mention the words *poison* or *murder*. And I followed, having made no such promise.

Madelaine had a private recovery room with a big window and whitewashed walls. She was propped up in bed, hooked up to an IV bag. A bouquet of flowers rested on the table beside her.

Cynthia squished her friend into a hug. The wad of tissues was back in her hand and she dabbed her eyes as she sat at her friend's bedside.

"Oh dear, what happened?" Cynthia asked.

"I must have eaten something wrong." Madelaine eyed me, sitting in a chair in the corner. "What are you doing here?"

"Oh, Humphrey." Cynthia waved a tissue. "He came with me. He's worried about you too."

"He is, is he?"

I didn't say anything.

"Cynthia," Madelaine said, grasping both of her friend's hands in hers, "would you mind checking on Teddy? He's in the waiting room with Agnes."

"Oh dear, of course!" Cynthia flailed her arms about frantically and then scurried out the door and down the hallway in search of Teddy. She went the opposite way of the painted arrows on the floor, but I didn't say anything. She would figure it out eventually.

That left just the two of us.

"Haven't you heard of an EpiPen?"

Madelaine stared at me. The long scar on her face was more noticeable now, as though the entire poisoning ordeal had reopened a prior wound. "As a matter of fact, Humphrey, I have. I usually keep it with me, but this morning I couldn't find it when I needed it. Gwynn and I both did a thorough search. Not that I owe you an explanation."

"You don't." I stared back at her. "What did you eat?"

"Do you want a list?"

"It would be helpful."

"Hmmm. Helpful how?"

"I wouldn't have to ask anyone else."

She amused me. "It's a short list. All I had was a terribly strong cup of coffee, a grilled cheese from the diner, and one of the muffins Brigid brought over to the shoppe."

Muffins from Brigid Dugdale? A cashew allergy? I stood up. I had to find Maharmallo.

"Humphrey," Madelaine said before I could leave. "That photographer friend of yours …"

Why did everyone always assume Logan and I were friends?

"I'm sure you're aware of his ... other job."

Other job? Good grief. I rubbed my head but nodded to her. "What about it?"

"It's easier to show you." Madelaine reached over and picked something up from the table—something flat, about the size of an envelope. She flipped it over and held it out to me. "Detective Maharmallo found it with Tedd's things at the motel."

I stared at it. It was a photo. A photo of Madelaine herself, the old Hollywood star, scantily dressed, with her back to the camera and her head over her shoulder, perched on a tall barstool with a greyish backdrop. I could only assume there were more—many more—where this came from.

"I don't know how Tedd got it," Madelaine said. "I didn't give it to him."

"Who did you give it to?" I asked.

Her face flushed, but it might have been from the IV in her arm or the lack of wine. "I didn't give it to anyone. I did it for myself. No one else knew."

Of course I was no expert, but my gut was telling me that most woman didn't take near-nude photos just for themselves. I inspected the photo, flipping it over to find the back was dated, but not in Madelaine's handwriting. The date seemed familiar to me, although I couldn't quite place it—

A nurse interrupted us. I handed the photo back to Madelaine and she stuffed it under her pillow.

I left the room to find Riggs still hovering in the hallway.

"Is Maharmallo here?" I asked.

He nodded down the hallway where Maharmallo was headed towards us, hand rested on his holster. He gave some nonverbal cue to Riggs, who walked away as his radio buzzed.

"Humphrey. We meet again."

"I brought Mayor McNally," I said.

"That's good. Madelaine will be happy to see her."

"Madelaine just told me about the photo."

"Ah." Maharmallo nodded slowly. "We found it tucked inside the motel Bible, between the front cover and Genesis. I don't think that has any significance." He paused. "I thought your friend was a newspaper photographer."

"He is," I said. "He's both."

"Busy man," Maharmallo replied, straight-faced.

"Something like that."

We started walking towards the waiting room. Beside me, Maharmallo took deep breaths and I stole a sideways glance at him. He seemed tired. He had bags under his eyes and his shoulders were heavy. I could hear him inhaling and exhaling, in and out, in and out, all the while his unsteady hand resting on his holster. I couldn't help but wonder if this was how police officers got trigger-happy, from all the tiring stress and unending crime. Maybe it was also how they developed drinking problems.

"Do you think someone purposefully gave Madelaine cashews?"

Maharmallo shrugged his heavy shoulders and repeated word-for-word what his sidekick had said to Cynthia. "We don't know if it was deliberate."

"She said Brigid Dugdale brought her muffins."

"What about it?"

I stopped. Maharmallo stopped too. We were at the waiting room.

"There's something you should know about Brigid Dugdale," I said.

"I didn't peg you as an amateur sleuth," Maharmallo replied, rubbing his tired eyes. "I should have. Reading too much Chandler will do that to a man."

"Ah. I blame you and Chandler." I shrugged a shoulder, stuffing my hands in my pockets.

"Me?"

"You said you needed my help."

"Spying and sleuthing are entirely different things."

"Maybe not entirely."

"What about Brigid Dugdale?"

"I want to know what happened to Teddy Archer first."

"Humphrey ..." Maharmallo hesitated for a moment. Then he sighed. "Teddy was hit repeatedly with a kid's toy. Some sort of rubber hammer."

"A mallet."

"Right. The one from an old arcade game."

"Whack-a-mole," I said, taking in a deep breath. "Tedd did it?"

"Allegedly."

"So Madelaine could have murdered him to protect Teddy?"

"She could have, but this complicates things."

"Then it was deliberate."

"I don't know, Humphrey. What about Brigid Dugdale?"

"Brigid's muffins have cashews in them."

"Banana chip?"

I blinked. "Cashew butter."

"They're banana chip muffins, Humphrey. I have them in an evidence bag."

I could feel my face redden, ashamed of my sleuthing skills—or lack thereof. I looked around the waiting room, spotting Agnes with Cynthia and Teddy. She gave me a tiny wave and held back a giggle. Cynthia was squishing Teddy in a blubbering hug and he was nodding with his bruised face. Gwynn sat across from them, anxiously biting her fingernails.

I glanced at Maharmallo again, his usual straight face pulled into a frown. I wondered what he was thinking. Maybe it was the same thing I was thinking, that strange things were happening in Pearl—murder, theft, blackmail, near-nude photos, and even poison.

But where did Tedd's murder fit? What did Madelaine's photo have to do with any of this? Why had Riley been fired for the missing antiques and not Gwynn? I wondered how much Maharmallo knew—if he knew about the missing antiques, especially that first edition of *The Big Sleep*.

"Have you ever read any Chandler?" I asked.

The detective tried to smile. "Yes, I've read him. I wouldn't pay thirty thousand for him, but I've read him."

Of course he knows, I thought to myself, shaking my head in exasperation. *What doesn't he know about? Why does he even need a spy?*

In fact, the only thing I was fairly certain Maharmallo didn't know about was Logan's blackmail letters. I wondered then if I should have confided in him, but he went on before I had a chance to speak.

"Do you know what I like about Chandler?"

"What's that?"

"He didn't write by the rules."

I thought about it and shrugged. "There are no rules of murder."

I let Agnes approach me as soon as the detective left. We'd gotten off to a bad start, I supposed, though I didn't really care to make things right. I didn't know the first thing about twenty-year-old women, particularly ones that giggled so much.

"Isn't it dreadful?" Agnes said. She'd gotten that word from her grandmother. "Gwynn said it happened right when she got to work. She was carrying her to-go mug and just dropped it on the ground. Coffee everywhere. She couldn't breathe."

"Ah."

"Did you know she fired Riley?"

There was something wistful in her eyes. I couldn't quite place it.

She gave a long sigh. "Riley's too good for her anyway. Do you know him?"

"Uh-huh." More than I wanted to.

Finally, she let out a small giggle. "You're just like him. Tall. Quiet. Except you're older, obviously. Not that you look old. How old are you?"

I hadn't meant to ignore the question, but her assessment of Riley surprised me. Riley, in fact, did indeed remind me of myself. I wondered if it was possible that Agnes was more perceptive than she appeared.

I decided against it. She was only Teddy's nanny. Just another one of Madelaine's employees. She couldn't have known the first thing about what was going on. She was, more than likely, oblivious.

"I wish he were here," she mused. "Riley. He makes everything better."

I woke up Sunday morning to the sound of the stray scratching at my fire escape. I swung my feet onto the floor and rubbed my eyes awake.

When I wandered to the window, the cat was gone. I peered down through the rusted-out steps and railings, twisting and turning and intertwining all the way to the ground. It was the perfect playground for a stray.

I threw on some clothes and went outside, taking in the morning air, and knocked on the door of Room 3.

Daphne opened it right away.

"Breakfast?" I asked.

She reached for her jacket. "Sorry, I'm heading home to help Tanner with another case."

"Who's Tanner?"

"My business partner, Tanner Redhill."

Of course. Tanner Redhill.

"Want to tag along?" she asked. "He won't mind."

Sunday was my day off, but I wasn't ready to meet Tanner Redhill, nice as he sounded. I shook my head and watched her twist her key in the lock and slip it into her pocket.

"Bye, Humphrey. See you tomorrow."

10

LETTERS

The best barber in Pearl was a man named Graham, and he also happened to be my cousin. He was my only cousin, as far as I knew, and I wasn't entirely sure if he was my first cousin or second. I only saw him five or six times a year when I needed a haircut, but he was, without hesitation, the best. Guy Russel was too old and shaky for my tastes. Just like Pope's bar, his barbershop was an old-timer hotspot. They huddled around a small table by the window, drinking black coffee with too much sugar, reading magazines, and reminiscing about the old days. Even if none of them needed a haircut, they were always there, like an old biker gang that couldn't ride their bikes anymore and didn't know where to go or what to do with themselves.

The door chimed when I walked into Rather Dapper, and everyone looked up at me.

First: Pope McNally, Cynthia's husband and a fellow bar owner. He was about as friendly as a cactus. Or a Doberman. When he saw me, he made a noise that sounded like the grunt of a pig and went back to flipping through his fishing magazine.

Second: Walter Ellis, my old English teacher, now retired and likely disappointed with where I had ended up in life. He was working on a crossword and whizzing through it, since he was a genius, even in his old age.

Third: Bartel Smith, who waved from the chair where Guy was working on his hair. Bartel was adamant that no one else could cut his hair like Guy, so the old barber probably wouldn't be allowed to retire until he dropped dead, which at this rate would be any day. I just hoped I wouldn't be there to see it.

I sat in the chair next to Bartel, who was drinking his coffee black while Guy trimmed his sideburns. Graham draped a barber cape over me and pumped the chair up.

"Long time no see, cuz." He was wearing a white tee that showed his tattoo sleeves. He also had a perfectly groomed beard and trendy haircut. I wondered if he cut his own hair. "I saw you walk by the other day. Thought maybe you were going for a shipwrecked look."

I looked at my tousled hair in the mirror and couldn't help but laugh.

Graham had a bunch of daughters, the newest of which must have been the photo pinned next to the mirror: a bald baby with a pink bow on her head.

"She's four and a half months," he said, beaming. "Born on Christmas Eve. There was so much snow, I had to borrow Guy's truck to get Marney to the hospital. Isn't that right, Guy?"

The old barber waved a scissor at him. "You almost hit the ditch."

"That wasn't the snow." Graham laughed despite himself. "That was panic."

Bartel suddenly turned to me. "Humphrey ... I saw you at the diner the other day with a blonde woman."

Ah.

"Who?" Graham asked.

"Nobody," I said.

"It doesn't sound like nobody. Sounds like a blonde woman," Mr. Ellis said without looking up from his crossword. I had forgotten how intimidating he could be. It was the first time he had spoken since I'd walked in. It might have been the first time he'd spoken to me since English class.

"Her name is Daphne Holland," I conceded. "She's from out of town."

Guy looked up. "I heard she's a private eye."

Apparently, word travelled fast among the old-timers.

"Huh?" Bartel put a hand to his ear.

"A private eye," Guy repeated. His smoker's voice was rough and gravelly. "She's from the city."

"What's a private eye doing in Pearl?"

Guy shrugged. "Why don't you ask Humphrey? She's his sweetheart."

"You're dating a private eye?" Graham stared at me in the mirror.

"No, we're not. Absolutely not," I sputtered, shaking my head.

Graham didn't seem convinced. Neither did Bartel.

"Did Madelaine hire her?" Guy asked.

I tried to sound nonchalant. "I don't know if it has anything to do with Tedd's murder."

The barbershop fell quiet.

"I almost forgot about Tedd," Guy muttered. He went back to trimming Bartel's sideburns.

"Weren't you the one who found him?" Graham asked hesitantly.

"What did he look like?" Bartel jerked his head sideways and Guy moved his scissors out of the way just in time.

"I don't know," I said. "There was a lot of blood."

Graham winced behind me.

"I heard he was stabbed six times," Bartel said.

"Shot," I clarified. "Three times."

Once again, the old-timers fell quiet. I had a feeling there was more to be said. The question was, which one of them was willing to say it?

"Tedd Archer was a menace," Guy finally said. It was the same word Wick Dugdale had used to describe him. "He thought he didn't have to pay for haircuts just because he owned the building. Madelaine gets her hair cut at Dollie's and she pays. But Tedd was cheap and greedy. Bad combination, if you ask me."

"Bad neighbour too," Pope grunted. He seemed to stare at me. Through me. I adjusted myself in the chair. He didn't seem to like me, although I couldn't think of any reason why not.

"Doesn't mean he deserved to be shot," Graham said.

"I heard he might have been involved in some blackmail," I said, shrugging casually under the barber cape.

I caught Graham's widened eyes in the mirror. Sure, my cousin and the old-timers at Rather Dapper didn't need to know about the blackmail, but if word did indeed travel fast, maybe they would have learned something useful.

"Blackmail?" Bartel jerked his head around. Guy let out a frustrated sigh.

I nodded. "Someone in town got a few letters."

Guy stopped mid-trim. "I got a letter."

Surprised, I turned to the old barber. "In the mail?"

"It was just a folded-up piece of paper on my doorstep. Not a blackmail letter. It was about that photographer friend of yours."

I straightened in my chair.

"Apparently Logan Griffith married our Ginny on a trip to Montreal," Guy said.

I swallowed nervously. "You don't say."

He nodded. "I called her up after I got the letter, thinking it was a joke. But turns out it's true. That whisky addict married Ginny when they were eighteen. The whole thing was in French, so she didn't understand a word of it. And when they got home, he paid big bucks for some hotshot lawyer in the city to end it."

"Montreal is Canada's city of love," Mr. Ellis said without looking up.

"Huh?" Bartel craned his neck around.

"Montreal is Canada's city of love. Like Paris."

"Says who?" Guy snapped at the old English teacher.

"It was one of the clues." Mr. Ellis flapped his crossword book in the air.

Guy shook his head, frustrated. He gave up trying to even out Bartel's sideburns and unleashed him from the chair. Besides, he needed a smoke break.

He fished a cigarette from his pocket and cocked a lighter. The door jingled when he walked out.

"Is he mad?" I eyed Graham in the mirror.

"Mad?" Graham shook his head. "Guy's not mad. Not anymore, anyway. He doused Logan's car in shaving cream and told him to find a fancy barber in the city because he wasn't welcome here. We've even got a sign on the door: *No Logan Allowed*. You didn't see it when you walked in?"

Good grief.

"He sprayed shaving cream on the Bentley?" I asked.

There were a few things Logan didn't let anyone mess with, chiefly his hair and his car. Guy may not have liked what was in the letter, but he had gone to war with the likes of Logan Griffith.

Unfortunately, I knew firsthand what it was like to wage war with Logan.

I sighed. "Logan's going to kill Guy."

It was an expression, of course. I hadn't meant anything by it, certainly nothing literal, but the look on Graham's face was enough to give me pause. He wasn't the type of man who could easily conceal his emotion. He wasn't as hardboiled as I was. He'd always been that way, even in our younger years. And he knew Logan.

"Well, what did Logan do?" I asked.

"Nothing." Graham shook his head. "He drove off. Probably to the car wash."

"Nothing? I find that hard to believe."

"Maybe he's changed." Graham grabbed his broom and did a quick sweep of the floor.

He swung the cape off, releasing me from the chair, but I couldn't move. A thought had flashed through my mind. A memory. The night we had broken into the church and disturbed the fake grave, Logan had assured me that it was a perfect hiding place. He'd had all kinds of things besides the rifle buried under the phoney headstone. He came from a long line of so many other Logan Griffiths that he figured nobody would notice another grave or two...

That had been the first time I saw the devilish grin on Logan's face.

The flashing lights. The chase that ensued. Logan had enjoyed every minute of it. And no doubt he'd enjoyed putting the gun in Wick's face. After all, he hadn't faced any serious repercussions. Just like he hadn't faced repercussions after what he'd done to Ginny.

The Manhattan Man hadn't changed. He had no reason to. I still saw that grin every night at the end of my bar.

I stood up, my legs like jelly, as realization slowly sank in. Logan and the blackmail. Logan and his side job. The photos of Madelaine.

I couldn't unsee the look that had spread over Logan's face when his eyes met Gwynn's that night at the bar. I knew that look. I knew Logan.

Graham rung me up at the counter. "You should stop by for dinner some time. See Marney. Meet the girls."

I told him I would. I always told him I would, but it never happened.

I left Graham a Logan-sized tip for his trouble, stealing a sideways glance at the old-timers' roundtable. Pope was still flipping through his magazine, and Mr. Ellis had started a new crossword.

Guy was loitering by the front door when I stepped out. The smoke break seemed to have calmed him down.

He took a puff of his cigarette as I passed.

"You knew?" His voice was coarse and rough. Dry, almost breathless, no doubt from years of smoking.

I ran a hand through my freshly cut hair. "About Ginny?"

"Don't play dumb, Humphrey." He took another puff. Smoke came through his nose. "Were you there in Montreal?"

"I sat that trip out."

"Too bad. I would have rather Ginny married you. I didn't like you much, but you were the Tom Sawyer to his Huck Finn. Anyway, that's what Walter always said. I think you still are."

"Thank you," I said awkwardly, dodging him and heading down the sidewalk. I shoved my hands in my pockets, knowing he was watching my every move. I hoped I wouldn't need another haircut for a long, long time.

I had been too quick to acquit Logan, my old friend, of murder. The man did have a dark side that I forgot about from time to time. The Logan I knew didn't simply brush things off, clean up and move on, forgive and forget. He wasn't that type. Logan Griffith fought back, unfairly at times, with his wealth and good looks and influence. I had experienced it firsthand, ever since his affair with Ginny. He'd toyed with her, manipulated her. And I hadn't been there to protect her. Any guilt I felt was shadowed by an overwhelming sense of anger. I had gone years without thinking about Ginny. I had gone years without thinking about our ruined friendship. At least, that's what I told myself.

But leaving the past in the past wasn't always possible.

The year after our blowup had been the worst. It had started with little things. Logan had come into the bar and ordered impossible drinks. He'd taunted me with the women on his arm, many of them bearing a striking resemblance to Ginny. Then he'd started his side hustle in one of the motel rooms.

And all the while, he disguised his emotions behind dark beady eyes and devilish grins. He fought subtly. He fought in the dark. But he didn't forget, and neither did I.

There was only one reason Logan hadn't retaliated against Ginny's grandfather. It meant that he already *had* retaliated, in some way. Somehow the problem had been dealt with. Subtly. Behind the scenes. With a dark, devilish grin.

That was the thing about Logan. Problems simply went away, mysteriously. Maybe it had something to do with his money. Maybe something worse.

Either way, I should have seen it sooner.

When I knocked on the door of Room 3, I only half-expected Daphne to be there. She opened the door in her aviator jacket and smiled. The red lips were back, but the ring was still missing from her left hand.

"Guy Russel sprayed shaving cream on Logan's Bentley in the middle of Main Street and kicked him out of Rather Dapper," I said.

Daphne raised an eyebrow. "What are you talking about?"

"Logan. He didn't do anything about the shaving cream. He just let it happen."

I suddenly felt strange, roping Daphne into this mess. She didn't know about Ginny or my old man or the trouble Logan and I had gotten into. She didn't know the Manhattan Man like I did.

I muttered half an apology and turned, cutting across the grass. But she followed me, struggling to keep up.

"Did you talk to Mayor McNally?" she asked.

"Uh-huh." I tried to fill her in on everything she'd missed. "Turns out Tedd bashed his son with a rubber mallet. Madelaine's allergic to cashews. Maharmallo's read Chandler. I don't think he knows about the blackmail."

"Who doesn't know about it? Maharmallo?" She shook her head. "Humphrey, slow down. What's going on?"

"You'd know if you hadn't been off in the city with Redhill all weekend."

"It was one day. What's eating you?"

I stopped and turned around. "Why isn't Logan mad at Guy?"

"For what?"

"Good grief—for the shaving cream!"

"Should he be?"

I shook my head, frustrated. "I want to see those blackmail letters."

"And I want to know what happened to you."

"I got a haircut."

"I can see that. Where are we going?"

I just turned and kept going, moving one foot in front of the other. And for some reason, she followed. I let her. After all, it wasn't really Daphne I was angry with.

Logan's house on Cigare Street wasn't only the biggest house on Pearl's oldest and most prestigious street, but the biggest house in all of Pearl, rumoured to have originally been built by the town's first millionaire, which surprisingly hadn't been Logan's granddad. Logan had moved in shortly after leaving the family business for the fifth and final time, but it had no doubt been paid for by Granddad Griffith.

Although vacant and on the market for nearly half a decade, the price hadn't gone down, and I didn't think Logan made enough — either as a newspaper photographer or his side hustle — to buy the front door, let alone the entire house. It was over a hundred years old, but both exterior and interior had been beautifully updated while maintaining its original bones.

I had only been inside once or twice, but I remembered a big kitchen and a pool in the back yard. The home was built on a corner lot, with a large front lawn and curved driveway where Logan's Bentley was parked.

I stole a quick glance over my shoulder at the private eye. She had followed me the whole way without saying a word. I couldn't tell if she was angry or confused or both. Perhaps I had gone too far with the whole Redhill thing.

Still, she was right next to me as I rang Logan's doorbell. The photographer opened the door, balancing a comb in his teeth while he fastened the top buttons of his collared shirt.

"What do you want, Humphrey?" he asked through gritted teeth.

"I want to see the blackmail letters."

He grabbed the comb and ran it through his hair. "I don't remember hiring you."

It was my turn to grit my teeth. "Fine. Daphne wants to see the letters."

"Daphne already saw them."

Daphne, deciding it was time to intervene, tossed Logan an eager look. "Humphrey thinks he knows who the blackmailer is."

He sighed and tucked the comb in his back pocket. "Then hurry up and tell me. I'm late for work."

"I want to see the letters first."

"I'll bring them by the bar later."

"I want to see them now," I said.

However messy Logan was at work, he was doubly so at home. When he let us in, I took in the house's high-vaulted ceilings, black-and-white trim, and arched doorways from one room to the next. Despite the opulence, my former friend's clutter had the entrance busting at the seams. The coat closet was so stuffed that it didn't close properly, and I stepped over a pile of various shoes, in and out of season. A tall, gaudy-looking mirror stood across from the door. It spooked Daphne, although I didn't understand why—that is, until I looked into it myself and saw what presided over us: a massive, taxidermized elk head hanging over the door.

"I have a cousin who hunts big game," Logan explained as we stared up at it.

I couldn't help peering into one of the open rooms as we passed the staircase. It seemed to be Logan's home studio. There was a camera on a stand and a neutral backdrop draped behind a couple of barstools. I pictured Madelaine Archer perched on one of the barstools while Logan flashed his camera. *Click-click, click-click.* I took in a breath and kept going.

The kitchen was a disaster. Dishes were piled high in the sink and on the cooktop. Stains splattered the counter and tiled backsplash. A glass bowl with runny egg yolks had been tipped over by the weight of a whisk.

The small breakfast nook by the window, however, was set neatly with two platefuls of steaming scrambled eggs and hashbrowns.

"Expecting someone?" I asked.

"Why does it matter?"

For the first time since he'd opened the door, I really paid attention to him. He looked awful. He had buttoned his shirt wrong, missing a button at the bottom so it was all bunched up at the top, and he had forgotten to brush out his eyebrows. Something was off.

"Where are the letters?" I asked.

He muttered something under his breath and wandered over to one of his kitchen drawers. He tried to open it but found it jammed. He shoved his hand in the narrow opening, trying to rummage through the contents. Finally, he pulled out a bundle of papers held together with a rubber band and handed the stack to me with an irritated look on his face.

There were four letters in total, all typed on white paper and folded into thirds.

The first turned out to be the one that had gotten him kicked out of Rather Dapper.

> **Darling Logan,**
> **One thousand cash. Bardakci's garage. Twenty-four hours.**
> **Or Guy Russel finds out you married Ginny.**
> **Sincerely,**
> **I-Know-What-Happened-In-Montreal**

The old car dealership on Second Street, Bardakci's to us locals, was as rundown as the rest of town, even if its owner was energetically young at heart. I doubted Emre Bardakci sold used cars on the daily, but the repairs alone would've kept him in business. Nobody could fix a car like old Emre. At least that was what Seth always said whenever he had tried to encourage me to resurrect my old man's Shelby from the alley.

I had to admit, Bardakci's was the perfect drop-off point. The garage out back stood on its own, separated from the uneven lot of used vehicles. It was a known fact that Emre Bardakci never locked his garage at night. His rental units across the street had better security. But he liked to say that folks in town were honest as the day was long. He'd never had a break-in. Until now, I supposed. Although technically he still hadn't.

It seemed Logan's blackmailer was using Bardakci's unlocked garage to their advantage. It was easy entry and exit, both for Logan and his blackmailer. Since it was on Second Street, it was off the main drag, which meant there was less chance of either party being seen. And Emre himself was never around come five o'clock. He didn't live on the property, nor across the street where he had tenants.

Assuming Logan's blackmailer had indeed been Tedd, he could have dropped the letters on Logan's doorstep and retrieved the money twenty-four hours later, somewhere inside Bardakci's. It was clever.

I only saw one flaw. "Emre must have seen him. Tedd. Loitering around. Four letters and he doesn't slip up once? I find that hard to believe."

Logan ripped the stack of letters from my hand, tossing them carelessly on the counter. "It was Tedd then. That's what you came to tell me?"

But I could still feel the paper between my fingers, soft and thin— strangely thin. It felt almost like newsprint, and the ink was dull in spots. And there was something old-fashioned about the typeset.

"That's your big revelation?" Logan went on, flashing a devilish grin. "I already told you it couldn't be him, Humphrey. I doubt he knew anything about my at-home photography, and if you'd read the second letter you'd see—"

He bit off whatever else he was going to say when he saw me shaking my head.

"Oh, I think he knew," I said.

A glare. "What's that supposed to mean?"

"I think Tedd knew about your photography, Logan. And I think you knew he was blackmailing you."

"That's ridiculous," Logan said with a laugh. "If I knew it was Tedd, why would I hire a private eye?"

I glanced at Daphne. She had seated herself at the breakfast nook and only stared back at me, wide-eyed.

"Daphne's your alibi," I said. "And you didn't think she would solve it."

Her wide eyes narrowed. She hadn't liked that.

"Solve what?" Logan sighed. He still looked terrible.

I ignored him, picking up the letters and forcing the stack back into his hands. "Feel that? That's typewriter paper. And that's a typewriter font. A 1970s typewriter, I'm guessing. If I can figure that out, so can you."

"Thank you, Humphrey. I'm flattered."

"A typewriter is one of the antiques that went missing. You knew that."

"I didn't know until I saw her list," Logan said, waving a frustrated hand in Daphne's direction.

I shook my head. "I think someone told you before then."

"Really? Who?"

"Gwynn Grant."

Logan frowned. "I'm sorry?"

"Gwynn overheard Tedd talking about a missing typewriter. She told you about it. She knew you were being blackmailed."

"How would she know that?"

"You showed her the letters."

Logan took a step back. "That's ridiculous. I don't even—"

"There's something going on between you two," I cut in. "I knew it the second she sat across from you that night at the bar, and then you couldn't say her name when I asked you about the motel's reopening."

He began to protest, then gave up and started rebuttoning his shirt. "You're right. There *was* something going on between me and Gwynn, but not anymore. I broke up with her."

"Did she tell you that Tedd accused her of stealing?"

"No—I don't know. I don't care about Gwynn, Humphrey. Like I said, we broke up."

"But because of Gwynn, you knew it was likely that Tedd had stolen his own typewriter. And that he was using it to blackmail you."

A devilish grin. "That's insane."

I turned towards Daphne and she stood, suddenly spooked. Her green eyes seemed to be searching mine and then quickly averted them as she inched away. She didn't want to end up between us. That much was obvious.

I turned back to Logan. "Why don't you tell us what happened at Rather Dapper?"

My former friend, thoroughly annoyed, rubbed his head in his hands. "What are you talking about, Humphrey?"

"Guy Russel covered your Bentley with shaving cream."

"Who told you that? Mag?"

"Why didn't you say anything?"

"I didn't hire you."

I looked at Daphne. "Did he tell you?"

She shook her head.

Logan sighed. "I didn't think it was relevant."

"So you got kicked out of Rather Dapper because you ignored a black-mail letter and you didn't think it was relevant?"

"I'll find a barber in the city. Maybe visit Darling Daphne while I'm there."

This time, we both looked at her. She hadn't moved. She still looked a little spooked. Maybe it was the elk head.

"You did nothing," I said to Logan. "You let Guy Russel toss you around and spray shaving cream on your car and all you did was drive off into the sunset."

"What's wrong with that?"

"You knew it was Tedd who told Guy about Ginny. That's why you weren't mad about what happened at Rather Dapper. You were mad at Tedd."

"So what? You think I murdered him?"

When I didn't answer, he stormed out of the kitchen, past Daphne and me. He turned around when he reached the hallway. His beady eyes glared at me. His devilish grin disappeared.

"Really, Humphrey, we have our differences, but a murderer?"

"I saw a photo of Madelaine," I said calmly. "One of your photos. Tedd had it with him at the motel. So he knew about your side job, Logan. Everybody does."

He shook his head. "I was with you the night of the murder, Humphrey."

"You weren't there the whole time," I said. He'd left after midnight. He'd been gone fifteen minutes.

"Neither was Daphne!" Logan said.

We both turned to look at her. She stared back, wide-eyed still. She bit her lip, but she didn't say anything. Of course, Logan was right. There had been a moment that night when even Daphne hadn't been around. I had assumed she'd gone into the ladies' room.

"But you left *after* midnight," I said to Logan, "to get Daphne's room key from the Bentley. Or had it been in your pocket all along?"

He swore under his breath just as a loud *thud* sounded from the staircase, like the stubbing of a toe. Then we heard limping footsteps across the hardwood and the click of a door.

"Someone's here," I said.

I caught Logan's dead-eye stare. He tried to stop me as I dashed out of the kitchen, but I broke free from his grasp, stumbling over the messy pile of shoes and feeling the invisible weight of the overhead elk as I pulled open the front door.

EMILY B. KERROS

The woman I was pursuing must have heard it open, because she stopped running instantly. She turned around slowly and scowled.

I had to hand it to her. She had almost escaped, barefoot on the lawn, wearing nothing but Logan's oversized shirt with her brown hair tied up in a knot.

11

A GUY WALKS OUT OF A BAR

"Well, if it isn't Miss Sunshine," I said.

Gwynn Grant threw the first punch. It wasn't really a punch. More like a slap, with her hand wound up in a fist. She marched right up to me and batted her hand across my face and said something bad-mannered. I should have expected it from her, but I held my jaw in shock and spit on the ground.

I turned to Logan, who was standing in the doorway. "You call this a breakup?"

"I call it none of your business."

"I just made it my business. You lied to me."

"I fudged a little." Logan grinned, then called out to Gwynn. "This isn't a bed-and-breakfast, darling. I'm late for work."

"Shut up, Logan," she hissed. "I was just leaving."

I grabbed her by the arm and smelled booze in her hair. "You're not going anywhere until you tell us about the typewriter."

"What typewriter?" She tried to wriggle free.

"The antique typewriter that went missing. Tedd stole it from himself. He used it to write Logan's blackmail letters."

Gwynn gave me a bewildered stare.

Logan grinned at her. "Humphrey thinks I'm a murderer."

She started to laugh hysterically and I let go of her arm.

"Maybe Logan had help," I said.

Her face turned into a scowl. "I didn't have anything to do with Tedd's murder."

Logan walked up behind her. "Never mind Humphrey, darling. He's in one of his moods. Where are your shoes?"

He caught Gwynn with one arm and redirected her towards the front door. She wandered off in another fit of laughter.

Logan tried flashing me one of those devilish grins, but it wasn't quite the same.

"I'm late for work, Humphrey," he said. "Mag's probably going to tattle on me. I'll see you tonight at the bar."

I dug my feet into the ground. "I'm telling Maharmallo about the blackmail."

He turned around. "What?"

"The photos you took of Madelaine, the photos you take of other women … it's motive for blackmail. And blackmail is motive for murder. I have to tell Maharmallo." I stared him down. "I know you, Logan. I know what you're capable of."

The photographer swung a right hook with surprising force. I tried to duck, but his fist landed in my eye and I fell backwards. I pawed at him, pulling him with me, and we both landed on the grass with a thud. I managed to get up on my knees, blinking and trying to see straight, but Logan didn't give me a chance. He grabbed me by the shirt and socked two punches to my nose. As he leaned over me, his hair dangled overtop the smug look on his face.

I tore the comb from his back pocket and swiped it across his face. He let out a yell as it snapped in half. I threw a punch under his chin, feeling my knuckles crack as my fist connected with his jawbone. It propelled him sideways, the wind knocked out of him.

He choked for air but landed with another thud and tried to get up, crawling on his hands and knees on the grass, wheezing for breath.

Daphne rushed over to him. Gwynn stood in the doorway with a complacent look on her face, but she was watching me instead of Logan.

I scrambled to my feet and left Logan behind. Staggering down Cigare Street alone, I felt my eye begin to swell up. Blood dripped from my nose and onto my shirt. I wiped my sleeve across my face, hardly caring what it looked like.

It had been a long time since Logan and I had fought like that.

Somewhere halfway down the street, I realized that Daphne hadn't followed me. I didn't blame her.

I barely remembered the walk home. In some sort of daze, I stumbled into the bar and grabbed the first bottle I saw. I glanced down at the label. Griffiths. Of course.

Crashing through the back door into the alley, I lurched towards the car, covered by the weathered tarp. It had been parked there for fifteen years, and I doubted I had even looked at it in five. It used to purr like a kitten. Now I didn't think it would run.

That didn't matter, though, since I didn't even know where the keys were.

Nonetheless, I stepped towards it and pulled off the tarp. There it was: my old man's classic Shelby with a luxurious coat of pearly white paint and classic black stripes. It wore the stripes like war paint, dividing the hood and dipping across the fenders. Somehow it looked new.

The door creaked open and I slid into the dusty driver's seat. It smelled like stale whisky and old books. I leaned my head against the headrest. Every bone in my body ached and my heart still pounded.

I popped the bottle open and took a swig. I gagged it down. It didn't feel good.

I thought about Logan, keeled over on his front lawn. Perfect Logan. Manhattan Man. Devilish grin. Charming smile. Logan, who got away with everything.

He had convinced me to steal the Shelby once when my old man had passed out after a midnight shift. Logan had rode shotgun with Ginny in the backseat. We had stolen some whisky to take with us. We drove to the city and talked about Montreal. When my old man found out about it, he had been furious. Logan's, somehow, hadn't. Logan had gone to Montreal as planned. Logan had married Ginny.

Somewhere in between it all, my old man had died. And Logan had gotten away with digging a fake grave in the cemetery. For how long? I didn't know. And he'd pointed a hunting rifle at Wick Dugdale. He had been trying to help. I knew that. But I hadn't asked Logan to take it that far. I hadn't seen the devilish grin on his face before then.

I supposed I hadn't known him then. Not really.

Perhaps Cynthia was right. We were foolish to hold on to the past.

But Logan's past had caught up to him. Nobody would be fooled by his charm anymore. He had messed up this time. He'd gotten away with a lot over the years, but he wouldn't get away with murder.

I waited for the pounding in my chest to stop. I didn't know how long I sat there waiting for it to calm down. Eventually it did. But the nagging feeling in the pit of my stomach wouldn't go away, even after more whisky. I supposed that was why I didn't drink. It didn't work for everyone.

I stumbled out of the Shelby, slammed the door, and covered it again with the tarp. I shooed away a stray, smashing the whisky bottle against the brick wall. Stripping like a madman, I tore off my shirt and tossed the whole bloody thing in the dumpster.

He wouldn't get away with murder.

"I'll have two Manhattans."

I looked up from behind the bar. It wasn't Logan. It was a man with an orange beard, and I didn't recognize him. He did a double take at my black eye but didn't ask any questions. Maybe he thought it was just a shadow. At times like these, I was thankful for the dimly lit bar.

I flipped over two cocktail glasses and turned to my backbar. There was an empty space where the bottle of Griffiths had been, so I used another brand for the Manhattans. After sliding the cocktail glasses across the bar to Orange Beard, I pulled the hatch behind the backbar and ducked down the short flight of rickety stairs into the cellar where I stored my extra bottles. I ran my hand along the shelves, but the familiar bronze label was nowhere to be found.

Good grief. I had smashed my last bottle of Griffiths.

Defeated, I climbed back up the stairs and closed the hatch. When I came back around, someone was sitting at the sidebar.

"How's the eye?" Daphne asked as she flipped open the menu.

"I've had worse."

"You should see the other guy."

"The other guy started it," I muttered, grabbing a dishrag.

"Well, you accused the other guy of murder."

"He lied to us."

She folded the menu. "You're really going to tell Maharmallo about the blackmail?"

"Why shouldn't I?"

"It's my case."

She was right about that. It wouldn't be fair.

I watched her pick up the menu again and run a long, pointed finger through all the options. I mixed another Manhattan for Orange Beard and brought out some orders for Seth. She was still studying the menu when I returned with a cup of black coffee.

"Fine. I won't tell Maharmallo," I said, and she smiled. "You know, Seth is famous for his cheeseburgers."

She ordered one—hold the pickles.

"I don't doubt you," I said.

She looked puzzled.

"I know you were gone for a bit the night of Tedd's murder. I couldn't help noticing." At this, she smiled again. "But I only meant to say that Logan used you. That's what he does. He uses people. And I'm sorry about what I said earlier. About Tanner... uh, Redhill."

"It's all right, Marlowe," she said, smiling once again. I liked her smile. But by not agreeing with me, she might as well have been defending Logan. Admittedly, I admired her confidence in my former friend. I only wished I felt the same.

The barstool next to hers remained empty the rest of the night. I found myself glancing at the door every so often, waiting for Logan to walk in. I supposed it was a good thing he didn't. I was fresh out of Griffiths. But somehow it felt like the longest shift of my life. And the nagging feeling in my stomach wouldn't leave. If Logan had been insufferable since the first day he'd walked into Humphrey's, why did it feel so strange now that he had finally walked out for good?

12

THE BIG SCOOP

"Where's your father's car? Don't tell me you've traded it in for … this."

We were tired of walking, so we'd taken Daphne's beat-up SUV to Bardakci's. Evidently the old man didn't approve of the colourless paint and dents in the door.

"The Shelby's fine," I assured him. "Emre, Daphne. Daphne, Emre."

"I'm only teasing," the man chuckled, steering Daphne into the garage, but he gave me a look behind her back.

Emre Bardakci was a short man, usually dressed in grease-stained coveralls and a ballcap. During the day, the doors to his garage were wide open. He'd let the sun in while he slid around the floor on a creeper or rattled through the assortment of tools and parts on his workbench. When he felt lonely, he'd play a little music on the radio and sometimes he'd whistle along. And he refuelled with a lot of coffee breaks.

"Coffee?" He lifted a pot from his desk. It must have been fresh. It was still steaming, as though he had been expecting us.

Daphne nodded eagerly.

As he poured, he leaned closer to her. "Did Humphrey tell you about his father's car? How he hides that beauty behind a dumpster? It's a shame, really. I don't know how he lives with himself. And I never see him anymore. I have to go all the way to his bar if I want to see him, and even then he's too busy." He offered me a cup. "When's your off day?"

I declined. "Sunday."

"Sunday I'm in church. And I don't see you there either."

Good grief.

"Emre, have you heard about Tedd?" I asked.

He took a sip of coffee and smoothed his greasy moustache. "Unfortunately. Shot, wasn't he? Your neck of the woods?"

"Uh-huh. We think he was blackmailing someone."

Emre bit his tongue.

"What is it?" I asked.

"That new detective was poking around here the other day."

Daphne shot me a look.

"I didn't tell him," I said, hands in the air. I had promised her I wouldn't tell Maharmallo about the blackmail and, as far as I knew, I was a man of my word.

"No, no," Emre cut in, wiping the edge of his coffee cup on his coveralls. "He wasn't here about Tedd. His son bought a car. That one, at the end of the lot. I have to replace the gasket, then it's all his. I only got the sense that the detective had seen better days. He looked dog-tired. All this murder business must be wearing him thin."

I tended to agree. Although the detective had looked tired from the moment I met him.

"You also look like you've seen better days, Humphrey."

Instinctively, I raise a hand to my bruised eye. I had almost forgotten about it.

"It's nothing," I said. Emre knew better than to believe me. But he didn't say anything. I glanced at Daphne before shifting the conversation back to the reason we'd come to Bardakci's. "We think Tedd was using your garage to collect his blackmail money."

Emre choked on his coffee. "You're kidding!"

"Did you ever see Tedd loitering around?"

"No. Tedd didn't do business here. Too good for little old me."

"What about Logan?"

"Logan Griffith? He hasn't been back here since he bought the Bentley. Remember his first car? I only just sold it to the crusher. It was rusting out behind my garage for years. I always thought he'd want it back if the Bentley became too rich for his blood."

Evidently it hadn't. Still, I appreciated Emre's sentimental side.

"Just the same," Daphne inserted, "maybe you should start locking your doors."

"I haven't locked my doors in thirty years!" Emre said stubbornly. "And Tedd's dead, isn't he? He won't be causing any more trouble."

That was that. There was no use arguing with him, set in his ways. And he had a point, even if he hadn't been much help.

He walked us out, around his workbench and past the car he was working on.

Once outside, he leaned close to Daphne again. "Tedd wasn't the only landlord in town. See those houses across the street? I had a tenant move out last week. It won't be available for long."

Taking the hint, Daphne smiled politely. "Oh, I'm not here to stay."

"Pearl grows on you," he replied with a wink.

I wasn't sure about that. It hadn't grown on me.

Emre watched us leave in Daphne's SUV before disappearing back into the garage. I realized, as I stared at my black eye in the passenger mirror, that not only had Pearl not grown on me, it was in fact lost on me. The buildings passed as we drove through town, each one as familiar as the next. Great Pearl, the church. The cemetery. Maharmallo's police station. When we turned onto Main Street, there was Bartel's Used Books and the post office.

The town hadn't changed. Perhaps, I thought to myself, I hadn't either.

I had never liked losing things. As a kid, I had lost endless games of slapjack to Seth. I had lost my favourite sweater once at the park. I had lost my family at eighteen, my old man to a terrible accident and my mother as a consequence. I had lost sight of the man I wanted to become before tragedy had struck. I had lost Ginny—and because I had lost Ginny, I also lost Logan.

Strange as it was, it felt like I had lost Logan all over again.

We stopped at the light, the *Gazette* offices up ahead. It was too soon to stop in, surely. Better to wait until the incident on his front lawn had blown over.

But I wondered if anything between Logan and I had ever blown over.

I asked Daphne to pull over, the words out of my mouth before I really knew it. She nodded wordlessly and, as if reading my mind, parked right outside the *Gazette*. I exited the vehicle and turned to look at her. There was something in her eyes I couldn't quite place. Had she lost interest? Yet another thing I'd lost, I supposed, though I couldn't tell for certain. More likely it was doubt that I would actually make things right with Logan. *"I don't doubt you,"* I had said. But evidently, she doubted me.

"Should I wait?" she asked.

"No, go on back to the motel. I could be a while."

But she hesitated at the curb until I waved her off.

I hesitated myself, at the bottom of the steps. I hadn't planned on stopping in at the *Gazette*. I had no idea if Logan was at work or the extent of his injuries. Perhaps he'd taken a sick day. If he was there, I wasn't even sure I wanted to see him. What was I supposed to say to a man I had accused of murder?

Finally, I shoved my hands in my pockets and gathered my wits, forcing myself to take the steps one at a time. I nearly bumped into Pearl's star reporter at the door.

"Humphrey?"

"Mag. Heading out?"

"Not if you're heading in," she said, smiling. She backed up. "Logan's not here. He told me to tell you that."

"Ah."

So he didn't want to see me either.

"That's quite the eye." Mag hardly had to look at my face.

"It's nothing."

"Quite the brawl yesterday too, I heard."

I looked up. "Did Logan say something?"

"No, but he showed up late again, with a scratched face and a bottle of whisky. The rumour mill filled in the rest."

"Good grief."

"It was his front lawn, Humphrey. Bound to be news. I even came up with a headline: 'Humphrey vs. Griffith: Old Friendships Die Hard.' What do you think?"

"I think it definitely died hard."

She pushed her glasses up her nose. "Do you want to talk about it?"

"Aren't you busy?" The offices seemed quiet. But she was pretty much Pearl's only reporter. And clearly she had places to be.

"Nothing that can't wait," she said, pointing me in the direction of her office. It was identical to Logan's but with a feminine touch. Less messy. A coatrack by the door. Framed photos on the wall. A vase of flowers by the window.

She sat me down in one of her chairs and disappeared, returning with two glasses of water from the watercooler.

"Off the record?" I asked.

She nodded. Despite her job as a reporter, I had no doubt Mag could be discreet.

"I thought Logan murdered Tedd Archer."

Her jaw dropped. She pushed at her glasses again. "You can't be serious?"

"I was. I told him as much."

"Oh, Humphrey …"

To my own shock, I began at the very beginning. Mag, having grown up in Pearl and being roughly around the same age as me and Logan, remembered our friendship well. She remembered, in fact, the very day it was formed; we had started sitting together on the bus to and from school. She had the memory of an elephant, which, given her professional excellence, didn't surprise me. She knew about our falling out. Logan's failed marriage. Ginny. Montreal. The works. She knew about Logan's complicated history with his family and his side hustle. She even knew about his recent relationship with Gwynn. According to Mag, it had been short-lived yet seemed unusually serious.

But she hadn't known about the blackmail.

"Wait," Mag interrupted. "Daphne is a private eye?"

I nodded. "Logan hired her."

"Why?"

"I thought you knew he was being blackmailed."

"I knew he was hiring a private eye. He never said anything about blackmail." She leaned back and removed her glasses, rubbing her eyes. The mere mention of Logan being blackmailed seemed to upset her. Perhaps "Mag the Nag" didn't dislike her photographer as much as she let on.

"We think Tedd was blackmailing him," I went on, telling her about the money Daphne had found in Tedd's wallet and how it was the exact amount that had been asked for in all the blackmail letters. "Logan left the bar that night, right around midnight, and there's a witness who heard two men arguing about money."

Mag collected herself, replacing her glasses on the bridge of her nose. "So he had both motive and opportunity. The only question is: is he capable of murder?"

I sat back, nodding slowly. That was indeed the question, the one that had caused the nagging feeling in my stomach. As much as I thought him capable, Logan was no murderer. Sure, he lived a little on the dark side, possessed a devilish grin, but that didn't make him a devil himself.

"If not Logan," Mag said, interrupting my thoughts, "then who?"

There were still so many unanswered questions. Madelaine's so-called poisoning. The rubber mallet incident with Teddy. The missing antiques. And there was something about the motel's reopening, something I had noticed while looking through Logan's photos …

I leaned forward. "Was Madelaine at the reopening?"

"No," Mag answered confidently. "She was supposed to be there for the ribbon-cutting but never came."

"What about your interview with Tedd that day? Did he seem like himself?"

"He bragged about himself all day. I'd say that was usual for him."

I stood up. So did Mag.

"Humphrey, I think you should know. That freelancer who's staying at the motel? He was here yesterday talking to my editor."

"Cosmo Clarke?"

She nodded. "I think he wrote something for the paper but my editor wouldn't take it. He wasn't too happy about it. But I overheard them talking about Tedd's murder."

So Cosmo had written something for the newspaper? Something about Tedd's murder? That seemed odd. It certainly would have been a change from polar bears and giant tortoises. Admittedly, I was curious to read it. But the *Gazette*'s editor likely already had a story lined up for the front page, and if anyone was going to write about a murder in town it was going to be our star reporter.

"Thank you, Mag," I said.

"Anytime. Anything else I can help you with?"

Maybe I wasn't known for good ideas, but the idea that popped into my head at that moment seemed to be a pretty darn good one.

"Actually, I'd like to place an advertisement."

That night, Cosmo walked into my bar. At least, it looked like Cosmo. He took a seat at the empty sidebar, wearing his Panama hat, though everything else about him seemed different. He appeared dejected, his shoulders slumped.

He sighed audibly when I approached. "Humphrey."

"Cosmo."

"How do you like your whisky?"

I looked at him and blinked a couple of times. "I don't."

"Fancy that."

He picked up Seth's menu and flapped it open. Unlike his previous visits, he didn't proclaim his name far and wide. He didn't brag about his adventures and accomplishments. He didn't go on and on about his hat collection. He just sat there at the bar, flipping through Seth's menu. Gone was the cocky, babbling dud of a writer. In his place was a sighing mess of a man. He was positively depressed.

"Humphrey?"

I looked at him again.

"You *have* heard of me, haven't you?"

"Not before I met you," I replied, honestly.

"That *Gazette* editor said he'd never heard of me either. He wouldn't take my piece on the dead guy in Room 7."

I leaned on the bartop. "I didn't know you were writing a piece on Tedd's murder."

He sighed. "Waste of time, now that I'm looking back. But I couldn't really stop myself." He folded the menu. "I'll just have another one of those Manhattans, if it's not too much trouble."

I slid a Manhattan in front of him minutes later. His only response was another long sigh. I shook my head in disbelief. Who was he and what had he done with the exasperating Cosmo?

"What did you write?" I finally asked him.

"I can't tell you here. Meet me at Room 6 in an hour."

I glanced at the clock. "Midnight. I have a bar to run."

He nodded slowly, downed his drink, and left.

Midnight. Another foggy night. The crickets were chirping and I listened for the last few vehicles rolling out of the parking lot before knocking on the door of Room 6, entirely unsure of what awaited me.

Cosmo poked his head out, still wearing his Panama hat. "Are you alone?"

"I think so," I said. I hadn't seen anyone besides my own shadow.

He peered out the door and checked both ways, just in case, before letting me in. Room 6 was just like the other motel rooms. Queen-sized bed. Nightstands. Wardrobe. But there were hats all over the place and an overstuffed suitcase in the corner. Cosmo offered me a seat in one of the two chairs by the window. He perched himself on the chair opposite me, removing his hat and placing it carefully on his lap.

"Now, why did you want to meet with me?' he asked.

"I didn't. I wanted to know what you wrote. You told me to meet you."

"You think the *Gazette* was wrong to turn me down." He hadn't phrased it as a question and it was a poor assumption on his part, but he gave me a toothy smile and I went along with it.

"Fame such as yours … how could they?"

He flashed another smile. "Someone once gave me some advice, Humphrey—can I call you Humphrey?"

I didn't see why not. He already had, multiple times. I insisted he go on.

"Yes, the advice! 'Write the big scoop and nothing but the scoop.' The greatest advice I've ever received. And so I had to write about the murder next door. I had to, you see, because I had the big scoop."

"What big scoop?" I asked.

"I'm afraid I heard—I saw—more than I thought!"

I stiffened. What could Cosmo possibly have heard or seen that he hadn't shared with Maharmallo? He had admitted that he "fudged" here and there, but outright omission was something else entirely. It didn't make sense that he would withhold information about Tedd's murder for his article.

Pale moonlight beamed on the sidewalk, and the light above the doorway swayed gently in the breeze. I had left my shadow outside. I almost wished I'd stayed out there with him. Ah, but I was all in. Whether I liked it or not.

"What do you mean?" I asked, trying to focus on the freelancer.

Cosmo cocked his head. "I remembered a few more things. Two things, actually. Both could be significant but one is more significant than the other, though I suppose it's not for me to determine—"

"You lied?"

"I didn't lie! Everything I told you is true. Except I'm not really deaf in one ear." He fingered the brim of his hat. "One of those voices belonged to Tedd. The other? Oh, I don't know, I would guess a young man, or possibly a woman. I heard them at midnight. I dozed off for a bit. But when I woke up again, I went outside and saw that the door to Room 7 was open."

"And then what?"

"Then I went in to try on the coat," he admitted sheepishly.

"I'm sorry?"

"The Italian coat. I just wanted to see what it felt like."

I stood up. "You did what? You didn't think to call the police?"

"He was dead! He didn't know any different. And it's not like I took it."

Good grief. I shook my head and headed for the door.

"You can't think I murdered him!"

The outburst from Cosmo was sudden, desperate even. He was still perched on the edge of his chair, elbows propped on either side.

"The detective searched my room, remember? If I'm such a murderer, where do you suppose I hid the revolver? In the drawer with the Bible? Under my hat?" He lifted his Panama for effect. "I didn't do it, Humphrey. I wouldn't fudge about that."

I didn't for a moment think he had murdered Tedd. He hadn't known Tedd, after all. He was from out of town. He hardly had business being in Pearl anyway. He had no motive besides the fact that he had admired Tedd's Italian coat, and he hadn't even bothered taking it. He'd made a mess of the crime scene instead.

But he had been in the room next door. He'd heard voices arguing. He could have seen anyone coming or going.

I turned around. "So what have you magically remembered, Cosmo?"

"I saw a woman that night."

I eyed him. "You saw a woman?"

"A brown-haired woman leaving Room 7 after midnight." Cosmo stood up, pointing out the window with his hat. "I saw her right there. It's the only room she could have come out of."

"Did you see her face?"

Cosmo shook his head. "It was too dark, and she had her back to the light."

"Where did she go?"

"I lost sight of her halfway up the sidewalk. But she had brown hair. I thought it was a dream."

There was no hesitation in his answers, but he could still have been lying. If he was telling the truth, then we were no closer to finding Tedd's murderer. There were lots of brown-haired woman in Pearl. Madelaine Archer, Brigid Dugdale, and Gwynn Grant, just to name a few. It could have been anyone.

Dream or not, he should have told Maharmallo.

"And that curly-haired fellow ..." Cosmo began.

"Riley Dugdale?"

"That's it. He's in love with the young wife."

"Madelaine?"

Cosmo nodded.

"How do you know that?" I asked, sceptical.

"It's rather glaringly obvious. Don't you think?"

I didn't know what to think. Riley Dugdale, in love with Madelaine Archer? I thought of the nickname he'd used for her. *Maddy.* But what did that have to do with Tedd's murder?

"Can I read this article of yours?" I asked.

"You might as well." Cosmo sighed. "It'll never see the light of day."

13

LA FEMME DANS LE NOIR

Cosmo got up, tossing his hat onto the bed. He produced a few thin sheets of paper from the nightstand and handed them to me. I settled back into my chair and scanned the article.

> The murder of Ted Archer is Pearl's biggest mystery, seconded only perhaps by the mysterious woman in the dark. She was seen leaving Room 7 that foggy, fateful night, not a trace of her face, only her brown hair.

He had spelled Tedd wrong, with one *d* instead of two. I wasn't surprised. I kept reading.

> This maddening mystery of murder is a rarity in Pearl. Mr. Archer was Pearl's hero, a husband, a father, a wealthy philanthropist ...

I squinted. Philanthropist, really? The freelancer evidently hadn't done any research.

> ... filled with community spirit, pride, and vigour. He saved Pearl's only motel from definite destruction and he cute the ribbon just weeks before his deadly demise.

Cute the ribbon. That was cute.

I skipped over Cosmo's continued praise of the man he had previously described as "an odd duck" and "rather rude."

Far be it for a humble journalist to suggest an illicit affair, but is Mr. Archer's deathly stay at the Pearl Motel not suggestive of woe at home? Could it be that Mrs. Archer had caught the attention of a younger man, an admirer? Perhaps it had been harmless. Perfectly innocent. An affair from afar. The truth of the matter might never be uncovered. But how Pearl's hero must have suffered in the end knowing his very own wife …

I put down the article and looked at the freelancer.

"No wonder they didn't print this," I said.

Horrified, Cosmo tore the pages from my hand. If he had been depressed after the *Gazette*'s rejection, he was likely to be even more so now. I thought I might have permanently deflated his ego, but he doubled down.

"I saw her!" he crowed. "I saw the woman in the dark!"

And in that moment, I had no doubt that he had.

"You have to tell Maharmallo," I said.

He slumped back down and sighed. "I suppose I will. Do you think it could wait until morning?"

"Good grief," I muttered as I exited the motel room. The door closed behind me, rattling the overheard light, and I moved quickly down the sidewalk towards the bar. I could hardly make heads or tails of what had happened.

I entered the bar, locking the door behind me and shutting off all the lights. Seth had long gone home and the entire bar was quiet and still.

I darted upstairs, collapsing into my armchair. My shoulders ached. My feet ached. I could barely keep my eyes awake, yet my mind was reeling.

If I thought about it long and hard, I supposed that evidence about Riley and Madelaine had been there all along. After all, I had seen something in Riley's eyes the night of Tedd's murder, in the way he had looked at Madelaine. The way he'd stood by, looking concerned, when she'd entered the bar, and the way he'd said her name. *Maddy*. And then there had been the way he'd jumped to her defence against Cosmo, a total stranger at the time.

Cosmo was right. The young man's head was turned, albeit by a married woman, but it wasn't like he was the first. I supposed the feeling itself wasn't a crime. Unless of course he had acted upon it ...

It still didn't explain Tedd's stay in Room 7. An affair, at this point, was all speculation, regardless of what Cosmo's unpublished article suggested. After all, hadn't Tedd had a photo of Madelaine? Maharmallo had found it among his things at the motel. There had been a date written across the back, not in Madelaine's handwriting. It had been rougher. Chicken scratch, really. I assumed it was a man's, likely Tedd's.

Then again, if there had indeed been an illicit affair between Tedd's own wife and his employee, then that was motive. Plain and simple.

But was Riley capable of murdering Tedd Archer in cold blood? He reminded me of myself in a lot of ways. Awkwardly tall. A loner. With an unbearable old man. Still, he seemed rather unmotivated. He lived in his parents' basement and, at least according to Gwynn, would've rather played video games than show up for work.

I wasn't sure Riley had it in him. Not the guts. Certainly not the gumption.

I was still completely out of Griffiths. I checked the cellar twice over in case I had missed any lonely bottles. I even searched Seth's kitchen, rummaging through crates full of bottled sauces and cooking wines, but couldn't find a single bronze label.

So when Logan walked into Humphrey's towards the end of my shift, I felt a surge of panic. I stuffed my nose in a book behind the bar and pretended I didn't see him.

Logan leaned over the bar. "Relax, Humphrey. I'm not staying."

I tried not to look disappointed. I snapped my book shut and saw his scratched face. His stare seemed to linger on my eye.

"I thought you should see this." He slapped a copy of the *Gazette* onto the bar.

It was Thursday's edition, a day early. I peered at the front page which, as expected, was plastered with Tedd's face and headline surrounding his death.

"What about it?" I asked, drying a few glasses and sliding them under the bar. I tossed the dishrag over my shoulder.

"Not that." Snatching up the newspaper, he flipped through several pages. When he found what he was looking for, he turned the paper around to face me and pointed at an advertisement.

I didn't have to look down. I knew what it was—the advertisement I had placed in the *Gazette*. Glancing at the ad, I decided that it looked good. It should have. It had cost me enough, especially being printed last-minute.

WANTED:

Rare, collectable, preferably first edition, classic crime novels.

If willing to sell, please contact Neal Humphrey.

Humphrey's bar at the Pearl Motel.

"I thought you didn't read advertisements," I said.

"I don't. Mag showed me."

"So?"

"So … do you have a death wish?"

"Not particularly." I shrugged at Logan, trying to seem nonchalant. Truthfully, I knew my advertisement was a longshot at best. Whoever had stolen the first edition of *The Big Sleep* would hardly be so foolish as approach me with it. But if they did, I'd be ready.

I looked up to find Logan scanning my backbar in suspicion. He had noticed there was no Griffiths.

I felt suddenly sick again, that nagging feeling in the pit of my stomach. I had made a mistake in concluding that Logan had killed Tedd. Devilish grin and beady eyes aside, he was no murderer. I owed him an apology.

I opened my mouth, but strangely nothing came out.

Instead I picked up a cocktail glass. "Manhattan?"

He fixed me with a stare. He wouldn't drink a Manhattan without Griffiths. But just then his phone vibrated in his pocket. He glanced at the screen before picking it up.

It was a quick conversation. I couldn't help but overhear the demanding voice on the other end. There was little dispute on his part.

"Gwynn," he said when he hung up, as if that explained everything. He turned to leave as though expecting me to go with him. But I still stood there, cocktail glass in hand. "Are you coming, Humphrey, or not?"

"Still stalking me, I see," Gwynn said when I arrived at her house with Logan. She lived, as it turned out, in one of Emre's rentals across from Bardakci's. She held the door, wearing more clothes than the last time I'd seen her. She scowled at me and Logan with bloodshot eyes.

"You drink too much, darling."

This coming from the Manhattan Man.

Gwynn didn't dignify his opinion with a response. She led us into the house, a ransacked mess. Stuff was everywhere. Some things were completely broken, smashed on the ground. A table was upturned. Potted plants were spilled onto the floor. A few cupboards in the kitchen had been emptied out recklessly, doors hanging open. I supposed, in this case, her foul mood was understandable.

She barely had time to explain before Emre showed up, still in his coveralls even though it was well after five o'clock.

"Your blonde friend tried to warn me. Locked doors and all that," he said, greeting me. Then he turned to his tenant. "At least this place has a tight perimeter. I'll check the security cameras."

"There's no need," Gwynn replied, frowning. "I know who did it ... I let him in. He said he just needed a friend, needed to talk ... and I believed him. His old man can be overbearing."

"Riley?" I hazarded a guess.

Gwynn nodded. "We only had a few drinks. Next thing I knew he had torn my whole place apart."

"What was he looking for?"

"How would I know?"

She appeared genuinely distressed. And rightfully so. What had Riley been thinking? As much as I sympathized with the young man, I couldn't deny he'd crossed a line.

"I didn't know who else to call," Gwynn added, glancing at Logan. "When he heard you were coming, he took off."

The photographer grinned. "I have that effect on Riley."

I let the two of them be, finding Emre at the door inspecting one of his security cameras. Despite Gwynn's protests, he seemed genuinely concerned.

"Young people are menaces nowadays," he said.

"I wasn't aware Gwynn was one of your renters."

"Oh, I didn't mean Gwynn necessarily. She's not bad. Keeps to herself. Sometimes she's a tad short when the rent's due, but she always makes up for it."

"Do you know Riley Dugdale?"

"Not personally. But he sounds like a menace, doesn't he?"

We helped Gwynn clean up as best we could. Logan offered, more than once, to straighten Riley up. I didn't even want to know what he meant. But Gwynn insisted that she didn't want any trouble with Riley. After all, she had to work with him.

"I thought Madelaine fired him," I said.

Gwynn laughed bitterly. "She did. And then she gave him his job back. Just like that. After he stole from her and everything. And now this ..." She motioned to the ransacked house behind her. "Madelaine's got to be out of her mind. I'm about ready to tell her that it's me or Riley."

"A no-brainer, darling," Logan assured her with a grin.

On the way back to his car, however, he changed his tone. "They're all crazy, if you ask me. Every last one of them."

I had to agree. Madelaine, Gwynn, Riley ... I could barely keep up. Who was firing who, who was blaming who, who was in love with who.

"Is Riley in love with Madelaine?" I asked.

Logan stopped short. "It's obvious, isn't it? I could see it from the start, that night in the bar. I'm not surprised you noticed, Humphrey. You caught me and Gwynn red-handed." He let out a laugh.

"Cosmo noticed," I said.

Logan rubbed the side of his scratched face. "You talked to Cosmo?"

"He also said he saw a brown-haired woman coming out of Tedd's room that night."

"*La femme dans le noir*—the woman in the dark," Logan nodded. He kept walking. "The whole town knows about it. He was trying to write a story for the paper. You don't actually believe him?"

"I think I do."

Another laugh. More devilish. "He's a liar. He probably made it up."

"Or you're just saying that because Gwynn has brown hair."

That ruffled a feather. "Give it a break, Humphrey."

We didn't talk on the way back to the bar. I didn't offer Logan another drink. I doubted he would have taken me up on it. He drove off in a huff and I headed upstairs, settling into the armchair and picking up the manuscript.

But my mind could only focus on one thing: if Madelaine had rehired Riley, then Gwynn was right—she was out of her mind. Either that, or she was in love with him too.

14

THE SMOKING GUN

The stray cat had a death wish. Scratching. Pause. Scratching. Pause. I slid open the window and it made a mad dash for my kitchen. I shooed the stray back outside and it darted down the fire escape with a few hissy meows. I watched its black tail sway back and forth, helping it balance its way down the rails.

It had scratched incessantly all night, with occasional outbursts of wild energy. I had covered my head with my pillow, trying to block out the noise. I told myself I'd never have a cat. Not if I valued my sleep at all. Not if I valued my sanity.

It didn't tire until morning, sunlight cracking through the blinds. Then, as if it knew I was sleeping in, it started up again. That was when it finally let itself be shooed away for good.

Between yawns, I ducked downstairs and flicked on the bar lights. Ah, there was nothing quite like the empty bar—still and calm.

I turned on the light in Seth's kitchen and moved across the tiled floor, my feet landing unwittingly in a puddle with a tiny *splash*. I looked down.

Darn that leaking sink.

There was a sharp *tap-tap* on the glass door. I came out of the kitchen, checking the clock. I wondered who would be visiting me this early. It wasn't Seth, since he always came in through the back door. And Humphrey's wasn't open for a couple more hours.

I found Maharmallo at the door, alone, carrying a copy of *The Pearl Gazette*, crisply folded and tucked under his arm. He raised his hand in a small gesture when he saw me.

"Ah. Humphrey." He held up the paper. "Have you seen this? Grue-some, isn't it? Although I heard it could have been worse."

So Logan had been right. News of Cosmo's "woman in the dark" had broken out among the townsfolk. But the detective didn't strike me as the type of person to listen to gossip. I decided the leaking sink could wait and pulled out two barstools for us to sit on.

"Tess was accosted at the library by a group of old women. Asked her what colour we're painting our bedroom. Previous owners went with a boring sort of beige apparently." Maharmallo shook his head, the hint of a smile pulling at his mouth. "Small towns."

"You'll get used to it," I said, not for the first time. It suddenly reminded me of Emre. *It grows on you*, he'd said to Daphne. But I had to disagree. And I wondered if anyone ever truly got used to the small-town rumours.

"Anyway, we're painting. And Tess says she has a constant headache from the fumes. I don't, but she says that's because I'm never home. And I'm never home because of this." He flicked the front page of the newspaper, laying it down on the bartop. He turned to me. "And Ethan bought his first car from some guy on Second Street."

The look on my face was a dead giveaway.

"You already knew that."

"Emre Bardakci," I confessed. "Don't worry about it. He's a good guy."

But I couldn't help but wonder why the detective was suddenly involving me in his personal life.

"What brings you in?" I asked.

Maharmallo seemed to snap out of whatever personal turmoil he'd been in. He adjusted his tie, back to his professional self. "I wanted to ask Cosmo Clarke a few more questions. I knocked on Room 6, but he doesn't seem to be in. You haven't seen him?"

I shook my head.

"He hasn't checked out?"

I doubted that. "You'd have to check at the motel office."

Of course. The detective hadn't, in fact, listened to the gossip making its way around town. He had heard about the woman in the dark directly from Cosmo. I was glad the freelancer had done the right thing and told Maharmallo about what he'd seen. Although it seemed strange that the detective would act so casually in regards to a man who'd walked all over his crime scene without bothering to report it.

"This so-called woman in the dark? Cosmo told you he saw her?"

Maharmallo nodded.

"Me too," I said. "But he said he saw her *after* he went in to try on Tedd's coat. So Tedd was already dead."

Maharmallo's tired eyes creased at the corners. "He tried on Tedd's coat?"

Apparently the detective didn't know everything. It seemed Cosmo had yet again fudged a few details.

Maharmallo stood up. I watched his broad shoulders stiffen and then relax a little, the way they had the first night when I'd met him in the fog. I was used to seeing it now. It seemed to happen when he had trouble focusing. He took deep breaths, in and out. His hands were shaking. He rested them on the bar, grasping his newspaper again.

It was just like Cosmo to tell a lie. Or a partial truth. Or omit the truth altogether. It was exasperating for the detective, no doubt. Especially since, as he had already alluded to, Tedd's murder investigation was consuming his life. He was hardly home. Clearly, he hadn't been sleeping well.

I looked at his shaky hands. Maybe he was drinking, just to cope.

But wasn't Maharmallo an experienced detective? Hadn't he handled plenty of murder cases back in Vancouver? He had asked me for help. He had asked me for my opinion on folks in Pearl. He had claimed it was because he didn't understand small towns. But it was obvious he was exhausted, too tired to try anymore. Perhaps he'd been a great detective once, but there was nothing left.

I watched him breathe in and out.

"Did Cosmo tell you about the argument he overheard?" I asked.

"Yes, he did." Maharmallo nodded. "Something like 'she doesn't love you' and 'where's the money.' I haven't been able to figure it out."

Neither had I. Not completely. Although I had realized an interesting connection. The "money" must have had something to do with the money in Tedd's wallet. One thousand dollars in cash, which we believed was Logan's blackmail money. It had made perfect sense when I suspected Logan of the crime. Except, of course, for the fact that the money hadn't been taken. It had still been there when Daphne and I had found him.

"It seems like it's about the money in Tedd's wallet," I said.

Another deep breath. Maharmallo looked puzzled.

"What money?" he asked.

"The money in Tedd's wallet. Ten separate hundred-dollar bills."

"What?"

"It was there when we found Tedd's body. Daphne counted it and then put it back."

Another disturbance of his crime scene. But the detective's mind was on other things.

Maharmallo shook his head. "There wasn't any money in Tedd's wallet."

He seemed to stop breathing altogether. He hadn't known about the money. He hadn't seen it. Which meant someone had taken the money before the police bagged it up. Someone had been in Room 7—after the murder, after Cosmo, even after Daphne and me.

Good grief. Someone like the woman in the dark.

Maharmallo's shouldered stiffened and his straight face turned into an apprehensive frown. He didn't move, leaning on the bartop and staring down at Tedd's face on his newspaper. He had missed something. Perhaps it was nothing, I thought to myself. But it was hitting him hard. He was taking it personally. He looked old suddenly, with his weathered face and his weary eyes.

He stood there for a while, even as a I started polishing cocktail glasses and flipping over chairs, even as Seth arrived and headed for the kitchen. For a moment, I thought he might stand there until Humphrey's opened, until my lunch rush came barrelling through the door. How would I explain the shaky, broad-shouldered detective in their way?

But finally he muttered something unintelligible and left, crossing the parking lot to his police cruiser. Through the window, I saw him almost bump his head as he ducked into the driver's seat.

It wasn't until after he'd gone that I picked up the copy of the *Gazette* he'd left behind, tucking it into my back pocket. I realized that he hadn't even mentioned my advertisement.

Perhaps the detective wasn't as thorough as I'd thought.

My old man's toolbox had to be somewhere. I could picture it—bright red metal with a solid black handle and latch. I hadn't seen it in years, certainly not since his death. Admittedly, I wasn't handy with a hammer—or any tool, for that matter—but if it had been good enough for my old man, then it was good enough for me.

After rummaging through the cellar for the better part of the morning, I finally found it at the back of the small storage closet under the stairs. It was on the bottom shelf, on top of a folded cardboard box, covered in dust. I wiped off the dust and cracked open the latch. It even smelled like my old man. Well, booze anyway.

I was heading outside, toolbox in hand, when I met Daphne at the door. She was wearing her aviator jacket with her hair pulled back. I caught a trace of her lemony scent as I greeted her.

"Hello, Mr. Fix-It," she said back, smiling. "What's with the toolbox?"

Good grief. I really liked that smile.

I told her about the leaking sink in Room 1. She proceeded to follow me.

"Do you need me to break in?"

I had to admit, her skill for breaking into things was impressive, but I hadn't broken into anything since the church at eighteen. I was a respectable citizen now.

"I have my own ways," I said, swinging open the door to the motel office.

The motel office was nothing more than a door and four walls, with laundry behind the desk and a vending machine in the corner.

"Morning, Ayda," I called. "Can I borrow the key to Room 1? Darn sink's leaking again."

"Again?"

A round head popped out from behind the desk. Ayda Bardakci was folding a stack of white towels. She had been the motel's part-time clerk and cleaner for years. It wasn't busy enough to employ someone full-time, but it kept Ayda occupied during the week when her husband was at the garage fixing cars. She was just as friendly as Emre, though she usually came and went quietly. She always said she liked living behind the scenes.

"Seth's going to have a cow," Ayda said, pulling a brass key out of the drawer. "If he hasn't already."

I took the key from her. "Ah, Seth's mellowed in his old age."

"That toolbox says otherwise. Who's your friend?"

I stepped aside to let Daphne introduce herself.

"Daphne checked in last week," I said.

"I remember," Ayda nodded, smiling at the private eye. "I have a daughter about your age, all grown up. My, doesn't that make me feel old." She laughed and swatted a towel at me playfully. "Next thing I know, you'll be calling me mellowed!"

"Never."

"Go on then. Bring the key back when you're done."

I promised I would, emerging from the office with Daphne behind me. We walked to Room 1 and I inserted the key into the lock before entering.

The water was coming from the bathroom sink. There was a puddle directly under the sink and on the floor, but it seemed like most of the water had seeped under the wall into Seth's kitchen on the other side.

I set the toolbox on one side of the sink and cracked it open. Daphne propped herself up on the other side.

"Ayda seems nice."

"She is. Emre's wife," I said, as if that explained it. I picked up a wrench, turning it over in my hands to examine it. It was old and a little bit rusty. I wondered if it still worked. I supposed I was about to find out. I ducked under the sink.

"Everyone in Pearl is so … lovely." She hesitated on her word choice, but I could hear the smile in her voice. She thought everything was lovely. She knew I'd tease her about it. "It's hard to imagine anyone being a murderer."

I didn't relish the thought of Tedd's murderer being someone I cared about. Seth. Emre or Ayda. Even Cynthia or Logan. But I had to agree with Logan's assessment of Madelaine, Gwynn and Riley … they were all crazy. Something more sinister was going on at Archer's Antique Shoppe. Thefts. Affairs. Murder wasn't so hard to imagine.

"Did you talk to Logan?" Daphne asked, as if reading my mind.

The last time I'd seen her had been when she dropped me off outside the *Gazette*. Of course, a lot had transpired since then.

"Sort of," I said. I clamped the old wrench around the pipe and turned. "We were at Gwynn's house last night. Riley ransacked the place."

"Ransacked?"

"Pretty much. She'd had a few too many and he took advantage of the situation."

"What was he looking for?"

"I don't know." I let out a sigh, rolling over to get a better look at the pipe. Daphne's legs were dangling over the edge of the sink. "Also, there was no money in Tedd's wallet when the police bagged it."

She raised a curious eyebrow. "That's strange. Do you think Riley took it?"

"I don't see how. He was with us that night. We never let him out of our sight." I hit my head on a pipe, letting out a grunt.

"Maybe he went back to Room 7 before he left. All right down there?"

"Uh-huh." I slid out from under the sink, pipe in hand. It smelled awful. I covered my nose with the back of my hand. "Have you read the *Gazette* this morning?"

"No. Why?"

I tossed her the copy I had tucked in my back pocket. "You might want to before we leave."

"And where exactly are we going, Marlowe?"

"After the sink is fixed, antiquing. Riley has his job back."

She flipped open the paper while I tinkered away at the pipes. She didn't say anything about my advertisement either. I supposed she had missed it, not that it bothered me. I didn't particularly feel like explaining it anyway.

But I couldn't help but notice the diamond ring was back, glittering on her left hand. I inhaled a deep breath but nearly choked on her lemony, whisky sour scent. I supposed it didn't mix well with jealousy and stinky bathroom pipes.

Riley Dugdale was back indeed. He was unloading a bunch of half-price Persian prayer rugs from the bed of his pickup, parked in the alley behind the antique shoppe right next to Madelaine's yellow car. The back door was propped open.

I called out to him just as he heaved a rug out of his pickup and over his shoulder. "Riley!"

He swung the heavy rug around, which was no easy feat, seeing me and Daphne approach. But he chose to ignore us, heading instead for the propped-open door. He lowered the rug carefully so as not to unroll it, setting it down inside the shoppe. Then he turned and walked back to his pickup.

"I'm k–kind of busy," he said as he passed me.

"I can see that. Nice of Madelaine to give you your job back."

"She h–h–had to," Riley stuttered. "I d–didn't do anything wrong."

He heaved another rug onto his shoulder and swung it around, missing me by an inch. With the massive rug in between us I couldn't get a good look at his face, but something seemed different. I moved around the rug, pacing myself with him.

"Good grief, Riley! What happened to your nose?"

Riley's nose was swollen, almost double its normal size. It looked bruised or broken, or both.

He shifted his lanky body under the weight of the rug. "Oh, uh, I th–think I bumped it."

"Bumped it how?"

"I d–d–don't remember. Probably when your photographer f–f–friend attacked me."

"A week ago? That looks pretty fresh. Is it broken?"

"I don't know."

"You didn't see a doctor?"

"I d–d–didn't need to."

Riley lowered the rug just inside the door, next to the first one. He repeated the process a couple more times while Daphne and I lingered around his tailgate.

"What were you looking for at Gwynn's?" I asked on one of his rounds.

He let out a sigh. "I was d–d–desperate. Even though Maddy g–gave me my job back, I d–didn't want her to th–think I was the one that was stealing. I thought if I f–f–found one of the missing antiques at Gwynn's place ..."

Perhaps the young man had more gumption than I originally thought.

"The night of Tedd's murder, did you take money from his wallet?"

Riley looked confused. "No. What m–money? Why would I t–t–take money from him?"

"Because he took it from you," I tried.

It was a hasty assumption, I supposed. I still maintained Riley that hadn't had an opportunity to take the money. But Daphne's initial suspicion had fallen on him and I trusted her instincts. *The type that takes*, Madelaine had said when describing the kind of man Tedd had been. It made sense.

I helped Riley lift another rug and steady it on his shoulders. "You said you went to the motel to get something back from Tedd."

"I d–d–don't know anything about any m–money," he said, shrugging it off. Carrying the rug, he started for the shoppe.

But Daphne stopped him. She had been admiring the prayer rugs in the back of the pickup and now pointed at one, made visible by the rug we had just lifted away.

"That isn't a Persian prayer rug."

Riley turned. "What?"

"The one in the middle. The pattern is too plain, like the ones at the motel. And the edges are overstitched. There's no way it's authentic."

I moved around Riley's pickup, inspecting the rug Daphne had spotted. The edges felt fine to me, but I was no rug expert. There was, however, a strange odour coming from the pickup bed. I wondered how I had missed it before.

Before Riley could protest, I hopped up into the back of his pickup and heaved the rolled-up rug diagonally across the others. It did bear a resemblance to the rugs at the motel.

It was heavier than the authentic prayer rugs and didn't appear to be rolled up neatly at all. The thick bundle was harder to unravel. Heaving the rug onto the tailgate, I grasped the edge with both hands and in one swift motion gave it a kick.

Daphne darted out of the way just in time. Riley turned pale, as though he was about to faint.

There on the ground beneath the rusted pickup was the body of Cosmo Clarke, Panama hat and all. And lying next to him was a small black revolver.

15

TWOS AND THREES

"This is getting to be a habit, Humphrey."

Maharmallo's so-called office was nothing more than a tiny desk in a cramped corner of the police station. It was cluttered with paperwork, an ancient-looking computer, and various file folders. Behind his desk was a crooked filing cabinet and a smudged whiteboard. I couldn't help but wonder whether he had given up a skyscraper office in Vancouver—and if so, how he felt about the obvious downgrade.

It was midafternoon and Officer Riggs had walked me over to Maharmallo's desk. Upon my arrival, the detective shrugged out of his suit jacket, hanging it on the back of his chair. He rolled up his shirtsleeves, grabbing one of the manila file folders and tucking it under his arm.

"Follow me," he said.

He walked quickly and seemed to be breathing normally again. I supposed that was a good sign.

We headed down a short hallway with a bright room on either side and glass windows so I could peer into them. Interrogation rooms. The room on the right was occupied. I could see Riley, hands folded on the table in front of him. Wick Dugdale was with him. The window was likely one-way glass. They couldn't see me or the detective walking by. They appeared to be having some sort of disagreement. Riley lifted a hand to his banged-up nose.

Maharmallo opened the door on the left and ushered me in.

"Take a seat, Humphrey. I'll be right back."

He shut the door behind me with a *click*. I thought about checking to see if the door was locked but decided not to. I didn't want to know.

The room looked the same as Riley's. There was a small rectangular table and three chairs, two on one side and one on the other, otherwise the space was completely bare.

Instead of sitting, I waited next to the door and listened to the rushed footsteps and bolstered voices of the officers. I thought I heard Maharmallo's voice among them and began to wonder if the detective had forgotten about me. I had left Seth alone to manage the bar while I was gone, which was almost certainly too much for him at his age. I had told him I wouldn't be gone long.

The door swung open and Maharmallo was back, carrying an evidence bag. Again, he told me to take a seat. I sat in the lone chair and he settled in across from me.

This was it. This was the scene I had imagined the first time I'd met Maharmallo: "Well, well, well, if it isn't the bartender who hated his landlord. Shot him in the head and left him for dead. What do you say to that, Humphrey—what do you say to that?"

But no, Maharmallo wasn't a fist-on-the-table kind of detective.

He tossed the evidence bag on the table. "How well do you know your revolvers?"

"I don't," I replied, but that was a revolver if I had ever seen one—black with a brown handle and a short, stubby barrel. Traces of dirt lined the bottom of the bag.

"It's an old Smith & Wesson snubnose. Model 10," Maharmallo said. "An American revolver. Popular in the mid to late 1960s."

There was a bit of a pause.

"It's an antique," I remarked.

"Ah. A revolver like this is small. It's easy to hold. It's easy to conceal. It has little to no recoil, making it easy to shoot. But how easy is it to procure?"

I didn't know. "Do you think it was procured loaded?"

Maharmallo nodded. He tossed the file folder on the table and flipped it open, turning it around so I could read what it said. "My guys searched Tedd Archer's office and found this. Some of the paperwork is questionable ..."

I scanned the file as the detective went on.

"Looks like the revolver was procured from an antique firearms dealer along with the compatible cartridges. Madelaine says she didn't know anything about it, but Tedd could have bought it as an expensive paper-weight."

"So Tedd procured his own murder weapon?"

"See this?" Maharmallo pointed to a long black cylinder sealed in the bag with the revolver. "It's a suppressor, or silencer. In theory, it would make the revolver absolutely silent."

"In theory?"

"Silencers don't work very well on revolvers. Gas can still escape the muzzle, so the sound of the gunshot is reduced but not eliminated. The question is, why would a paperweight need a silencer?"

"It wasn't Tedd. Someone else procured this weapon."

Maharmallo seemed to agree. "Which suggests that Tedd's murder, at least, was premeditated."

I took in a breath. "No fingerprints?"

"Nothing. The revolver was wiped clean. Except for the dirt in every crevasse."

"What about Riley?"

"Riley swears he doesn't know how Cosmo's body got in his pickup. He's lawyering up."

No doubt on his old man's advice. It seemed unlikely that Riley knew nothing about the body in his pickup. After all, hadn't he loaded and unload-ed the rugs himself?

Maharmallo went on. "Whoever murdered Tedd Archer also murdered Cosmo Clarke. It's not a coincidence that he was murdered after all that 'woman in the dark' business. And based on what we know about the silencer, it's possible he not only saw a brown-haired woman but also heard a gunshot. He could have seen who the murderer was."

I tapped my fingers on the table, trying to think. There was no way the lanky Riley Dugdale could have lifted Cosmo's dead body into the back of his pickup, rolled up in a rug, at least not on his own. It was impossible. He had barely been able lift the rugs. Which meant he would have had help.

"Where'd you get the shiner, Humphrey?"

I looked up. The detective hadn't noticed my black eye before. I assumed he hadn't thought it pertinent.

"Logan," I said.

"Funny. That's who Riley says broke his nose. I seem to recall him getting hit on the back of his head." Maharmallo leaned back, adjusting his tie. "He's hiding something. Riley. But my hands are tied. I don't have any physical evidence or fingerprints or anything to tie him to either murder. And it doesn't help that he's got a former bigwig policeman as a father."

I felt bad for Maharmallo, having to deal with Wick.

"What about Madelaine?" I asked.

"Madelaine claims she has no idea how Cosmo's body got in that rug. She sent Riley to the city to pick up the rugs just to get rid of him. I sense some regret over hiring him back."

"Gwynn?"

"Gwynn started work at eight o'clock and was busy all morning, dusting shelves, ringing up customers, sorting through the sale items ..." Maharmallo sighed and closed the manila folder. "What happened this morning, Humphrey?"

"Riley was looking for something at Gwynn's place. I went to ask him about it."

"I can't have you turning up at all ends of my investigation. I'm sorry I ever asked you to help in the first place, although I'm starting to think sleuthing is in your nature. Anything you aren't telling me?"

"Uh-uh," I said, meeting his tired gaze.

Logan's blackmail was the only thing I hadn't told him about. It was Daphne's case and I had assured her that I wouldn't tell Maharmallo.

"Putting aside your criminal record, Humphrey, I believe you." He stood up to leave. "Incidentally, when I talked to your friend Daphne, she mentioned that the rug Cosmo's body was rolled up in looked an awful lot like the ones at the motel. I sent my guys to check Room 6 this afternoon and I'd appreciate it if you and your private eye respected my police tape this time."

Good grief.

"I almost forgot," he said, turning around. He pulled a smaller evidence bag from his pocket and laid it on the table. It was filled with bean-sized metal shells. "I have six empty cartridges. There were two bullets in Cosmo Clarke's body and three in Tedd Archer's."

"Two and three is five."

"Exactly. Where's my sixth bullet?" His face hardened.

I looked down at the bag of shells. A loaded gun. Six empty cartridges. Where was the sixth bullet? It was a good question. One that held an obvious implication. I met the detective's gaze again. "You think there's been another murder we don't know about?"

His response was cryptic.

"Murders are like good friends. They usually come in twos and threes." With that, he walked out, leaving the door open for me. "You're free to go, Humphrey."

I felt surprisingly relieved to be let go. For the briefest moment in the interrogation room, I hadn't been sure they would let me walk out.

Across the hallway, Maharmallo was in with Riley. To his credit, he had somehow gotten Wick out of the room.

I thought about what the detective had said about murders usually coming in twos and threes. Sure, one murder could be used to cover up another, then another. But murders being like good friends? What on earth was that supposed to mean?

I supposed that was about me, the lone bartender. He didn't think I had friends. Or if I did, two or three at most.

Admittedly, he wasn't wrong.

Daphne was waiting for me outside, pacing back and forth, wearing out a small radius on the red sidewalk. Something was wrong. Her pale skin was flushed and her hair unkempt, falling out if its ponytail. She didn't know what to do with her hands, tucking and untucking them in the pockets of her jacket.

"Daphne, what's wrong?"

"My ring is missing."

I stared at her. "What ring?"

She lifted her hand, wriggling her bare fingers. "My diamond ring. It's gone!"

Personal feelings aside, I wanted to help her. I took her by the shoulders, trying to calm her down.

"Daphne, when did you notice it was missing?"

"Just now, in the police station, when the detective was talking to me. I felt for it and it was gone!"

"We've been all over town. It could be anywhere."

She shook her head. "I had it at the antique shoppe."

"Are you sure?"

She nodded.

"Then we'll go back," I said.

"The police probably have it closed off by now."

"That hasn't stopped you before," I teased, but she didn't laugh.

She rubbed her hand anxiously, her green eyes flitting around, avoiding mine. She appeared grateful for the distraction when her phone rang. By the time she pulled it out of her pocket and turned to answer it, she had mostly regained her composure.

I waited for her outside the station. A police officer—not Riggs—exited and gave me a nod as he walked towards a police cruiser. I nodded back, somewhat awkwardly.

Daphne came back, slipping her phone back in her pocket. "That was Brigid Dugdale."

"What did she want?"

"Riley's being blackmailed."

Brigid set down her garden shears as soon as she saw us. She was alone. We'd beaten Riley and his old man back from the station. Riley was understandably being detained longer than Daphne and me.

"You didn't tell us you were a private eye," Brigid said to Daphne.

"I told Riley. Obviously he told you."

"Actually, he didn't." Brigid sighed as she pulled off her gardening gloves. "I don't normally snoop through his things, but after Riley got that blackmail letter … I found your business card and called you."

"When did he get the letter?" I asked.

"A couple days ago. It was left on the doorstep and it wasn't in an envelope or anything. Just a folded-up piece of paper. I thought it seemed threatening, but he didn't want to talk about it. You know how kids are. So secretive." She smiled nervously.

"Did he pay it?" Daphne asked.

"I don't think so." Brigid looked down at her hands, trying to rub dirt off her wrists. "I don't know how he'd get that kind of money that fast. It said something about twenty-four hours."

"How much?"

"A thousand dollars. Wick said we shouldn't take it seriously, but I …" She let her voice trail off, breaking slightly. She wrung the gardening gloves in her hands.

"Can we see the letter?" I asked, glancing at Daphne. I couldn't tell if she was thinking the same thing I was: that Riley's letter sounded an awful lot like Logan's.

Brigid nodded and went inside to retrieve Riley's letter, swatting the screen door.

"Good grief," I muttered aloud.

Daphne sat down on the steps. "Two days ago? Whatever it is, his time's up."

I wanted to sit down next to her. I shoved my hands in my pockets instead.

"I don't get it," I said. "Why Riley? It's not like he's rich."

Daphne didn't have a chance to answer. Brigid came back with the letter—a thin, folded slip of paper—and handed it to the private eye. She had only lifted a corner when we were interrupted.

"Humphrey!"

I turned.

Wick Dugdale had pulled up in the driveway, slamming the door of his pickup and starting for the porch. I watched his son exit the passenger side, although he closed his door more gently. Riley's own pickup was likely locked up somewhere in evidence.

"What are you doing here?" Wick bellowed, an angry look on his face.

I felt eighteen again. The former policeman still carried himself with the same arrogance and moved at nearly the same pace, although his back seemed to be giving him more trouble than usual. He swore fiercely.

I didn't move. "Your wife called us."

"She shouldn't have," Wick sneered, giving Brigid a look. "Is this about that letter?"

"I had to do something. Poor Riley—"

"Poor Riley?" Wick interrupted again, letting out a snort. "Poor Riley's spent the afternoon at the station being questioned about some dead out-of-towner from your motel, Humphrey." He turned to me, eyes narrowed into slits.

"It's not my motel." I wanted to say more, but Daphne was eyeing me, clearly suspicious of any interaction between myself and the former police-man. Wick was dismissive of Cosmo's death, unsurprisingly so. He'd been dismissive of my old man.

"I thought I told you to stop pestering my son."

"I haven't been pestering him," I said.

"He said you were snooping around this morning."

I hated to state the obvious. "He had a dead body in the back of his pickup."

We were talking about Riley as if he wasn't there. I watched him linger behind his old man, shoulders sagging miserably. I wondered if Maharmallo had been hard on him. He certainly didn't trust him. I wasn't sure if I did anymore.

Then again, another blackmail letter turning up out of the blue, this time addressed to Riley … I wasn't sure what to make of it all.

Riley's eyes briefly met mine. Brigid, concerned mother that she was, hadn't said anything about his broken nose.

"Do you know who sent you the letter?" I asked over Wick's shoulder.

But Riley only shook his head, avoiding my gaze.

"There," Wick snorted. "He doesn't know and it doesn't matter. Now get off my property, Humphrey, before I file a trespassing report."

Brigid wrapped her arms around Riley and led him towards the screen door while Wick stood at the bottom of the porch, watching us leave.

Once we were down the driveway, he spoke to his wife. "Where's the letter?"

"I gave it to them."

He swore. "You gave it to them? Of all the stupid—"

But when he looked back, we were long gone, having taken off down the street. We slowed around the corner, passing the cemetery and the church. I half-expected Wick to chase after us. Half-expected red and blue flashing lights, followed by his hand and his voice, *"Get comfy, Humphrey."*

But by the time we turned down the alley behind Rather Dapper, a dif-ferent voice, a different phrase, was ringing in my ears.

"His time's up."

I stopped Daphne, leaning my hands on my knees. I was out of breath and so was she. We collapsed in the alley, resting our heads on a brick wall. Sunlight peaked through between the tops of the buildings. Birds flew back and forth, making a lot of noise. Beside me, Daphne was breathing heavily and I looked down to find her reading Riley's letter.

"So our blackmailer strikes again," I said after a minute.

"It's the same at Logan's. Same writing style. Same drop-off. But if he got the letter two days ago ..."

"It couldn't have been Tedd."

As much as I didn't want to admit it, it was true. Which meant I had been wrong. About almost everything.

Daphne handed the letter to me. She moved to rest her head on my shoulder and I inhaled her lemony scent. I hadn't forgotten her missing ring. Evidently neither had she, as she played with her bare finger. I wanted to wrap an arm around her. Tell her everything was going to be all right. But I was distracted by the letter in my hands.

> **Riley Dugdale,**
> **One thousand cash. Bardakci's garage. Twenty-four**
> **hours.**
> > **Or I tell the police.**
> > > > **Sincerely,**
> > > > **I-Know-What-You-Did**

"What did he do?" Daphne wondered aloud.

I shuddered to think of it. "Isn't that the rub."

16

STRANGER THINGS ...

Logan's office door was open, so I didn't bother knocking. He was leaning back in his chair, throwing darts at the wall, tossing one with extra vigour when he saw me. It missed my head by an inch. Did I deserve it after scratching the bloody murder out of his face? I supposed so, but that didn't stop me from arming myself with one of the darts, lifting it from his desk, and feeling the sharp point with my fingers as I took the chair across from him.

"What do you want, Humphrey?"

I wanted a lot of things—where did I begin?

"Mag said you were drinking at work."

"She did, did she?" Logan opened the top drawer of his desk, taking out a bottle of Griffiths whisky and a couple of glasses. "I wonder why."

His tone dripped with bitter sarcasm. The fact that he tolerated my presence in his office was remarkable, although he wasn't doing it very well. He threw another dart; it struck the wall directly above my head before falling to the floor, but he hadn't intended to hit me. If he had, he wouldn't have missed. Perfect-bullseye-Logan never missed, even on a bad day.

Luckily, I hadn't flinched.

"You keep whisky in your desk?"

"I do now. I'm not going back home."

Griffiths Distillery. He still called it home.

"Pope's is closed," he added. "Apparently he's gone fishing."

Why he would even want to hang out with all the old-timers was beyond me.

"And I can't go to your place anymore." He let out a sigh.

Of course not. I had accused him of murder, and instead of apologizing I'd doubled down. He wouldn't forget that anytime soon. His combed face seemed to be healing, though.

"Want a swig?" he asked, offering the bottle.

I rotated the dart in my hand. "No thank you."

"Mag won't drink with me either," Logan said. "Because I said something insensitive about her husband. Did you know he died last year?"

I stared at him. "Didn't you?"

"I don't read obituaries."

"Do you read anything?"

"I'm just a photographer, Humphrey." He poured his glass half full and downed it in one swift swig. He poured another before tucking the bottle back in his drawer.

He threw another dart. Perfect bullseye.

"Riley got a blackmail letter," I said.

"Really? Did Tedd come back from the dead and deliver it to him?"

There it was. The nagging feeling returned, as if Logan himself was twisting a dart into the pit of my stomach. We weren't friends anymore—no amount of whisky or perfect bullseyes could cover that up—but I knew I owed him an apology. I simply didn't know how to say it.

"I got another letter too," Logan said casually, taking a sip of whisky.

I leaned forward. "When?"

He shrugged.

"What did it say?"

"Sorry, Marlowe. Last time I checked, it was a woman that I hired. You've seen her. Blonde. Green-eyed. Answers to darling." He took another slow sip.

"Did you tell Daphne?"

"Not yet."

He threw another dart just as I stood up. I felt it whizz past my face, pulling back just in time. When I looked back at him, I expected a devilish grin. But he was simply sipping his whisky. And in that moment, I realized that he was every bit as pathetic and lonely as I was. Maybe more.

I turned the dart over in my hand. Perhaps I didn't know Logan as well as I thought. He hadn't been blackmailed by Tedd. He wasn't involved in

Tedd's death. He wasn't a murderer. And years ago, he had only been trying to help me. He'd only wanted justice for my old man, for my mother's sake. And Ginny … it hardly mattered about Ginny anymore.

I set the dart down. I didn't want to be at war.

"Logan?"

He sighed, sounding annoyed. "What is it, Humphrey?"

"You can come back to my bar anytime. I'm told I mix a mean Manhattan."

"Who told you that?"

"Someone I used to know. How about a pair on me?"

"I'll think about it."

When he looked away, his eyes were glassy, but it was probably just the whisky.

It was later in the morning by the time I walked up the driveway to the tall white house on Lilac Lane. I had barely lifted the brass knocker when the door flung open and Cynthia squished me into a giant hug.

"Humphrey, dear, how are you?"

"Squished." I heard Pope's voice from inside. "He's probably squished."

Cynthia let go and I did a doubletake to make sure I was at the right house. It was supposed to be Madelaine's. What were the McNallys doing here?

"Is Madelaine home?" I asked. I had already been by the antique shoppe, which was closed for the second time in a little over a week, this time taped off and swarming with police officers.

"Come on in." Cynthia stepped aside and shut the door behind me. Then, whispering, "How are things with that gorgeous private eye?"

I shrugged off the question. I didn't want to give Cynthia too much to gossip about. But just the mention of Daphne brought me back to the alley, the feeling of her head resting on my shoulder. I shook the thought quickly, finding Pope standing in front of me. His arms were folded across his chest, a frown affixed to his face. Something about the old man always made me feel uneasy. I supposed he hadn't gone fishing after all.

"Wiley!" Teddy's voice called out as he dashed to the door, but he slowed when he saw me, bumping into the back of Pope's leg. The old man let out a grunt and Teddy backed up. Cynthia laughed and took the boy, small enough to pick up, in her arms. Now, closer to my height, I could see his big eyes sizing me up. I wasn't a stranger anymore, but I wasn't his beloved "Wiley" either. He mopped his runny nose with his sleeve. The bruise on the side of his face had turned yellow.

Finally, Madelaine strolled out of the kitchen. She was holding a glass of wine but appeared to be a bottle deep already. Which explained Pope and Cynthia's presence, I supposed.

As if reading my mind, Cynthia lowered the boy and said cheerily, "We're taking Teddy for the day. Maybe we'll go to the park!"

"Will Wiley be there?"

Puzzled, Cynthia shook her head. "I don't think so."

They left in a hurry. Backpack. Shoes. One-eared rabbit. Madelaine blew a kiss to her boy from afar, cradling the glass of wine in her arm. The concerned look on Cynthia's face was the last thing we saw before the door clicked shut behind them.

"If this is about Mr. Clarke, I didn't even know the man," Madelaine said.

Nobody had known Cosmo, but he'd still been murdered. She waited for me to say something and I decided not to. With Madelaine, I had learned it was best to simply listen. Eventually she would let everything pour out. Probably had something to do with the wine.

I followed Madelaine back to the kitchen. "Where's Agnes?"

"I don't know. She didn't show up today. She's terribly unreliable."

"You're lucky to have good neighbours."

"Lucky." She let out a laugh, setting down her glass. She didn't offer me any wine. Maybe she knew I would refuse. More likely, she didn't want me to stay. "What's this about, Humphrey?"

"The revolver was an antique."

"Hmmm, I've heard."

I eyed her. "How come it wasn't on your list of missing antiques?"

"I didn't know about it."

"Would you have been able to procure it, if you wanted to?"

"If I wanted to. But I didn't."

"What about Riley or Gwynn?" I asked. "Could either of them have procured it?"

She nodded, with pursed lips. "They both know the tricks of the trade."

I could picture the revolver in Maharmallo's evidence bag. He'd said there'd been dirt in every crevasse. It was strange, now that I thought about it, and I considered asking Madelaine if that was how an antique might normally be procured. It seemed to me more likely to be procured in a clean, polished condition. If so, what had happened to it?

"You hired Riley back?" I asked instead.

"What of it?"

"I thought he was stealing from you."

"I thought so too." She swirled the wine in her glass. "But he begged for his job back, practically on hands and knees. What choice did I have?"

"You didn't hire him back because he's in love with you?"

She took a step back. "What?"

"You heard me."

"It's not what you think."

"And what do I think?"

"You think it's some kind of mad affair, but it's not."

"Ah."

"It's not," she insisted.

"What is it then?"

"I hired Riley back because I needed someone to pick up more rugs for the sale. That's all there is to it."

"And he came back with a dead body."

"I don't know anything about that." Madelaine tucked a strand of hair behind her ear, lifting the glass of wine to her lips with an unsteady hand. The old-Hollywood actress seemed to be breaking character, ever so slightly. Far from being indifferent, she now seemed to be on the defence.

"I know what happened with Teddy," I said.

"Hmmm." Her voice was hoarse, almost lost. "But it's nobody's business."

It was subtle but, as my old man used to say, I got her drift. So her affairs, whether they involved Tedd's death or not, were nobody's business. But somehow it had become mine. I hadn't asked for it.

"What do you want from me, Humphrey?" she asked again.

Still, I wanted a lot of things.

"I want the truth," I said. And surprisingly, I meant it.

"I told you the truth."

"About the photo?"

She held the empty glass against her chest. "What do you mean?"

"Are there others?"

"No."

I found that hard to believe. "Logan only took one?"

"He took more. I only wanted one."

"Tedd didn't know about it?"

She shook her head.

"Then how did he get it?" I pressed.

"I don't know."

"He must have found it somehow, and taken it. You said he took things."

She let out a sigh, frustrated. "He saw Gwynn with some money and thought she was selling his missing antiques, so he took it from her and wouldn't give it back. That's what I meant when I said he took things."

"What did he take from Riley?"

"How should I know?" She lifted her glass again, gritting her teeth on the edge.

"And what did he take from you, Madelaine?"

"Everything." She turned away, squeezing the glass in her hand. She set it down so harshly I thought it might shatter, but I was halfway to the door before I heard anything—the sound of glass against the wall. She had picked it up and thrown it, letting out a tiny scream as she did so.

No, she wasn't indifferent.

I closed the door quietly and turned, nearly bumping into someone who had come up the driveway.

"Agnes?"

"Oh. Hello, Humphrey."

"I wouldn't go in there if I were you."

She giggled and reached to open the door.

"No, I'm serious. A little late, aren't you?"

Agnes bit her lip. "Is she really mad?"

"She's been better."

"She deserves it. After what she did to Riley."

I had written Agnes off as oblivious to the goings-on in Pearl, but I had been wrong before. Perhaps she knew more than she was letting on.

"What did she do to Riley?" I asked.

Agnes tucked her hair behind her ear. "Nothing, that's what. She just let the police take him in. He must have been terrified. Don't you think? But Madelaine doesn't care what happens to him. If I'd have been there, I would've done something. I would've done anything."

And just like that, she was blubbering like her grandmother. I steered her away from Madelaine's house. It didn't seem like the two women were particularly fond of each other. And I assumed Madelaine needed some space. I didn't care to see Agnes getting pelted with yet another household item.

"You think Riley's innocent," I said.

"Yes." She batted her eyes at me. "Don't you?"

That was indeed the question.

I sent her home. Turning one last time to look at the tall white house, I caught Madelaine watching from the window. She had seen the exchange between Agnes and me. She had very likely seen Agnes arrive late and me turn her away. There were tears on her face, I was sure of it. Angry tears. The hysterical fit she'd thrown after I'd left the kitchen hadn't been an act.

I wasn't sure about Riley, but Madelaine ... whatever she was, she wasn't innocent.

I could feel her watching me as I walked away, her big eyes boring into my back. She'd had too much to drink. I'd give her that. Sober people didn't throw wine glasses at the wall. Just like sober people didn't throw kitchen knives at nannies. They had been cut from the same cloth, Tedd and Madelaine. Angry. Unhappy. Spoiled.

Perhaps I had seen the similarities between Tedd's murder and my old man's. Both of their untimely deaths had proved to be rather convenient for the wife and son left behind. With my old man out of the way, my mother and I had finally been free from his drinking, his violent fits of rage. I thought of Teddy's bruised face and arms. Perhaps the same was true for them.

If I had been hesitant to judge Madelaine, it was only because of the unfair speculation my mother had faced. But Madelaine was nothing like my mother. She was part of the problem. She was just as bad as Tedd.

Maybe she was worse.

Back at the bar, I used the old landline to call Cynthia.

"Humphrey, dear, it's you!" she exclaimed. "I thought the number looked familiar. I didn't know that old bar phone still worked. How mysterious! Pope, it's Humphrey."

It wasn't so mysterious. The bar phone was nearest to my backbar and I was making room for a new bottle of Griffths.

"If Agnes loses her job, it might be my fault," I said.

Cynthia was quiet on the other end. "Oh dear, that would hardly be your fault."

She was right, I supposed. I had nothing to do with the nanny being ditzy and unreliable.

I picked up a shiny bronze labelled bottle, turning it over, feeling the weight of it in my hand.

"Humphrey, are you there?"

"Ah. Sorry, I'm here."

"I thought the line cut out. You never know with these old phones. What is it you called about?"

I could almost see my reflection in the bottle. I thought of Madelaine in the window.

"Are you sure Madelaine has an alibi for Tedd's murder?" I asked.

To my surprise, Cynthia hesitated. I had assumed she would be quick to come to her friend's defence again. She wasn't as quick as I thought.

"Pope would've seen her leave, Humphrey," she said. "Maybe you don't trust Madelaine, dear, but you can trust us."

I had no reason not to believe Cynthia. Sure, she was a busybody, but, for the most part, she wasn't in the habit of telling lies. If Pope hadn't seen Madelaine leave her house the night of Tedd's murder, then it couldn't have been Madelaine at the motel with her husband. She couldn't have murdered Tedd. After all, Pope had been on neighbourhood watch.

Good grief. That meant he hadn't been at his bar.

"Pope's bar couldn't have been open that night," I said.

I heard Cynthia say something, presumably to Pope.

"Pope says no."

But Gwynn and Riley had claimed to be at Pope's bar the night of Tedd's murder. Which meant they have lied about their alibis. Pope's bar had been closed the night of Tedd's murder. He was Madelaine's alibi. He couldn't be both.

Cynthia went on, blubbering about one thing or another. Listening to her voice, I couldn't help but think of Agnes. She seemed to have an infatuation with Riley. Riley this, Riley that. I wondered what had brought that on. I didn't wonder why the feelings hadn't been reciprocated.

Strangely enough, she didn't seem to be the only one. I didn't know Teddy Archer—or many five-year-olds, for that matter—but it seemed to me that the mysterious "Wiley" he so eagerly wished to see at his front door could only be Riley.

And it begged a new question: why did Madelaine's son keep mistaking me for Riley Dugdale?

I made a deal with the devil, trading two Manhattans for a little advice. I already regretted it.

"It's just like you, Humphrey, to let a beautiful woman make you all tongue-tied."

"Tongue-tied?"

"You never could talk to Gin either." Logan raised the cocktail glass to his nose and sniffed. In a moment, he would ask me if it was Griffiths and I would tell him he was losing his taste. It would be just like old times.

I took in a breath. "Daphne's not Ginny."

"You're right. Gin liked me. Daphne likes you," he said. "Why don't you just ask her about the ring?"

"I did. She couldn't find it."

"No, Humphrey. Ask her who it's from."

"I can't do that."

Another sniff. "Why not?"

"What if it's from Redhill?"

"Who's Redhill?"

"Tanner Redhill. Her business partner. Another private eye. You're the one who hired him."

"Redhill?

"Daphne said you wanted him, but he was busy with another case."

He finally took a sip and grinned. "Then Granddad Griffith hired him."

I raised an eyebrow. "Do you do anything yourself?"

"I take my own photos."

"Really. Are you sure Mag doesn't do that for you?"

"Mag would never."

The door opened and Wick Dugdale walked into the bar. He moved slowly, as though every step was painful, and he had one hand gripped behind his back. Eventually, he made his way over to the bartop, leaning over it.

"Humphrey," he growled.

"Can I get you anything, Mr. Dugdale?" I doubted it. He never drank at my bar. Something was up.

"You can get me something all right, but it's not a drink." He jerked his head towards the back door. "I think we should talk outside."

I tossed my dishrag over the edge of the tub sink and followed the former policeman outside. Logan watched us leave, sipping his drink. I tossed him a shrug as I passed. I didn't know what Wick wanted.

I should have, I supposed.

No sooner had the door swung shut behind us than Wick overtook me, pushing me backwards and pinning me against the door, his thick arm pressed against my neck.

"Where's that letter?"

I tried to swallow. "Mr. Dugdale—"

"Where is it?!" He slammed me against the door again. I tried to pry his arm away from my neck, but he pushed back harder. He was strong. He still had it.

"Give me that letter, Humphrey!"

He thrust me into the door again.

"All right," I gasped, letting go of his arm and extending my hands in the air. He eyed me as I reached into my pocket and pulled out the folded piece of paper.

He ripped it out of my hands, unfolding it to make sure it was Riley's letter.

"It *was* blackmail," I huffed. "Why did you lie?"

The words were barely out of my mouth before I was pinned against the door again, with even more force. My head made a *th–thunk* sort of noise as it cracked against the door. This time, his fist drilled into my neck.

"Get comfy, Humphrey, you—"

The door opened behind me, propelling me forward. Startled, Wick released his grip and backed away. I kneeled over, coughing and gasping for air, as Logan emerged from the bar, a devilish grin on his face.

"How about that?" he said. "It's just like old times."

Too much like old times.

Wick swore, tossing each of us a disgruntled look.

"You leave my son alone, Humphrey!" he bellowed. He crumpled the letter in his fist and brushed past Logan. "That goes for you too, Griffith."

We watched him hobble off around the corner of the building and back to the parking lot.

"Thank you," I said as we headed back inside.

"Don't thank me. I needed another drink and you weren't around."

Ah, of course. How could I have thought he actually cared?

"Seth said he doesn't do cocktails," Logan added. "You should really hire another bartender."

I laughed quietly as I watched the photographer reclaim his spot at the sidebar, thinking to myself something I scarcely would have admitted out loud: it was good to have him back.

17

... HAVE HAPPENED

I awoke the next morning, too exhausted to get up. My neck was still sore from Wick Dugdale's rather unpleasant visit. It still felt swollen. Between that and my black eye, I was definitely the worse for wear. I turned over in bed, letting myself doze in and out of sleep, until I heard a noise downstairs. Someone knocking on the door.

I let out a groan, threw on a shirt, and ducked down the stairs. I was still rubbing my eyes awake when I unlocked the door.

It was Ayda and Daphne. I couldn't think of a better combination. Except, perhaps, it could have been better timed.

"What time is it?" I groaned.

"After ten," Ayda replied. "My, Humphrey, what happened to you?"

I ignored the question and the look of concern spreading across Daphne's face.

"After ten?" I gasped, coughing. Good grief! I turned back into the bar. Humphrey's would be opening in two hours, Seth arriving even sooner.

The two women, unsure what to do, joined in as I hurriedly flipped chairs off the tables. Before I could do anything else, Ayda sat me down in one of them.

"Humphrey, sit for a minute. Let us get you a drink. Not that kind of drink, I know. Just water. Daphne?"

Daphne nodded and hurried off to fill a glass behind the bar.

"She's lovely like Leyla, isn't she?" Ayda said when she'd gone, lowering her voice.

Leyla was Ayda and Emre's daughter, about Daphne's age, but she had moved out of town.

I smiled at the thought of Daphne being called lovely. I wished she had heard it.

She came back with a glass of water and I guzzled it down. It hurt to swallow, but it felt good to drink something. I couldn't remember the last time I'd eaten.

"What's gotten into you?" Ayda scolded.

"He thinks he's Marlowe," Daphne teased, but there was still a concerned look on her face.

Ayda rested her hands on her hips. "I don't like it. You're going to get yourself killed." She looked at Daphne. "I don't even think I should tell him."

I blinked. "Tell me what?"

They exchanged a knowing glance before Daphne explained.

"Ayda found something. You'd better come see."

I followed them back outside, down the sidewalk to Room 6. Cosmo's room.

The police tape was gone. Ayda entered first, producing from her pocket the key ring she used for cleaning. The first thing I noticed was the hardwood floor, completely bare. The usual rug was missing. Evidently, Cosmo had been murdered the same way as Tedd. Shot in the doorway and dragged onto the rug. Only his body had been rolled up and somehow loaded onto the back of Riley's pickup.

The policed had already searched the room, otherwise it looked the same. It lacked Cosmo's belongings, obviously bagged up by Maharmallo's officers, and it appeared Ayda had already cleaned up after them. There were fresh linens on the bed and clean towels on the rack next to the bathroom.

But in the middle of the room, on the floor next to the wardrobe, something stood out: a single metal shell. Not large, but big enough to see from where I was standing.

"What is it?" I crouched down.

"A bullet casing," Daphne said. "Ayda found it sweeping under the wardrobe. The police must have missed it."

Good grief. A bullet casing?

"Look, see that?" Ayda jingled her keys in my direction like some sort of jailer. "That glint in his eye. I knew I shouldn't have shown him."

I stood up. "Glint? There's no glint, Ayda. And you should call Maharmallo."

Ayda frowned. "You think it's from the gun that killed that poor out-of-towner?"

"Cosmo? Likely."

"That's the thing," Daphne said, turning to me. "Revolvers don't eject casings. They stay in the cylinder until they're manually removed."

"Even antique ones?"

"Especially antique ones."

"Why would Cosmo's killer empty it here, in the room?"

"Accidental?" Daphne shrugged.

"The gun was wiped clean," I said. "So were the casings, most likely. On the off-chance they weren't, there'd be fingerprints on this." I looked up at Ayda. "Did you touch it?"

She shook her head.

"You should call Maharmallo," I said again, standing. If there weren't any fingerprints, I hardly saw how it was useful to the detective. He'd mentioned something about a missing bullet but nothing about casings. I mulled it over.

"Did *you* touch it?" I asked Daphne as we headed outside. I'd meant it as a joke, to tease her, but the look on her face suggested otherwise. "Good grief, you did!"

"Barely. I only rolled it over with the back of my hand. Just to get a good look." She let out a laugh, pulling me away from the doorway. Ayda was still inside. I imagined she was already on the phone with the police.

"You can't help yourself, can you? You know, Maharmallo already warned us to stop messing with his crime scenes. You're not helping our case."

"Technically, this isn't a crime scene anymore."

"He's going to arrest us for obstructing."

A pause. "Humphrey ..."

She'd gone straight to Wick Dugdale. I could see it in her face, the careful way she thought things through. And she was wondering how to ask me about it. She didn't want to pry.

I saved her the trouble. "Wick Dugdale frequented the bar back when my old man owned it. There was some stuff that happened that may or may not have involved him. I never could prove it. But he's not my biggest fan."

I supposed that would have to do. For now.

"Actually," I added, "he paid me a visit last night."

Almost unconsciously, I lifted a hand to my throat.

Daphne's eyes widened at the sight of the injury. "He did that to you?"

"He wanted Riley's letter back."

"Did you give it to him?"

"I didn't really have a choice. He almost choked me to death."

She stared at me. Her green eyes were unreadable, somewhere between concern and ... there it was again—interest.

"Oh, Humphrey," she simply said.

I didn't like her pity. I managed a small smile. "It still hurts to swallow and I'm dog-tired, but otherwise I'm fine. Ayda's right, maybe. I'm in over my head."

She nodded, understandingly. "Me too. Tired, that is. I don't think I've slept a wink since Tedd's murder. And now Cosmo. I can't help but feel like I'm next."

Good grief. How could I have missed it? So far, Daphne was the only guest at the motel who hadn't been murdered in her own room.

I looked down at my feet, suddenly unsure of what to say, except that she couldn't be next. She just couldn't be.

"Well, Humphrey, what's keeping you up?" She suddenly slipped her arm through mine, guiding me back towards the bar.

It felt good, her arm in mine, so I kept it there.

But what *was* keeping me up at night? Not Daphne, surely. I wasn't that fickle. And not Logan. No, I could never lose sleep over him. Perhaps Tedd's murder, but the man was like fog, after all. Dense and incredibly thick, and by all accounts another version of my own old man. I cared for the truth, of course, but not for Tedd's sake. I doubted he was the source of my sleeplessness.

"There's a stray that keeps scratching at my fire escape," I said.

"It's probably just lonely."

That made two of us, I supposed, although the last place I expected to find a kindred spirit was a stray cat. I wondered if Daphne ever felt lonely. There was Redhill obviously, and whoever had slipped that diamond on her finger. Perhaps they were one and the same. But for some reason, she was walking next to me, arm in mine, with her enveloping lemony scent. I hardly wanted to think about anything else.

But I had been mulling it over. The single casing. Then the missing bullet.

"Do you have time for breakfast?"

I almost didn't hear her. I pulled away and turned. Behind us, Ayda was coming up the sidewalk. She'd seen us walking together. She'd seen us break apart.

I looked back at Daphne, my eyes meeting hers. I didn't want to pass up another breakfast at the diner, but truthfully I didn't have time. I had a bar to run. And then there was that bullet. That darn missing bullet.

"No, uh, sorry ... I mean, there's something I need to do."

Later on, just before opening, I wandered back outside, tracing my steps back through the grass and trees towards the river, the same way Daphne and I had gone to dispose of her unwanted roommate the day she'd arrived at the motel.

I stood at the edge of the riverbank and looked down. I knew it was a longshot. A shot in the dark. There was a good chance I was wrong. But we'd found a bullet casing in Cosmo's room. The murderer had slipped up. And maybe, whoever it was, they'd slipped up before.

A black stray darted out of the trees and I wondered whether it was the same one that had taken a liking to my fire escape. It hissed, startled to see me, but I ignored it. I wasn't looking for a stray.

At least not one that was alive.

I could count on one hand the number of times Bartel had walked into Humphrey's. Once he had borrowed a book from my mother and had needed to apologize because he'd lost it. Once he had come to offer his sympathies when my family had fallen apart. And another time he had popped by to wish me a happy twenty-fifth birthday on my twenty-seventh birthday.

So when I looked up in the middle of mixing a couple of highballs, I couldn't help but feel a little unsettled, especially when I saw what he was holding: a copy of *The Pearl Gazette* and a brown-wrapped bundle.

"Bart?"

"Humphrey, is that you?"

Good grief. Was he going deaf *and* blind?

The old man saddled up on the barstool closest to me, already fiddling with his hearing aid.

"I saw your ad." He presented the newspaper. "You know, Humphrey, if you wanted a rare book, you could have just asked me."

"I know, Bart—"

He handed me the brown-wrapped parcel and I forgot all about the highballs.

"What's this?" I asked.

The old man winked. "Why don't you open it?"

I tore at the paper, listening to the satisfying shred as I peeled it back. I stared at the book in my hands and couldn't breathe. It had nothing to do with my bruised neck.

"Is that the one?" he asked.

He wanted to know if it was the one he had borrowed from my mother. It wasn't. It didn't have her name handwritten inside the cover and it definitely wasn't *Playback*.

Still, I nodded. "Sure is. Thank you, Bart."

He smiled ear to ear.

"What do I owe you?" I asked. After all, my advertisement had said I'd be willing to pay.

He waved a hand. "Owe me? It was me who owed you."

I swallowed. I couldn't stop staring at the book, handsomely bound, and feeling its dust jacket, in perfect condition.

"Bart, where did you get it?"

"Huh?"

"Where did you get the book?"

"It was in one of the donation boxes."

"Do you know who donated it?"

"I shouldn't." The old man chuckled. "But I do."

I leaned over the bar. "Can you tell me?"

He fiddled briefly with his hearing aid. When he was certain no one would overhear him, he gave me a name I wouldn't have guessed in a million years.

"Brigid Dugdale."

He left after that. I offered him a drink, but he just told me that the bar was too noisy for him and he had to get back to the bookstore. He had piles of books to sort through. Spring was busy season for used books. Who would have thought?

When Bartel was long gone and the highballs were finally served, I snuck behind the bar and held the book in my hands. The more I stared at it, the more surreal it became. I wasn't just staring at any old novel. I was staring at a 1939 first edition of *The Big Sleep*.

"What are you reading?"

"Nothing," I said, snapping the book shut and adding it to the stack on the backbar.

Logan took his seat. He eyed the stack of books curiously but didn't say anything. He wasn't too interested in books. Evidently, he didn't read anything.

He tapped his fingers on the bar. "Where's our private eye?"

"Upstairs."

"Sorry, I thought you said upstairs."

"I did."

Logan grinned. "She's moved in already, has she?"

"It's not like that."

"What *is* it like, Humphrey?"

I flipped over two cocktail glasses. "She happens to be staying at a motel that doesn't have the best track record with guests. I think she has a right to feel a little uneasy."

"So she *did* move in."

"Just until the murderer running rampant around here is caught."

"I don't suppose she's couch-crashing."

Bronze label, bitters, dry and sweet vermouth … I stirred it together and poured. "I don't have a couch."

He nodded slowly. "You gave her the bed. I should have known. You always were the gentleman. Where are you going to sleep? Do you have a cot down in the hatch?"

"I have my armchair."

"That old thing?"

"I always sleep in it."

"Ouch. That must be why you're always so tired."

"Actually, it's quite comfortable," I said, setting both glasses in front of him just as Daphne came down the stairs. Underneath her aviator jacket, she had changed into a black tee and jeans. Her hair was pulled back and she wore her red lip. She looked like she had the first night she'd walked into the bar. I couldn't help but feel a little speechless, which didn't matter, because Logan, as per usual, was not.

"Daphne, darling," he said, setting down his glass. "I brought something for you." He reached into his pocket and retrieved a folded piece of paper. All three of us knew what it was.

"You got another letter?" Daphne took the paper from him and unfolded it.

I read over her shoulder.

> **Darling Logan,**
>
> **One thousand cash. Bardakci's garage. Twenty-four hours.**
>
> **Or Gwynn Grant bears it all.**
>
> **Sincerely,**
>
> **I-Know-What-Happens-On-Cigare-Street**

I shot Logan a glare. "You took photos of Gwynn too."

The Manhattan Man sipped his drink nonchalantly. "She asked me. Don't look at me like that, Humphrey. I've taken photos of half the women in Pearl. It's what I do."

"You're a *Gazette* photographer."

"By day."

"By night?"

"Whatever kind of photographer they want."

Good grief.

Daphne flapped the letter. "Logan, when did you get this? And why didn't you say anything?"

"More than twenty-four hours ago." Logan tipped his glass towards me. "And I told Humphrey."

"Humphrey's not your private eye."

"He seems to think he is." After taking a slow sip, Logan grinned devilishly, his face shadowed in the dim bar. Or perhaps he wasn't as clean-shaven as usual. He reached into his pocket once more, retrieving something small and flat that easily fit in the palm of his hand. He held it face-down on the bar. "Before I show you this, you should know I really am just a photographer."

Don't shoot the messenger, my old man used to say. I wasn't sure it applied now.

"My blackmailer is nothing if not insistent," Logan said. "I got another letter today. It was the same, granting me another twenty-four hours, since I ignored the last one. Only this time it came with proof."

He flipped up a photo on the bartop. Gwynn Grant. Perched on the barstool. A strikingly similar pose to the one Logan had taken of Madelaine.

"Who else would have these photos?" I asked.

"I don't know," Logan said. "I don't keep copies."

"Well, someone has them," Daphne said, fingering the photo with a look of horror on her face. "What do we do?"

Logan shrugged. "You're the private eye."

"I know, but Logan—"

"I'm not paying up," he interrupted. "I don't care about Gwynn, not enough to hand over another thousand."

But Daphne's expression of horror only grew. I gave her what I hoped was a reassuring smile. Logan would come around. I knew him, and if there was one thing I had underestimated about Logan, it was that despite any side hustle, he was in fact a gentleman. He would have taken Daphne in the same way I had.

If I needed any proof of his undying chivalry, it came when he finished his Manhattan and looked at Daphne with his trademark grin.

"You could have stayed with me," he said. "Cigare Street doesn't have any strays. Or cynics."

To which she replied, "But it does have a creepy elk head."

"And me, darling. Don't forget about me."

18

PEARL

The police car was just pulling into the parking lot as I looked up from my armchair. I'd been trying to read without much luck. The manuscript in my hands was interesting, but not as interesting as my new roommate.

It was Sunday, my night off, and the bar was closed. I was getting used to sharing the loft with Daphne, who had attempted to brew a decent cup of coffee downstairs and had now taken over the entire loveseat, her feet propped over the back, trying to conceive of a clever plan to catch Logan's blackmailer once and for all. Gwynn's reputation was on the line. I wasn't entirely sure if Gwynn even cared about her reputation, but I was hesitant to voice my doubts, not that I could have gotten a word in edgewise.

"A stakeout," Daphne was saying. "We'll wait outside Bardakci's until the blackmailer shows up."

I nodded absentmindedly, watching through the window as Maharmallo emerged from the driver's seat of the police car, alone again. His sidekick Riggs was nowhere in sight. Moments later I heard the familiar *tap-tap* on the glass door.

Grateful for the interruption, I excused myself to duck downstairs, although I wasn't sure Daphne even noticed.

I ran across the empty bar and let the detective in. He unbuttoned his suit jacket with one hand; the other rested unsteadily on his holster.

"Guess what the cat dragged in," he said.

"The missing bullet?"

"In a dead stray ..." Maharmallo shook his head. "I don't get it. Why shoot a cat?"

I didn't know. "Practice, maybe?"

The dead stray from Daphne's room had been easier to locate by the river than I had thought. Evidently my instinct had been correct: Maharmallo's sixth bullet had been lodged into its odd leg wound.

"Cats aren't particularly easy targets. They're small. They move quickly." The detective took a seat at the bar, in what had become his usual spot. I watched him fold his hands, shakily, on the bartop in front of him. "If it was a practice shot, it was a darn good one. And the shot in Tedd's forehead. Point blank." He took a deep breath. In and out. "This was no amateur, Humphrey. Whoever it was, he knew how to shoot a gun."

He was right, of course. A stray cat wouldn't be easy to shoot. He—or she—would have to be someone with good aim. Someone who knew their way around a revolver, antique or otherwise. Yet if they had known their way around the revolver, why hadn't they known better than to empty the cylinder in Cosmo's room?

"What about the casing Ayda found?" I asked.

"No fingerprints. Not even a partial." Maharmallo sighed, rubbing his tried eyes. He glanced at my bruised neck. "Was that Logan too?"

"Wick Dugdale," I corrected.

Another sigh. "Wick Dugdale is a thorn in my side. He did that to you?"

"I'm sure he'd deny it."

"He's awfully protective over Riley. I've seen helicopter parents. I am one. But I can't tell if this is just fatherly love or something more."

Good grief. "You mean you think it could be him?"

"Ah. That's where things get a little ... foggy."

Unfortunately, everything seemed foggy. The dead cat. Logan's blackmail letters. The antique revolver. Cosmo's body in Riley's pickup. Gwynn's indelicate photos. The woman in the dark. Even Tedd himself had turned out to be something of an enigma. After all, how had he ended up with Madelaine's photo after she supposedly threw it away? And why had he been in possession of Logan's blackmail money if he hadn't been the blackmailer?

Maharmallo was seemingly lost in thoughts of his own. He rubbed his eyes again with his shaky hands. The focused breathing, in and out, compensated for whatever unsteadiness seemed to be overtaking him, a big man in a small, simplified world.

I pulled a bottle of Griffiths from the backbar and poured a glass, sliding it in front of him. "You look like you need a drink."

His eyes widened. "I don't drink—"

"It's fine. My old man relapsed all the time."

"Relapsed?" he said. "Relapsed from what, exactly?"

I didn't answer but caught his stare apprehensively. His eyes were suddenly more awake and alert.

The floorboards creaked above us. It was Daphne, of course, walking around, but I wasn't used to hearing anyone up there. I broke eye contact, if only for an instant, and Maharmallo half-laughed.

"I was going to say I don't drink on-duty," he clarified.

"Ah."

"You thought I had a drinking problem?"

"I didn't—"

"Close, but no cigar, Humphrey. *Workaholic* is more like it." He half-laughed again. It was a sad, dreary sort of laugh. "You know, they laughed when I resigned. They told me nothing ever happened in small towns. They said I'd be bored out of my mind."

"They?"

"My higher-ups in Vancouver."

Ah, Vancouver. So the big-city detective was a workaholic and he had come to Pearl for a change of pace. He had come to Pearl because of all the things I disliked about it. A simple, dull, quiet life. His shaky hands and tired eyes represented a different kind of withdrawal than I was used to. He was exhausted, having worked an entire career before he was even close to retirement. And now he was here, in Pearl of all places. The middle of nowhere, where nothing ever happened. Only something had, the moment he arrived. Perhaps work simply followed a workaholic, as was the case for so many vices. A man could run, but he could never hide—another one of my old man's pathetic sayings.

I had never been good at meeting new people, less so at making new friends. I didn't have a lot of those, as Maharmallo well knew. But I considered the detective something like a friend. An acquaintance, perhaps. A familiar straight face. I liked him, even if at one point I had been certain he suspected me of killing Tedd Archer. I hadn't been sure of him then, but something about two men in a dim bar, with a glass of whisky in front of them, brought the truth to the surface. He wasn't an alcoholic. I wasn't a murderer. Perhaps we could be friends.

The clock ticked on the wall and I heard Daphne's footsteps again upstairs. Evidently, so had Maharmallo.

"You have company?"

"Daphne's staying with me. Just until the motel feels, uh, safer."

The detective nodded. "Tess says motels are never safe."

Tess had a point.

"Maharmallo," I said.

"Ah."

"Can I ask you a question?"

"Shoot."

"What happened in Vancouver?"

He didn't answer at first. He leaned forward and rested his hands firmly on the bar.

"I worked too much," he finally said. "And I saw too much. And over time it turned me into someone else. And I lost sight of who I was and what was important."

I watched him breathe, in an out. I had no doubt the detective in front of me had changed from the man who had first roamed the streets of Vancouver. But I connected with his words more than I wanted to. In a way, I'd lost sight of who I was. For fifteen years I'd been lost, living my lonely life behind the bar. No family. No friends. No life outside my own four walls. And I was tired. Tired, like the detective.

Maharmallo laughed his dreary laugh again. "I met Tess at a football game. It was love at first sight. Actually, football was my first love. I played in high school and university and always wanted to play professionally. But my old man was a homicide detective and for some reason we always grow up to be just like our fathers, no matter how hard we try not to."

If I was anything like my old man, I might have agreed.

"I had two tickets for the game that night. My friend bailed on me last minute and I almost didn't go, but I showed up halfway through the first quarter with my jersey and a cowbell and my face painted orange. I guess you could have called me a superfan."

Looking at him now, in his suit and tie, I couldn't picture it.

"Somehow we ended up in seats next to each other. She was talked into going with some friends from church and didn't know a thing about football. By the end of the game, I had her ringing that cowbell so loud I thought I was going deaf. But I didn't care. I would have given anything for her." His face broke out in a smile. It was the first real smile I'd seen on him. "We got married a few months later. When you know, you know. We both wanted a big family, as many kids as our house could hold, but after Ethan was born ... well, it just wasn't going to happen for us, and then the years went by."

He paused and closed his eyes, breathing in and out. Focused. He hands were less shaky.

"Tess was hurting, but I didn't notice. A detective doesn't sleep in a city like Vancouver. I threw myself into work and what little sleep I did get was haunted by the things I had seen—the bodies, the smells ... it never goes away."

"So you quit?"

"I had to. Tess couldn't take it anymore. And given the choice between a woman who loved me and a job that didn't, I'd make the same decision all over again."

"She gave you an ultimatum?"

"Not in so many words."

"What did she say?"

"She told me I needed to stop and breathe once in a while." He smiled again, fondly. "And then we decided the small town, the fresh prairie air, was just what we needed."

"Do you miss the city?"

"Ethan does, I think. Tess and I haven't looked back." He thought about it. "Actually, I had a brief moment of regret when Mayor McNally brought over a pie. I thought I'd never get out of that hug."

I let out a laugh.

He slid the glass of whisky across the bartop. "Your turn."

"I don't drink," I said.

"No?"

"I never acquired the taste. My old man drank enough for the both of us."

"Ah. But he left you the bar."

I shrugged. "He had no other option. And he died before he could arrange anything else. Sometimes it feels like I'm his stand-in. Like everyone's just waiting for him to come back."

"What happened to him?"

I had a feeling the detective already knew. Surely it was in a file somewhere. My old man had been murdered, after all, even if it was accidental. I wondered if Maharmallo had come across it during my background check. He'd found everything else associated with it. Gravedigging. The other infractions Wick Dugdale had concocted as payback.

"My old man used to have these poker nights," I explained. I reached for the whisky glass and held it in my hand instinctively. Maybe I didn't drink, but it felt like reassurance. "He was always drunk afterwards. But one night he passed out in the parking lot and got run over. A hit and run, I suppose."

"Did they ever find out who did it?"

I shook my head. "Everyone thought it was my mother."

The detective nodded slowly. He didn't ask me to elaborate.

"Small towns," he muttered instead. It had become an expression of his. Something he said in exasperation. Like something he didn't quite understand.

I wasn't sure I totally understood small towns either. Lonely, but never really alone. Rumours, but always rooted in some truth. I had wanted to run away. Anywhere but a small town. Anyplace where someone wouldn't know my name, or my family, or my past. Small towns never forgot those things. Townsfolk had memories as old as the hills. They had eyes that watched every move.

Pearl was very different from Vancouver. Maharmallo had said so himself.

"Why Pearl?" I asked. The question had been on the tip of my tongue for too long.

"Tess had a good feeling about this place. She said it was meant to be." He let out a laugh. "If you were from the west coast, I'd use my oyster analogy. Maybe I still will."

I must have looked sceptical.

He went with it. "A pearl is a symbol of tragedy transformed into beauty. When a single grain of sand finds its way into an oyster, its natural defence is to cover up the sand, layer by layer, until eventually it turns into a pearl. Perfect. Round. It's remarkable, really. But you have to crack open the oyster to find it."

There was a lesson in there somewhere. I decided right then and there that my mother would've liked Maharmallo. Chandler might have been fun to read and Marlowe might have been a sleuth for the ages, but Maharmallo was a real detective. He lived and breathed the truth. Justice. Integrity. It all ran in his blood. He'd taken a stand against a life that had nearly eaten him alive. He'd lost himself but was determined to find himself again. Sure, there was Tedd Archer. And Cosmo. And a dead cat. Maybe Maharmallo's job hadn't changed. Maybe the workload had indeed followed him from Vancouver. But he had changed. Maybe he'd cracked open the oyster and found his pearl.

"Amateur sleuth that you are, I'm surprised you never found the culprit," Maharmallo suddenly said, and I realized he was talking about my old man again.

"I never said I didn't."

"Ah." The detective smiled to himself.

"Wick Dugdale," I said. It didn't matter anymore anyway.

And just like that, the conversation had circled back to the former policeman.

"How do you know?" Maharmallo asked.

"He played poker with my old man. And the tire treads matched his police cruiser. In hindsight, I suppose I just assumed. But when we confronted him, he all but threatened us to keep quiet."

"Us?"

"Me and Logan."

"Did Wick admit it was him?"

I shook my head. "No. We thought he might've skipped town. But we found him, acting like nothing had ever happened. Logan pulled a gun on him and he didn't even bring us in."

"Where'd Logan get a gun?"

"It was an old hunting rifle from his cousin. He kept it buried at the cemetery."

"Hence the gravedigging."

"Hence the gravedigging," I repeated.

Maharmallo leaned forward on the bartop. He looked around the bar, lingering on the rows of sparkling bottles. He took another deep breath, no doubt inhaling the scent of poured whisky, still in the glass between us. If he was struggling to process it all, I couldn't tell. I wondered how I'd ever thought he was an alcoholic. His tired eyes were sober as a judge.

"None of that came up on your record check," he said. "Or Logan's."

"Wick knew he was guilty. He couldn't file a report without us telling the truth. I didn't have proof, obviously. It was my word against his. But I suppose he couldn't risk it. It would have ruined his career, his reputation." I shrugged a shoulder. "It ruined my mother's reputation instead."

"They really thought it was her?"

They, the townsfolk. Some of them had cared about my mother. They'd been her friends. They'd even known about my old man. The wild drinking. The yelling. The endless poker nights. Perhaps, in the end, that was why they'd suspected her. It only made sense she would want to get rid of him.

The bar was silent for a moment, before the detective said, "I'm sorry, Humphrey. For what it's worth."

It turned out it was worth a lot.

Maharmallo thanked me for the drink he hadn't drunk and glanced at the clock. "It's getting late. I should probably get going or Tess is going to think I'm still working."

"I won't tell if you won't."

He smiled and stood up, straightening his jacket and tie. "We won't be able to sleep until Ethan's home anyway. He's out with a girl tonight. First date. I know he's seventeen, but I'm not ready for it. It could be worse, I guess. Ethan at his age. He could be gravedigging."

I almost laughed but the detective was back to his straight face and I wasn't sure he'd meant it as a joke. It didn't matter anyway, because by the time Maharmallo had exited the bar and drove away, I was still preoccupied with the thought of what it would feel like to be seventeen with an old man who couldn't sleep because I wasn't home.

"Humphrey?"

I blinked and saw Daphne standing in the middle of the loft. Her hair was pulled back and she had changed into dark clothes. She thrust a dark Henley and a pair of black jeans into my hands.

"Here," she said. "Change into this."

I blinked some more, trying to process what was happening. "You went through my clothes?"

Daphne didn't seem to hear me. She was busy unpacking one of her duffle bags, spreading out random articles of clothing, including an out-of-season knitted scarf, a pair of what appeared to be combat boots, a pair of brass knuckles (which I was fairly sure were illegal), and a manual called *Private Eyeing 101*. Eventually she found what she was looking for: two heavy-duty flashlights.

"What did Maharmallo want?" she asked.

"Nothing."

He hadn't wanted anything, I supposed, expect to talk. Maybe we *were* friends.

When I didn't move, she came over to me and dumped a flashlight on top of my clothes, pushing me towards the bathroom. "Well, hurry up. Logan's going to be here any minute."

I turned around. "Where are we going?"

"Haven't you been listening? We're going on a stakeout."

Blackmail could be a funny thing. It could drive someone to a sort of madness, although I supposed a sort of madness ran in Logan's blood anyway. Whatever it was, Logan had had enough and told Daphne that this would be the last time he would part with his hard-earned money. Apparently Daphne had assured him that he would get it all back. Stakeouts were foolproof, according to the famous yet ever-elusive Tanner Redhill.

I wasn't sure I agreed.

According to Daphne, a proper stakeout would have included coffee, a box of stale doughnuts, and a pair of classic black binoculars, but the only place open in Pearl in the middle of the night was the gas station, and I didn't think we would find any of those things there. Except maybe a cup of coffee Daphne wouldn't approve of.

"You're late," Daphne said as Logan came up the stairs just before midnight.

I couldn't remember the last time Logan had been in the loft. His beady eyes shifted around. The place probably looked the same as it had when we were young.

"I had to gas up the Bentley, darling." Logan reached into the pocket of his jacket—a dark colour, Daphne had insisted—and pulled out an envelope. "And I had to visit the ATM."

By ATM, he meant Granddad Griffith. Logan had likely visited him at the distillery, since the old man in the wheelchair didn't get around much these days. But he was wildly generous, even with the black sheep of the family.

In that moment, as the three of us walked out of the bar and loaded into the Bentley—the photographer behind the wheel, the private eye taking shotgun, and an ordinary bartender crammed in the back seat—I thought of something Maharmallo had said. Something unusual. Something about twos and threes.

19

BLACKMAILERS DON'T SHOOT

"What now?"

"Now we wait," Daphne said to Logan.

He handed over his flashlight, having just returned from stashing the envelope stuffed with ten one-hundred-dollar bills deep inside the walls of Bardakci's garage. It was closed up for the night, the big garage doors bolted down, yet the main door on the side was, as per usual, unlocked. We'd watched Logan park the Bentley across the street and saunter through the lot of parked cars, entering through the side door. He'd stashed the envelope alone. Then we'd taken the Bentley around the block and returned, parking in the driveway of Emre's vacant rental. It was the perfect position to see anyone coming or going.

Logan cut the headlights and leaned back in his seat. Like Daphne had said, it was a matter of waiting.

And waiting.

Well past midnight, no one had entered Bardakci's. No one had even driven by.

"How long is this going to take?" Logan asked, growing impatient.

Daphne shrugged, covering a yawn with her hand.

So we waited some more, in silence, taking turns watching the garage, listening to the nighttime chirping of crickets, and watching the slight drizzle of rain perspire on the windshield.

After another half-hour or so, Logan spoke up. "Daphne, darling, Humphrey wants to know where you got your ring. The one you lost."

I couldn't see his face, but I imagined there was a devilish grin involved. I stared out the window. It suddenly felt very cramped in the back seat.

If Daphne was surprised by the question, she didn't show it. She answered right away. No hesitation. No reluctance.

"It's from my fiancé."

I had suspected as much, of course, but hearing her say it was another thing entirely. I couldn't breathe. Was it an appropriate time to ask Logan to crack a window?

"But he died," she added. "In a car accident."

I looked at her. So did Logan. She was staring out the window, but she must have felt our eyes on her. She turned her head, unable to see us in the dark.

"I'm sorry," I said.

"Sure you are," Logan muttered sarcastically. He got a swift kick in the back of his seat.

"It's fine," Daphne said. "It happened a while ago, but sometimes I still like to wear the ring. He bought it for me and he didn't have much, you know? It must have cost him a lot."

"Of course." I nodded in understanding, but I didn't really understand. I wanted to. At least, I thought I wanted to. It was quiet again. Before I knew what I was thinking, my voice came out almost in a whisper: "What was he like?"

She hesitated now. "Well, he was kind of like you, Humphrey."

I still couldn't breathe. What was going on?

"He liked reading old books." She laughed a little, despite herself.

But if she could have seen me, she would have seen a small smile appear on my face. It wasn't that I didn't feel bad for her. I did. Losing someone in such a sudden way was terrible. Gut-wrenching. I knew how that felt. Even if I hadn't cared all that much for my old man.

"We have action!" Logan said suddenly, springing forward in his seat.

I peered out the window between them. It was much too dark to see anything concrete, but the overhead streetlight had caught the glimpse of a shadow, some movement across the street.

"Good grief," I muttered.

Daphne pushed open her door and stepped out. Gentle rain splatted against her face as she zipped up her aviator jacket. "Let's go."

"Shouldn't someone stay here?" I asked.

I felt a sudden nervous feeling in the pit of my stomach. I wasn't scared. It was just that I had finally gotten comfortable in the cramped Bentley.

"I'll stay, Humphrey," Logan said.

"It's *your* blackmailer."

"It's my car. And rain wrecks my hair."

With that, he leaned lower behind the wheel.

Annoyed, I shook my head and crawled out of the Bentley. Then Daphne and I crossed the street side by side, armed with nothing but our wits and a couple of heavy-duty flashlights.

We were barely into the parking lot before Daphne pulled me down beside an old truck, motioning for me to stay low. I inhaled, breathing in the rain, feeling the splatter against my face, and knowing I would probably be soaked by the time we got back to Logan's car. Crouched behind the truck, we could see the door to Bardakci's garage open and the inside light flick on.

Two people entered.

They were young, judging by the sound of their voices, which carried through the open lot. A young man and a woman. I couldn't see well enough to recognize them, but the man appeared to have entered the garage first, broad-shouldered with a large hand extended to the young woman. She stepped gingerly over the threshold, letting him guide her inside. She giggled softly.

When the door closed behind them, Daphne turned to me.

"Did you see that? What do we do? Wait till they come out? Or is there a back door we can go through?" She looked down at the flashlight in her hand.

"You should have brought the brass knuckles," I said. They might've come in handy right about now.

It wasn't the time for teasing. Daphne trained her eyes back on the garage that had seemingly swallowed up the blackmailers. Two of them? That hardly seemed right.

They weren't inside for very long. They emerged minutes later, wandering into the parking lot. They talked in low voices, but the closer they got to the truck the more I could make out.

"I know it's around here somewhere," the young man was saying as they walked directly past us. "Maybe it's still on the lot."

It was then that I recognized the woman. Her dark curly hair and the low, soft giggle.

I stepped out, flicking on my flashlight. "Agnes?"

Startled, the young woman jumped back, letting out a scream and raising a hand to cover the blinding light.

I lowered it. "You're not Agnes."

Sara Swope let out a breath of relief. "Humphrey! What are you doing here?"

The nanny's younger sister no doubt recognized me from the diner. Her striking resemblance to Agnes had fooled me for a moment. But I could see her now. I ignored the question and spun my light onto the young man standing behind her. "Who are you?"

"Ethan Maharmallo," he replied. He was broad-shouldered with dark skin and deep sunken eyes. So this was the detective's son. He had a mature look about him for a seventeen-year-old.

"Ah. Nice to meet you, Ethan."

"Likewise," he said, but he didn't seem too pleased.

"Want to tell me why you're breaking in Bardakci's in the middle of the night?"

Ethan frowned. "We weren't breaking in. You sound like my father."

I didn't mind the comparison.

"Answer the question," I said. "Where's Logan's money?"

"What money? Who's Logan?"

"The money you took from inside," I said forcefully. I looked at Daphne. "Where'd Logan leave it? On the workbench?" I turned back to Ethan and Sara. "Empty your pockets."

But Daphne cut in, lowering my flashlight. "Humphrey, I don't think it's them."

"Ethan was just showing me his car," Sara said, eyeing me warily.

I recalled Maharmallo mentioning that Ethan had bought a car from Emre. I also recalled that Ethan was out on a date tonight. With Sara, I supposed.

Good grief, I'd made a total mess of things.

"Did you see anyone else in the garage?" Daphne asked Sara.

The younger Swope sister shook her head just as a light flicked on inside Bardakci's, a dark figure illuminated in the doorway. I only caught a glimpse of her out of the corner of my eye, but it was clearly a woman, her delicate figure and long hair disappeared into the garage.

Daphne had seen her too. She abandoned Ethan and Sara and, brushing past me, tore off towards the garage. I followed, picking up my strides to match her pace.

We were still a few paces from the door when the woman darted out. She'd had just enough time to rummage through Emre's workbench before taking off, leaving the light on and the door swaying.

The woman rounded the corner of the building. The grassy area behind Bardakci's was unlit and unlevel, but she managed it with a remarkable ease.

I sprinted ahead of Daphne, turning the corner and spotting the shadowy outline up ahead. The flashlight beam darted back and forth as I ran, sometimes catching a hint of the woman's face or hair tailing behind her.

She was quick, and I wasn't sure I was quicker. But eventually she would run out of grass and hit a fence or street. Once I had her cornered, we'd have her once and for all. And once I'd seen her entire face, I knew I'd recognize her.

But somewhere along the way I lost sight of her. Pulse pounding, I slowed to a stop, spinning my flashlight around. Where had she gone?

In an instant, I felt a pair of hands tug at the flashlight, jerking the blunt end towards my face and knocking me squarely between the eyes. The impact forced me backwards as my assailant escaped.

"Humphrey!"

Daphne ran up from behind, helping me fall gently onto the wet grass.

I blinked away the rain pelting against my face, trying to see straight. Eventually Daphne's face came into focus. Blonde. Green-eyed. Gorgeous. For a moment, I forgot what we were doing there, behind Bardakci's. It was just the two of us. And for some reason we were spinning, round and round.

The grass rustled behind us. I sat up. Daphne whipped her flashlight around.

"Don't shoot," Logan deadpanned, both hands in the air as if under arrest. He had a camera in hand, its strap wrapped around his neck.

"Good grief." I exhaled, falling back on the grass.

But moments later, settled into the back of the Bentley, I could finally catch my breath. It had to be well after midnight, the small hours of the morning. The sleek black Bentley as it crawled down Main Street was perhaps the only sign of life, and everything was quiet except for the crickets. Dark except for the lone headlights on the road.

Logan spoke first. "For a lifelong Chandler enthusiast and a professional private eye, the two of you are extremely disappointing."

"I'm sorry?" Daphne asked—a question, not an apology.

"I practically had to catch my blackmailer on my own." He grinned at me through the rearview, lifting the camera hanging around his neck. "Luckily, I have her right where I want her."

Of course Logan's blackmailer was a woman. The letters had been addressed to *Darling Logan* after all, a mockery of him, of the name he used for every woman he met.

"You have photos," I said.

"You have photos?" Daphne repeated, surprised.

"It's called a night lens, darling."

He passed the camera to her and we flicked through the pictures, one by one. I could hardly believe my eyes. The woman, entering and exiting Bardakci's garage with the incriminating envelope in her hand, was instantly recognizable. Logan's blackmailer was none other than Gwynn Grant.

Logan grinned. "She's still in love with me."

"Don't flatter yourself," I muttered.

"It's not easy having deep pockets."

I imagined, in almost every sense, that it was quite easy.

"What do we do now?" Logan asked.

It was too dark to see the sparkle in Daphne's eyes, but I knew it was there.

"Perhaps a little blackmail of our own," she said, taking the words right out of my mouth.

Back at the bar, I couldn't sleep.

I couldn't blame it on the stray. For the first night in what felt like forever, it wasn't scratching at my fire escape. Perhaps it was the knock to my forehead, in addition to my other aches and pains, that kept me awake.

We had returned from Bardakci's only a few hours ago and I still sat unsettled in the armchair, trying to get comfortable. I wondered if Daphne was having as much trouble sleeping. Somehow I doubted it, looking at the blonde head of hair poking out from underneath the sheets and the long, slender outline of her body, unmoving.

On second thought, it was no wonder I couldn't sleep.

Sunlight eventually filtered through the window and I closed my eyes, feeling the warmth on my face. Maybe it was the lack of sleep, but the events of the night were hitting harder than I thought they would.

Gwynn Grant was Logan's blackmailer. It all made sense. As Logan's former girlfriend, she'd known enough about him to use it to her advantage and, knowing the photographer, had likely been scorned by him in some way. She lived directly across from Bardakci's, a convenient drop-off point. Emre had even said that she'd fallen behind on rent a few times. Perhaps she'd been in desperate need of money. Easy money. Money Logan hardly would've been missed.

Driving back to the bar, Logan had admitted that he should have known it was Gwynn all along. But then, he wouldn't have needed a private eye and I wouldn't have met Daphne.

I watched her stir, ever so slightly, under the sheets.

I closed my eyes again, this time turning my thoughts towards the photos Logan had taken at the motel's reopening. I could picture them—Tedd and Cynthia cutting the ribbon amidst the gathering of townsfolk, like Bartel Smith, Wick Dugdale, Brigid, Mag, Gwynn ... but Madelaine had been noticeably missing. And she wasn't the only one.

It was barely morning when the old landline began to ring, the sound echoing throughout the bar and upstairs. I sat up, accidently knocking a pile of paper from atop a nearby pile of books: the unfinished manuscript. The thick stack landed mostly with a *thud*, although some sheets of paper scattered further, catching air and fluttering to the floor.

I looked at Daphne, still asleep, and carefully rose to gather the manuscript, replacing it in the armchair where I'd been sitting. The phone downstairs was still ringing, the caller persistent. With a final glance at Daphne, undisturbed in my bed, I ducked downstairs and pulled the phone off the hook.

"Hello?"

"Humphrey."

"Maharmallo?"

The detective's voice sounded groggy, as if he'd just woken up himself. "Is this that old phone on the wall? Funny you never disconnected it."

"How do you know?"

"I'm a detective."

Good grief.

"I'm calling," he said, "because I know about your little escapade last night."

Ah. I assumed Ethan had told him. Although, looking at the clock, I wondered when he'd had time to.

"Did my son break into Bardakci's to show his car off to that girl?"

I doubted Ethan had told him that.

"Bardakci's is always unlocked," I said. I felt like I owed the kid some help. "So technically he didn't break in."

"And why were you there?"

"It's a long story."

"I'm ready to hear it. Oh, and Humphrey," he added, "have you ever worn a wire?"

20

THE WIRE

The sign on the door of Archer's Antique Shoppe read OPEN. Flanked by Daphne and Logan, I entered and led the way past the prayer rugs, nearly getting lost among a cluster of Griffiths whisky barrels. I squeezed between them, ducking under a plethora of dangling windchimes and around the book cart, which seemed to have moved since my last visit.

When I finally found the piano in the middle of the shoppe, I knew Gwynn was nearby.

"You look terrible," Gwynn said, looking up from behind the counter.

She was right, of course. I did look terrible. I supposed that was what happened after a fistfight with Logan, nearly being choked by a former policeman, and taking a flashlight to the forehead. Her face pulled into a frown when she saw Logan emerge from the windchimes.

"What are you doing here?" she asked.

"I have something for you, darling." Logan flapped the stack of printed photos in his hand.

"I don't want anything from you," she hissed.

"Oh, I think you'll want this." Logan laughed to himself as he laid the photos one by one on the counter. He grinned devilishly, watching her. He seemed to be enjoying it all a little too much.

Her eyes widened. "What's this?" she snapped.

"You've been blackmailing Logan," Daphne said.

"I never—"

"The proof is in the pictures, darling," Logan interjected. "You can't sweettalk your way out of this one."

I found it hard to believe Gwynn could sweettalk her way out of anything. She frowned again, stealing a glance at me. I didn't say anything.

"Why'd you do it?" Daphne asked.

"I needed money." Gwynn looked down at the photos again. "It wasn't that much. It's not like you needed it!"

"That's called extortion," I said. "It's a serious crime."

"Humphrey knows all about serious crimes." Logan tipped his head, grinning.

"How did you know Logan would pay?" Daphne asked.

Gwynn bit her lip. "I didn't. Not at first."

"The missing typewriter—you stole it," I said. "That's what Riley was looking for when he searched your house. He knew you had it because you tried to blackmail him too."

"I didn't steal anything," she insisted.

"But he didn't find it," I continued, "because you never took it home."

I moved around the counter and the piano, sliding the postcard rack out of the way and twisting the knob of Tedd Archer's office. The door swung open.

There on Tedd's desk sat a black 1970s typewriter, an antique that was no doubt in pristine working condition, without a single key askew. Maharmallo, in his search of Tedd's office, had overlooked the item as just another antique, unaware of Logan's blackmail letters.

Gwynn stepped into the office behind me. "See? I didn't *steal* it. It never left the shoppe."

"Tedd didn't use his office," I said, although I had to admit it was an assumption on my part.

But Gwynn confirmed it quickly. "I pretty much had the office to myself. The typewriter was hidden in plain sight ..."

"... and Madelaine and Riley had been none the wiser," I finished, mulling it over. Gwynn last night at Bardakci's. The brown-haired woman in the dark.

It seemed to me the two women were one and the same.

"You were with Riley at the motel on the night of Tedd's murder," I said. "Tedd saw you with some extra cash. He thought you were stealing antiques and the money was his, so he forced you to give it to him. But it was Logan's blackmail money and you went to get it back."

Gwynn didn't say anything. She could hardly deny it.

Daphne flapped one of the photos from the counter. "Tell us what happened, Gwynn, and we won't turn these over to the police."

"Extortion, darling, remember?" Logan grinned.

Gwynn bit her lip. "I told Riley that Tedd had taken money from me. He offered to get it back. He said he was going to see Tedd anyway. That's why we drove to the motel. The whole way there, he kept talking about how horrible Tedd was, how he didn't deserve Madelaine. Maddy, he called her. He was all jittery, like he couldn't keep his hands on the wheel. I thought he was drunk, but I've never seen Riley drunk."

"What about Pope's?" Daphne asked.

"They were never there," I said, turning to Gwynn. "Pope's was closed that night. You and Riley made up the alibi so neither of you would have to explain how long you were really at the motel."

Gwynn nodded. "Riley said he'd take care of it. I waited in his pickup for a while. When he didn't come back, I went to Room 7 myself. The door was open. Tedd was already dead."

"So you took the money."

"It was my money," Gwynn hissed at me. "It didn't matter if Tedd was dead or alive."

While Gwynn had been taking the money from Tedd's wallet, Riley had been held up unexpectantly, hit over the head with a whisky bottle, and then detained by Daphne and me as we waited for the police. Yet he had no alibi for midnight, and by Gwynn's account he'd been at the motel earlier. In fact, he'd been in Tedd's room before anyone else.

Gwynn's letter to Riley had indicated that she knew something. Something she was willing to tell the police. It was the only letter that had differed from the others, not addressed to *Darling Logan*, and the threat had been much more serious. *"His time's up,"* Daphne had said.

But Riley had long outlasted his twenty-four-hour deadline.

I wondered why Gwynn hadn't made good on her threat, especially when she'd made good on her threats to Logan.

"When you tried to blackmail Riley, you said you knew what he'd done," I said. Gwynn let out an irritated sigh. "What did he do?"

She frowned again, apprehensively, and looked down one last time at the photos. Finally, she gave in. "I think he murdered Tedd that night. And I think if he still had that gun, I'd be next."

Given the right incentive, Gwynn had sung like a canary. She wasn't too thrilled about it, but then again, she wasn't too thrilled about anything.

Satisfied, Logan gathered up his photos. We left the way we'd come, finding our way back out on the street where the Bentley was parked out front. Logan and Daphne would drop me off at the police station, just in time for me to get wired up with Maharmallo. The detective had let me keep my promise to Daphne. We'd solved her case start to finish. And we'd black-mailed the blackmailer into revealing the killer, although Gwynn would still have to give Maharmallo an official statement about Riley.

Now all we had to do find him. There was a chance he'd skipped town, I supposed, but if he was anything like his old man, I doubted he had.

The wire was a small device, no bigger than a bottle cap. Maharmallo gave me the rundown, slipping the wire into the front pocket of my jeans. As long as it was on me, it would transmit and record everything I said and did. They used them in Vancouver all the time. Undercover operations. Drug busts.

All I had to do was find Riley Dugdale, preferably without Wick, and get him talking.

This time his time really was up.

The Archers' house on Lilac Lane was still picture perfect, with its white picket fence and purple lilacs. As I walked up the driveway, I felt strangely alone. Despite the wire in my pocket. Despite Maharmallo listening in.

Agnes answered the door, followed closely by Teddy.

"Hello, Humphrey," she said with a giggle, batting her lashes.

"Is Madelaine here? Her car's in the driveway," I said.

Agnes pouted. "She's in the kitchen."

"And Riley?"

"He's not here yet," she replied, biting her lip.

Yet. I smiled at her despite myself.

The sound of a clattering glasses echoed from the kitchen, followed by the shutting of a cabinet door, swiftly, with unneeded force. Madelaine rounded the corner, looking a little lost without a glass of wine. I'd clearly interrupted her indulgence. She seemed surprised to see me, glancing between Agnes and me.

"What's going on?" she asked. Her voice was stilted. She took slow, careful steps towards me. I pictured a thick cigar and smoke rings. The whole nine yards, as my old man used to say.

"I was just talking to your nanny," I said. "She said Riley was coming over? Funny. I was hoping to talk to him."

Madelaine stared at me, defensive. "Agnes doesn't know what she's talking about."

Perhaps it wasn't meant to be insulting to Agnes, but it came across that way. The young nanny sucked in her bottom lip and blinked her eyes.

In an effort to prevent her from shedding poorly-timed tears, I turned back to Madelaine.

"Actually, I think she does. You pulled at least two glasses out of the cabinet. I heard it when I walked in. You're expecting someone. And I know it wasn't me."

There it was. A small giggle. Fluttering eyelashes. Agnes was back to normal.

Madelaine, on the other hand, kept staring. Her eyes turned cold like Gwynn's. "Hmmm. Agnes, would you take Teddy outside?"

Agnes did as she was told, taking Teddy by the hand and leading him to the door. The small boy looked back at me, only briefly, blinking his big brown eyes and trying to comprehend with his five-year-old mind what was going on, why there was so much tension in the air, why he was constantly being dragged off when I showed up at his house.

I let them pass out the door, although I caught a lingering look from Agnes. She missed her step, tripping over the threshold and stumbling forward. My instinct to catch her kicked in and I lunged in time for her to dip rather conveniently into my arms.

She let out a giggle that made me wonder if she'd planned it.

"Agnes, please," Madelaine said.

Agnes let me go. Rather, I let her go, watching as she led Teddy away from the house.

I turned back to Madelaine, catching the knowing smile fixed to her face.

"What?" I asked.

"You can have her, Humphrey."

"I'm sorry?"

"Agnes. She likes you. I don't know why. You don't strike me as a romantic. But she's not the sharpest stick on the tree."

At least Agnes hadn't been around to hear that.

Madelaine walked back to the kitchen and I followed. As I suspected, two wine glasses had been set aside and one of the doors of the wine cabinet still hung open. Madelaine, with a hardened expression, pulled out a third glass and a bottle of red. She poured all three, taking the fullest glass for herself before handing one to me.

"Here, Humphrey. If you insist on barging into my home, I might as well offer you a drink." She took a gulp and washed it down with another. Then she sat on one of the barstools. "Maybe I was expecting you."

Me. Madelaine. Riley. A nice little chat over wine. I was almost looking forward to it.

I set my glass down. "How long have you and Riley been having an affair?"

She didn't answer at first. She took another gulp of wine.

"How do you know?" she finally asked.

"The photo of you, the one Logan took," I explained. "There was a date written on the back. I knew the date was familiar, but for the longest time I couldn't recall why. Then I remembered. It was the date of the motel reopening. And it wasn't your handwriting. It wasn't Tedd's either. I believed you when you said didn't give the photo to him."

She took another sip of wine. It was a long sip.

"You weren't at the reopening," I said. "Neither was Riley. I think you were together that day and you gave him the photo."

"That's absurd, Humphrey. Really."

"I think Riley wrote the date on the back."

"Hmmm. He isn't that sentimental."

Maybe he wasn't normally, but it was Madelaine. Maddy. He was in love with her. So in love that it had been obvious to Cosmo, to Logan, even, if

I thought about it, to me, right from the beginning. I wondered how they'd ever thought their affair would stay a secret.

And I wondered what Madelaine saw in him.

She gave me another cold stare. "It's nobody's business what I do with—"

"Even if he murdered your husband?"

She was momentarily distracted, suddenly staring past me. I turned to follow her gaze out the window. She had seen a rusted pickup pull into the driveway. It parked behind Madelaine's yellow car, and Riley got out. He walked up the driveway just as he had undoubtedly done plenty of times before. I heard the front door open and close.

The first thing Riley did when he entered the kitchen was kiss Madelaine, pulling her into him with both hands around her neck. He thought, of course, they were alone.

When they pulled apart, he let out a breath he'd been holding.

"I hope you b–b–broke out the red. I'm d–dying for a drink."

Ah. So that was what she saw in him.

Then he realized that they weren't alone.

"H–H–Humphrey?"

Madelaine handed him the glass of wine he'd been desperate for. It was all she could do.

He took it with a suddenly shaky hand.

I had underestimated Riley Dugdale. On the night of Tedd's murder, I had argued with Daphne in favour of his innocence. I had recognized myself in the young man: tall, long-limbed, awkward, anxious. A bit cynical. Oppressed by his old man. He had feigned shock, with the stutter in his voice and the shake in his leg. He might very well have been shocked, but it hadn't been the shock of finding Tedd's dead body; it had been the shock of being spotted so soon after.

Something like shock spread across his face now. He set his wine down but refused to sit. He chose to position himself in front of me, almost exactly my height. We were level with each other. I supposed he thought we were even.

"Humphrey knows," Madelaine said to Riley. "I don't know how he knows, but he knows."

That frightened him. He looked back at Madelaine frantically and swore. It was the first time I was able to see a trace of his old man. It was his expression somehow, the way he set his jaw, grinding his teeth, and cursing under his breath.

"What d–d–do you want?" he asked.

"The truth," I said firmly. "I know the two of you were having an affair. I want to know why you were stealing from your own shoppe. And why you killed Tedd."

Riley looked away. His eyes met Madelaine's, briefly, then flitted to the floor. Eventually he gritted his teeth and snatched up his glass of wine.

"And th–then what? You'll l–let us go?"

"If you tell me the truth."

"My old m–man s–s–said you were nosy."

"Ah," I said, and I took a seat, making myself comfortable. I even picked up the glass of red, peering through it. "Here's what else I know. Gwynn Grant stole a typewriter from the shoppe. Well, technically she only moved it to Tedd's office, but she used it to type her blackmail letters to Logan. And then she sent a letter to you." I tipped my glass to Riley. "That's why you ransacked her house. You were looking for the typewriter. And you were desperate to find it and confront her. You couldn't have Gwynn telling the police what you'd done. What you'd done, of course, was murder Tedd Archer."

Silence.

"Tedd had quite the temper. You said so yourself." At this, I pointed the glass at Madelaine. "He took things. He threw things. He even hurt Teddy. When he found out about your affair, he was livid. And he found out because of a little photo taken by my friend Logan."

My friend? Perhaps it was an overstatement, but I thought it added a bit of flair.

"Somehow he found Riley with a photo of his wife," I continued. "And he did what any self-respecting husband would do. He was angry. He threw a fit. Then he checked himself into his newly acquired motel. Or was that your idea?" I asked Madelaine.

But she didn't respond. She made no movement, standing off in the corner as if guarding her precious wine cabinet. Riley looked lonely, across from me. He hadn't looked up. I was fairly sure his eyes were closed. He wasn't here. This wasn't happening. Denial was a powerful thing.

"I'm torn on whose idea it was to procure an old revolver. But it's quite novel, really, the way you planned to end him with one of his own antiques. He never would have saw it coming, I supposed, when he opened the door and saw Riley. And of course," I added, nodding at the younger man, "you had some practice with a stray cat, a brilliant way to test the silencer. Where'd you learn to shoot a gun anyway? Was it the video games?"

He had been hovering over me, but now he finally sat down. His leg started to shake again, nervously.

"Madelaine leads a fairly comfortable lifestyle. Full-time nanny. Italian coats. Imported red." I tipped my glass again. "Maybe Tedd could afford it," I said to Riley, "but you can't. So you started to steal things. Easy things at first. Stuff that would hardly be missed. A simple prayer rug here and there." I looked again to Madelaine. "I'm assuming you looked the other way. The thing I don't understand is why you fired him for stealing."

She finally dared to speak.

"A momentary lapse of judgement," she said. "I was having second thoughts."

"About the affair or the murder?"

"Hmmm."

"You have no p–p–proof of any of th–this," Riley suddenly said. Even his voice was unstable, his stuttering more prominent.

"And you have no alibi for Tedd's murder."

"I d–do have an alibi. I t–t–told you. I was at Pope's with Gwynn."

"Pope's was closed that night."

"That old man p–p–probably d–doesn't remember—"

"Pope was next door on the neighbourhood watch. So either he's Madelaine's alibi or he's yours. Can't be both. Which s it?"

Riley looked down, shaking his head. He was beat. He knew it. Finally, he lifted his head heavily. "It was s–s–self-defence, really. Him or me."

"Him or you? Tedd was angry about the affair, sure. I very much doubt your life was on the line."

Knowing Tedd, his life probably had been on the line. But that was neither here nor there.

"You d–d–don't know what it's l–l–like, Humphrey. You've never b–been in love." Riley stole a sidelong glance at Madelaine. "Not like us."

That was a bold statement. I was liking him less and less.

"Am I wrong?" I asked him. I hardly expected an answer. "Cosmo saw Gwynn leave Room 7 that night. You were worried he had seen you too. So you shot him the same way you had shot Tedd—in the doorway of his motel room. But you knew you only had two bullets left and you couldn't afford to miss. You tensed up. The revolver kicked back. That's how you broke your nose. Where'd you hide the gun in between?"

"I b–b–buried it by the river."

That explained the dirt on the gun. And under his fingernails. I noticed it the night we'd caught Riley at the bar. He'd shot Tedd and stashed the gun. Then came back for his photo and Gwynn's money.

"Ah. You cracked open the gun accidently, didn't you? In Cosmo's room. We found a bullet casing on the floor. We thought it might have your fingerprints on it. Or the person who helped you."

His eyes widened. "N–Nobody helped me."

"Nobody helped you? You lifted Cosmo's body, rolled up in a rug, all by yourself? I very much doubt that." I glanced at Madelaine.

"No." Riley stood up. "Not Maddy."

"Then it was your old man."

"How d–d–do you—"

I couldn't help but smile. "I didn't, but I do now."

So Wick Dugdale had been involved. He'd tried to help his son get rid of Cosmo's body, cover up his mistake. Like father, like son. I hoped Maharmallo had heard that one over the wire.

"I'm not s–s–sorry I shot him," Riley sneered. "Tedd d–d–deserved it. And Cosmo ... I d–d–don't know if he s–saw anything that night. I shouldn't have wasted those sh–shots on him."

For a moment, my mind flashed back to another time, another place. Perhaps it was the mention of the buried handgun, the mention of Wick, that took me back to that night at the church: me and Logan, the dark grave ...

"I can find him," Logan had said.

I had been holding a shovel. "And then what?"

It hadn't ended well.

But perhaps Riley was right. Maybe Tedd had deserved it. A fatal shot to the head, point-blank. Two more in his chest, just for good measure, to put an end to his fits of rage. Or maybe it had been the other way around. Two shots to the chest, then the final blow. He'd never hurt Teddy again. He'd never throw a knife at Agnes or damage Madelaine's wine cabinet. He'd never be obnoxious or angry.

Riley backed away. "I've leaving. M–Maddy?"

He seemed unsure of himself, certainly not as confident as when he'd first walked in.

It wasn't hard to see why. Madelaine had aligned herself with neither of us. She stood coldly in the middle of the kitchen, clutching her glass of wine. The colour had drained from her face, and the long scar beneath her eye seemed to pulsate.

"Maddy, c–c–come with me. Please." Riley reached for her.

But she only stared at him. "What about Teddy? I can't ..."

His begging was futile. She kept pulling away from him, shaking her head. He'd gunned down Tedd. She'd known that. They'd cheated and stolen and lied. But running away had never been part of the plan. She hadn't planned on leaving Teddy.

Admittedly, I was surprised her motherly instincts had finally kicked in.

Eventually Riley resigned himself to his apparent options: either he could stay with the woman he supposedly loved like no other, or he could make a run for it.

I certainly wasn't going to stop him.

I took my first sip of red. I'd forgotten how bitter it tasted. It suited the two of them. Mostly Madelaine. Riley was way beyond bitterness. He'd planted a simple, final kiss on Madelaine's lips. He was saying goodbye. He'd expected as much, I supposed, from the moment he'd murdered Tedd. And then Cosmo. He'd expected he'd be caught eventually. He had to have known he couldn't go on living the way he had.

What he hadn't expected was to run into two men at the front door, waiting for him, one in a black suit and tie and the other in a police uniform.

"Ah, if it isn't the man of the hour," Maharmallo said, standing alongside his sidekick, Riggs.

Riley tried pushing through, but his efforts were useless. Riggs caught him, slammed him up against the house, and slapped a pair of cuffs on him faster than I had ever seen Riggs do anything.

"Riley Dugdale," the detective said, "you're under arrest for the murders of Tedd Archer and Cosmo Clarke, as well as the illegal procurement of a firearm ..."

"*That* was I–I–legal," Riley protested, grasping for something, anything.

"We'll see about that," Maharmallo said, straight-faced. "In any case, what you did with it wasn't too legal, now was it?"

He nodded at Riggs, who took Riley away, stuffing him into the back of the police cruiser.

Another car door slammed. I turned to see Wick Dugdale storming up the driveway. Apparently word had travelled fast. He'd probably heard something was going on at the Archers' house on Lilac Lane, not far from Second Street, something about a police cruiser parked half a block away.

He swore something fierce as he approached the detective. Maharmallo, professional that he was, remained calm. He almost sounded cheerful.

"Mr. Dugdale, your timing is impeccable."

"What's going on?" Wick shouted. "Where's my son?"

The detective stepped between him and the cruiser. "Your son's being taken in on suspicion of murder, Mr. Dugdale. And with the evidence we've gathered today, I see no reason why he won't be spending the rest of his life behind bars. The question is whether you're prepared to join him."

Wick took one look at me and flew into a panic.

"That was an accident! And it was fourteen, fifteen years ago. I hardly see the point—"

Maharmallo held up a hand. "I'm referring to the murder of Cosmo Clarke, Mr. Dugdale. It appears you are referring to an altogether different incident, although I'll happily hear anything you have to say on the matter."

The former policeman went pale.

In all the chaos, I hadn't noticed Agnes emerge from the back yard with Teddy. They were watching the scene unfold at the edge of the driveway. The boy was clutching his one-eared rabbit, no doubt confused about why his beloved "Wiley" was being hauled off in a police cruiser. Agnes, on the other hand, looked downright miserable.

She sucked her bottom lip, a sudden wave of tears overtaking her.

"No, it can't be Riley," I heard her sob.

Agnes let Teddy run off to his mother, who had remained in the doorway of her tall white house. Deciding I was closest to Agnes, I walked over and tried to steer her away from Riley in the cruiser and Wick threatening Maharmallo with lawyers.

"It isn't him!" she sputtered, and in that moment, I realized he'd been more than just Teddy's beloved Riley.

"It's that horrid Mrs. Archer," Agnes cried. "It's got to be. I—"

But she had nothing else to say. The tears in her eyes did nothing to hide the truth. She'd already given herself away between her love for Riley and her hatred of Madelaine. If she liked me, it was only because Riley bore a resemblance.

How often I'd been wrong in my assessment of others. Agnes wasn't obtuse or oblivious. She was something else entirely.

Ah, Agnes, I thought to myself. *Poor, sweet Agnes. What have you done?*

"I'm sorry I hit you with a flashlight," Gwynn said. She'd pulled me aside at the police station. "You really do look terrible. You should get that looked at."

"Thank you. I will."

"I think you should have this."

To my surprise, I looked down to see her holding Daphne's diamond ring in the palm of her hand.

"I found it the other day in the alley behind the shoppe. I was going to keep it ... I don't know, it's probably worth a few thousand." She shrugged. "But I kind of like your private eye friend. She's ... interesting."

She dropped the ring into my hand.

"I didn't know you two were engaged," she said to me.

I should have denied it, but I didn't.

"Thank you," I said again. This time I meant it.

I closed my fist around the ring, holding it so tight that I could feel the edges of the diamond digging into my hand. The momentary pain would be worth it, if only to see the look on Daphne's face, the sparkle in her eyes, when I gave it back.

I just had to get Maharmallo's wire off me first.

21

M

Greenwood Cemetery. It wasn't particularly green, the grass was dry and dull, and the lone standing tree in the middle of the freshly cut grass could hardly be mistaken for woods of any kind. A white fence surrounded the graveyard. It had a tall arched gate, which the last pastor had jokingly referred to as the Pearl-y Gate. Needless to say, he hadn't lasted long.

Brigid Dugdale hadn't wanted to meet in too public a place, and I couldn't really blame her. She had picked one of the benches outside church, overlooking the cemetery.

As we sat there, side by side, watching blackbirds land and peck around the gravestones and then fly away, I couldn't help but feel eerily calm. I looked down at the book in my hands, the first edition of *The Big Sleep*. I had tried to give it back to Brigid. It had been a gift from Riley, she said. He knew she read old novels. She hadn't known how valuable it was. Not right away.

"You knew Riley had stolen it," I said.

"A mother always knows."

"You didn't say anything."

"I thought if I donated it, it would go away. I couldn't keep it, not knowing it was stolen. But I couldn't rat on my own son. And anyway, it's much too special to turn in to the police." Brigid signed, grasping both hands around her handbag. "I knew Bart would give it a good home." She met my eyes for a moment and smiled.

"Are you sure?" I asked. The book in my hands suddenly felt heavy.

But Brigid insisted. "I won't take it back, Humphrey. It was never mine."

She stood up to leave, turning her face as she swept away a tear. I wanted to ask her to stay a little longer. I wanted to ask if she'd known about

Wick all along. If she'd known that he'd run over my old man. If she'd played along when the rumours circulated about my mother.

But Brigid wasn't unscathed. She was holding back more tears as she nodded goodbye and walked away. She went through the cemetery, scattering the blackbirds. She'd lost her son—not to the clutches of death that had claimed Tedd Archer and Cosmo Clarke, but she'd lost him just the same. And, by association, she'd lost her husband, a man who had been harbouring his own terrible secret for fifteen years. She'd also lost her friend, Madelaine. I had no doubt that the whole affair between Riley and Madelaine would have ruined even the most kindred friendship.

Her life would never be the same.

I wondered, maybe, if mine wouldn't be the same either.

Something had shifted in Pearl. Perhaps, for the first time in forever, something had changed. The truth had been exposed. It hadn't mattered fifteen years ago, but it mattered now.

I could practically hear my mother's voice.

The truth always matters, Neal.

And suddenly the book in my hands, worth a small fortune, paled in comparison to the truth. I cracked it open, feeling the old, rough pages rustle in the spine. I flipped through the pages almost absentmindedly, letting my thoughts travel across the field of grass to a single gravestone. I could see it from where I was sitting, could pick it out from among the others. It was Logan's fake gravestone. Of course, the original grave hadn't survived. The police had torn it up after we'd been caught digging in it.

But there was another. A backup. I wondered what was buried underneath the grave marked *Griffith* these days. My money was on whisky. Backup whisky. A whole lot of it! Then again, the past week had proved I didn't know the Manhattan Man as well as I thought.

When I finally stood, I tucked my hands in my pockets, holding the book under my arm, and traced Brigid's steps though the cemetery. I only turned to look up at the church behind me, its little white steeple strong against the blue sky.

The detective was right. Remarkable things came from tragedy. And it didn't hurt to stop and breathe once in a while.

Daphne stood next to her beat-up SUV. She had loaded her duffle bag into the back seat and was waiting for me around the front. Room 3 was already locked up, the key turned in to Ayda at the motel office. I imagined that particular goodbye had been heartfelt. I was certain the next occupant of Room 3, whenever that might be, wouldn't be nearly so beautiful, so extraordinary.

A breeze blew her blonde hair across her face and she pulled it back with her hand as I approached, smiling up at me. I wanted to tell her to stay, but I couldn't find the words. Since I'd first laid eyes on her, I had known Daphne didn't belong in Pearl. She was too beautiful. Too free. She had her business in the city. She had Redhill.

She greeted me warmly. She didn't notice *The Big Sleep* still under my arm, or perhaps she pretended not to.

I'd nearly forgotten about the ring in my pocket. Reaching in and retrieving it, I grabbed her hand and slipped it back on her finger.

"You found it," she said.

I smiled. "Something like that."

She stepped back to admire the ring, letting it glisten in the morning sun.

I lifted the book I'd carried back from the cemetery.

"Here," I said. "You promised you'd read Marlowe if I showed you Pearl."

She took it from me. Her eyes widened as she realized what it was. She started to object, but I stopped her.

"I want you to have it," I said.

She hugged me then, on her tiptoes, throwing both hands around me and resting her head on my shoulder. I hugged her back, wanting more than anything to hold on and never let go.

When she pulled away, her eyes lingered on mine. Gloriously green. I decided I would miss those eyes.

She brushed her lips against my cheek before whispering, "Farewell, my Humphrey."

I watched as Daphne swung her aviator jacket over her shoulder. Then she climbed up into the old SUV and closed the door. I stood there, a trace of red lipstick on my face and some strange feeling dwindling somewhere in my chest. She waved as she pulled out of the parking lot.

And when she hit the dirt road, she didn't look back.

I almost didn't recognize the detective seated at the bar. He had traded his sleek black suit and tie for a plain grey tee. There was no holster, no badge, no cuffs, and no buzzing radio. If not for the fact that he was in his usual spot, I might have missed him altogether.

He had already ordered up an appetizer of Seth's famous waffle fries by the time I approached him.

"On or off duty, Maharmallo?"

"Off, this time," he said. "I thought I would try Pope's, but it was closed." He was making a joke—and with a smile, at that.

I couldn't help but smile myself. "Pope's probably gone fishing."

"So they say."

"What can I get you?"

"How about I try some of that local whisky ..."

I nodded, pouring from a bottle of Griffiths and sliding him a glass.

He took a sip. "Congrats on the engagement, by the way."

I winced. "You heard that?"

"Only me and Riggs." He looked around. "Where is your private eye anyway?"

"She went home."

I missed her already, finding myself looking at the door every now and then, willing her to walk back in. If I closed my eyes, I could see her there at the sidebar, in her usual spot next to Logan.

The truth was, I'd probably never see her again.

I took a breath, in and out.

"I'm sorry about Wick Dugdale."

I blinked at Maharmallo, shaking my head. "Did you say something?"

"Ah, Humphrey. I thought I lost you."

"You said something about Wick?"

"Only that I'm sorry I can't tie him to your father's death." The detective tipped his drink. "But with Riley's statement, he'll go down as an accessory for Cosmo's. That's some justice at least. I can't stand dirty cops."

Apparently, neither could Pearl's townsfolk. The detective might not have been able to officially connect Wick Dugdale to my old man's death, but the recent rumours around town suggested otherwise. Wick's fit of rage outside the Archers' home had caused quite the stir. His outburst about an "accident" that had occurred fifteen years ago had made its way around town.

Maharmallo was right. It wasn't much, but it was something. The truth had finally surfaced, even if it had taken fifteen years.

A new face walked through the door just then. A new face in my bar anyway. Her curly black hair and batting eyelashes were otherwise familiar. The sight of her sent a chill down my spine. I wondered how quickly I could escape through the back door before she noticed me.

She came up to the bar, hardly glancing at Maharmallo, who'd gone back to his whisky and fries. Maybe she didn't recognize him in the grey tee. There was no giggling, which at least made her bearable.

"I need to talk to you," Agnes whimpered to me. "Somewhere private. Maybe upstairs."

She was smooth. I had to hand it to her.

I led her out the back door into the alley. "What is it, Agnes?"

She collapsed on the ground, plopping her head in her hands. "You know, Humphrey, don't you? Somehow you must. I'm the one who tried to poison Madelaine last week. I don't know what came over me …"

Good grief. I sat next to her. Sure, I'd had a feeling, but I hadn't been prepared for her confession.

"It was the coffee, wasn't it?" I let out a breath. "Madelaine said it was too strong."

She nodded, wiping tears out of her eyes. "I made it strong on purpose so she wouldn't taste the cashews. I ground up a handful and mixed them in."

"You took her EpiPen too."

She nodded again.

"She could have died, Agnes."

"I know," she sobbed. "I just couldn't help it. I had to do something. Riley didn't even notice me. It was always all about *her*." She spat out the word with a particular distaste. "What do I do now?"

That was the question.

I watched her, knees curled against her body, her shoulders quivering with each sob. She had made a mistake—well, more than a mistake; she had attempted murder. But when I looked at her, I still saw a young, impressionable nanny. It wasn't her fault that her boss's affair had gotten so messy. And sometimes the truth hurt. That wasn't her fault either.

"I think you should quit your job," I said. "For your sake and Madelaine's, and forget about Riley Dugdale."

She gazed up at me with watery eyes. "I already have."

"Ah, good."

"Are you going to tell Detective Maharmallo about me?"

I thought about it, glancing back towards the bar. Then I thought about Cynthia. I'd made mistakes at Agnes's age. Mistakes I wasn't proud of.

"No," I said. "It'll be our little secret."

She breathed a sigh of relief. Before I knew it, she flung her arms around me and squished me into a hug—not quite so tight as her grandmother's signature hugs, but tight nonetheless.

I felt a few of her tears drip onto my shirt like raindrops.

"Thank you, Humphrey. You're a brick."

I was a brick, wasn't I? Whatever that meant.

Somehow I managed to wriggle out of the hug and send her on her way. Then I wandered back into the bar and picked up a dishrag, tossing it over my shoulder.

Maharmallo was gone, but he had finished his drink. When I reached for his empty glass, I saw that he had scribbled a note on the back of his receipt. I picked it up.

> Had to go. Tess is making salmon again. Ethan's bringing Sara.
>
> Your private eye will be back. Remember to stop and breathe once in a while. Don't go digging up any graves.
>
> M.

22

HUMPHREY'S MOTEL

It was raining on Thursday morning. The slight drizzle started to pick up on my way back to the bar. I'd been in town, running a few errands and picking up a copy of *The Pearl Gazette* from the bundle of new, freshly printed editions near the post office.

I entered the bar through the back door, eyeing the tarp-covered Shelby before letting the door close behind me. The gentle *pitter-patter* on the tin roof sounded louder than usual as I wandered across the bar and dropped the *Gazette* on the nearest table. I had managed to keep it dry.

Unfolding the paper, I read the front-page headline: *Caught! Pearl's Murderer Cuffed and Stuffed*. It was written by Mag, of course, accompanied by a black-and-white photo of Riggs stuffing Riley into a police car.

I was eager to read the full article, but I was long overdue for a phone call to my mother. I glanced at the clock. What time was it in Vancouver?

I crossed the empty bar to the phone on the wall, plucked the landline off the hook, and dialled a number from memory.

"Hello, Neal. How are you?"

It was good just to hear her voice.

"I mailed back the manuscript," I said.

Snail mail. We liked the classics, after all.

"What did you think?" she asked.

"There's no ending."

"Actually, there are two. I couldn't decide which one to send."

"I don't think it matters."

"That bad?"

"That good. It's very Chandler."

Silence on the other end. She was speechless. So was I.

"So you think they'll pick it up?"

"They'd be crazy not to," I told her.

"That's what Margot said. They'd be batty to turn it down!"

Batty was a good word. Nobody used it anymore.

Silence again. It had been so long, we'd seemed to have lost our footing. No matter. We'd find it again.

"You sound tired," she finally said.

"It's been a long couple of weeks," I said before relaying the events of Tedd's murder, right down to the nitty-gritty details of Logan's blackmail and Wick's involvement. I left out some parts about Daphne. This time, anyway.

But it felt good to talk to her the way I used to. She listened with the occasional input, bouts of shock and surprise. Mostly she couldn't believe it. Nothing ever happened in Pearl!

"Good grief, it's like a Raymond Chandler novel!" she exclaimed. "I should be writing this down."

And for a moment, I reverted back to my eighteen-year-old self, speaking the words into the receiver before I'd thought them through: "You can come home now."

Silence again. "Oh, Neal. I am home."

Ah. Of course she was. Vancouver was home. It always had been.

"Say hello to Seth," she said, her way of ending the call.

"Say hello to Aunt Margot."

No sooner had I hung up the phone than it began to ring. I waited for an instant. Maybe she'd redialled by accident. Or maybe she was calling back on purpose. Maybe she wanted to tell me that I'd been right, that she *could* come home. There'd be no more rumours. No more speculation.

But no. I shook my head. She wasn't calling back. She'd gone off writing, inspired by my Marlowe-esque brush with murder.

I picked it up, only half-expecting anyone to be there. "Hello?"

"Humphrey! How are you, dear?"

I steeled myself, fortunate that Cynthia couldn't squeeze me to death over the phone.

"Fine," I replied.

"Would you be able to come down to town hall for a jiffy? There's something we need to discuss."

I didn't have much choice. I had been summoned by the mayor herself, and she generally wasn't one to take no for an answer.

I took the stairs at town hall two at a time, heading down the long hallway and past Randy Something-or-Other's desk, assuring him that Cynthia herself had called me in. He seemed sceptical.

Cynthia's office door was open and she greeted me with a hug before ushering me to a chair. Her office was just as cluttered as usual and she had to move several things off the chair before I could sit down.

That was when I realized we weren't alone. The chair next to mine was already occupied.

Madelaine Archer was sitting there, with one leg crossed over the other. She looked up at me and curled her lips into a small smile.

I couldn't be bad-mannered. I gave her a small smile back.

Cynthia sat on the other side of her desk and clapped her hands together. "We would like to start by thanking you for coming, Humphrey. We know you're a busy man."

Did they? I stole a glance at Madelaine. She was still smiling.

"What's this about?" I asked.

Cynthia moved some papers out of the way and rested her arms on the desk. "Now, Humphrey, we really do appreciate you coming. This sort of thing has to be discussed in person, the good old-fashioned way. It just can't be done over the phone. It isn't proper."

"What sort of thing?"

She cleared her throat. "As you know, the Pearl Motel fell into Madelaine's hands upon the tragic death of Tedd …"

The small smile was still permanently affixed to Madelaine's face.

"However, Madelaine does not wish to continue owning the property." Cynthia rustled through the papers. She seemed to be unable to find the one she was looking for and gave up. "She would like to gift it to someone for whom it has, shall we say, sentimental value."

"Who?" I asked.

Cynthia dropped the papers and looked at me. "Why, Humphrey, you of course!"

I blinked. "Me?"

Just like that, Cynthia's office was abuzz. Well, mostly Cynthia was abuzz.

"Isn't it marvellous? It was all Madelaine's idea. Of course it's a historic site, so anything you want to change will have to be approved by town council first, although I don't see any reason why you wouldn't be able to spruce it up a little. I think it could use a little sprucing, don't you? Not that Tedd wouldn't have done it. I'm sure he would have eventually. I'm sorry, Madelaine, dear, is this too much for you?"

Madelaine had stood up to leave. "Not at all, Cynthia. It's just that I have somewhere I have to be, as long as we're about finished here."

Somewhere to be with a glass of wine, I thought to myself.

"Of course," Cynthia sputtered, but she looked at her friend with deep concern.

Madelaine gave me a brief nod on her way out. When she was gone, I hardly knew what to say.

Fortunately, Cynthia was rarely at a loss for words. "On another note, Humphrey. I was wrong about Laurel. We all were."

Laurel. My mother. I stared at Cynthia, more surprised than anything.

She let out a small cry. "Oh dear, I've startled you, haven't I?"

"Not really," I said, shaking my head. I stood up. "It's just … the motel. I might need some time to think about it."

"Oh, Humphrey." Before I knew it, she scurried around the desk and squished me in another hug. "Take all the time you need."

"Thank you."

"May I suggest fishing? Pope always says it helps him think."

What did Pope have to think about? It wasn't like someone had handed him a motel he didn't want in a town he hadn't particularly cared for.

Besides, I didn't feel like taking up fishing.

"Two Manhattans coming up."

Logan sat on his usual barstool at the sidebar, looking like his usual self. His hair was perfectly combed and he wore that devilish grin. His scratched face had healed up faster than my eye and neck and forehead combined. Of course. Perfect Logan. It figured.

He flapped a copy of the *Gazette*. "What did you think?"

"Another front-page story for Mag."

"Mag who? I was talking about my photos." Logan took a sip. "Did you ask Daphne about Redhill?"

I shrugged. "I didn't really have the chance."

"Of course you didn't."

"What?"

"Nothing. You probably would have got all tongue-tied anyway."

I poured two cocktail glasses, adding the garnish. "Did you?"

"Did I what?"

"Did you ask her?"

A devilish grin. "If I did, I'm not telling."

"Logan—"

"What? It's not like he's the one who gave Daphne the ring. We know what happened to her fiancé."

"But who exactly is Tanner Redhill?"

"Another mystery for you to solve. I thought you liked solving mysteries."

"I prefer reading them."

Logan raised an eyebrow.

"What?" I said.

"I doubt that."

I couldn't help but laugh a little. So maybe the Manhattan Man knew me better than I knew myself. I supposed that was the thing about being old friends, whether we liked it or not.

"I might own the motel," I added after a moment.

"You might?"

"I do. I think I do, anyway. If I want it."

"Do you want it?"

I shrugged. "I don't know."

He took another sip. "That's not a no."

"It's not," I admitted. "But I didn't even want to run the bar, remember? What am I supposed to do with the whole motel?"

"You can call it something else, for starters. Humphrey's Motel has a nice ring to it."

I shook my head, sliding his drinks across the granite. "I don't think so."

"You could put up a new sign. Trim the grass."

"No."

"Replace the windows. Paint the trim. Fix the lock on Room 4."

"Logan, no."

"Then you could have a reopening and cut a red ribbon with Cynthia, and I could take the photos."

"Absolutely not."

"We could invite Daphne."

That was tempting ... but even so, I shook my head. "I'll probably just sell it."

The Manhattan Man finished his drink and grinned. "That's what you said when your old man left you Humphrey's."

———————

It was well after midnight by the time I settled into my armchair, listening to the rain pattering against the window and trickling down the gutters. I was almost nodding off when I heard another sound. Scratching. Pause. Scratching. Pause.

The cat was back.

I slid open the window, startling the stray. It backed away to the edge of the fire escape and curled its tail anxiously through one of the rails. Before I knew what I was doing, I ducked under the window frame and climbed out onto the fire escape, trying not to look down as I stepped over a rusted hole.

I stretched my hand out to the small creature—and when it didn't run away, I grasped its soaking wet fur and lifted it. I tucked it under my arm. It didn't put up a fight or try to wriggle free. It didn't want to be free. It wanted a place to call home.

ACKNOWLEDGEMENTS

Writing a novel is so much fun, as I'm sure any writer will attest to, but it's a largely a solitary experience. I've spent hours alone, cross-legged on my bed, laptop in my lap, typing as fast as the words came to mind. I could only have imagined that one day it would find its way into the hands of you, a reader, and I'm thankful that what once was mine has become yours too.

But if writing a novel is a solitary experience, publishing a novel certainly isn't. As such, I am thankful to a great many people who have surrounded me throughout the process.

First and foremost, I'm thankful to my mom, Michelle, who is and always has been my biggest supporter. The dream of becoming a writer first belonged to you—I hope you don't mind that I inherited it. Thank you for inspiring me to read at a young age. Thank you for introducing me to *Nancy Drew* (hence my love for mysteries) and, of course, our beloved *Mitford*. Thank you for answering all of my ridiculous questions and your constant willingness to play the "name game." Above all, thank you for always letting me be myself and encouraging me to explore my talents and dreams. I love you most!

Thank you to my first ever readers: Courtney Bergsma, Erienne DeVries, Darlene Flokstra, Beth Derksen, and Melissa Unruh. Some of the early drafts of *Humphrey's Motel* were rough (to say the least), and each of you offered support and encouragement, along with the occasional much-appreciated critique.

Corina, my dear friend. You have no idea how much our friendship has meant to me over the years. Who knew all those photography magazines would inspire one of my favourite characters. I'm only sorry I don't write fantasy novels!

EMILY B. KERROS

Thank you, Marina Reis, and the entire team at Word Alive Press for believing in *Humphrey's Motel* from the beginning. Thank you for being professional yet personable, guiding me through the exciting yet unfamiliar process, and giving me the confidence to share my writing with the world. A huge thank you to Evan Braun and Kerry Wilson for your thorough editing skills and suggestions. And thank you, Sebastian, for the most amazing cover design—you brought *Humphrey's Motel* to life!

Of course, there are many others who have provided encouragement and various forms of inspiration (often without realizing it). To name each of you would make this list unbearably long, but I'm thankful to be blessed with such supportive family and friends.

Finally, I'm thankful to my heavenly Father. My own faith journey has not been an easy one, and I continuously struggle, but I believe it's through my writing that He is healing me, reminding me that He is faithful and His promises are good.

ABOUT THE AUTHOR

Born and raised in a small town in Manitoba, Emily B. Kerros spent her bus rides to and from school reading her mom's old collection of *Nancy Drew Mysteries*. Now there is nothing she loves more than a good mystery, especially golden-age classics. When she isn't reading or writing, she's working her day job in a dental office and enjoys puzzling, baking sourdough, and spending time with her family and her cat. She also loves browsing for hours in bookstores. *Humphrey's Motel*, her debut novel, was shortlisted for the *2023 Braun Book Awards*. Follow Emily on Instagram: @emilybkerros.